William Cullen Bryant

Orations and Addresses

William Cullen Bryant

Orations and Addresses

ISBN/EAN: 9783741186363

Manufactured in Europe, USA, Canada, Australia, Japa

Cover: Foto ©Andreas Hilbeck / pixelio.de

Manufactured and distributed by brebook publishing software (www.brebook.com)

William Cullen Bryant

Orations and Addresses

TO THE READER.

THIS volume contains several discourses delivered by me in memory of eminent men of our country, which I have put together not without some hope that they may thus attain a little longer life than they would in the pamphlet form in which they originally appeared. To these I have added a few addresses delivered on other public occasions.

W. C. BRYANT.

NEW YORK, March, 1873.

CONTENTS.

COMMEMORATIVE ORATIONS.

THOMAS COLE.

THOMAS COLE.

A FUNERAL ORATION, DELIVERED BEFORE THE NATIONAL
ACADEMY OF DESIGN, NEW YORK, MAY 4, 1848.

GENTLEMEN OF THE ACADEMY:

We who were not permitted to see our friend
laid in his grave, and to pay his remains the last
tokens of respect before they were forever removed
from our sight, are assembled to pass a few moments
in speaking of his genius and his virtues. He was
one of the founders of the Academy whose members
I address, as well as one of its most illustrious ornaments. During the entire space which has elapsed
since the first of its exhibitions, nearly a quarter of a
century, I am not sure that there was a single year
in which his works did not appear on its walls; to
have missed them would have made us feel that the
collection was incomplete. Yet we shall miss them
hereafter; that skilful hand is at rest forever. His
departure has left a vacuity which amazes and alarms
us. It is as if the voyager on the Hudson were to
look toward the great range of the Catskills, at the

I

foot of which Cole, with a reverential fondness, had fixed his abode, and were to see that the grandest of its summits had disappeared—had sunk into the plain from our sight. I might use a bolder similitude ; it is as if we were to look over the heavens on a starlight evening and find that one of the greater planets, Hesperus or Jupiter, had been blotted from the sky.

When the good who are not distinguished by any intellectual greatness die, we regard their end as something in the ordinary course of nature. A harmless life we say has closed ; there is one fewer of the kindly spirits whom we were accustomed to meet in our path ;—and save in the little circle of his nearest friends, the sole feeling is that of a gentle regret. The child dies, and we think of it as a blossom transplanted to brighter gardens ; another springs and blooms in its place ; the youth and maiden depart in their early promise, the old man at the close of his tasks, and leave no space which is not soon filled. But when to great worth is united great genius ; when the mind of their possessor is so blended with the public mind as to form much of its strength and grace, his removal by death, in the strength and activity of his faculties, affects us with a sense of violence and loss ; we feel that the great fabric of which

we form a part is convulsed and shattered by it. It
is like wrenching out by the roots the ivy which has
overgrown and beautifies and upholds some ancient
structure of the Old World, and has sent its fibres
deep within its masonry; the wall is left a shapeless
mass of loosened stones.

For Cole was not only a great artist but a great
teacher; the contemplation of his works made men
better.   It is said of one of the old Italian painters,
that he never began a painting without first offering
a prayer.   The paintings of Cole are of that nature
that it hardly transcends the proper use of language
to call them acts of religion. Yet do they never strike
us as strained or forced in character; they teach but
what rose spontaneously in the mind of the artist; they
were the sincere communications of his own moral
and intellectual being.   One of the most eminent
among the modern German painters, Overbeck, is remarkable for the happiness with which he has caught
the devotional manner of the old ecclesiastical painters, blending it with his own more exquisite knowledge of art, and shedding it over forms of fairer symmetry.   Yet has he not escaped a certain mannerism;
the air of submissive awe, the manifest consciousness
of a superior presence, which he so invariably be-
stows on all his personages, becomes at last a matter

of repetition and circumscribes his walk to a narrow circle. With Cole it was otherwise ; his mode of treating his subjects was not bounded by the narrow limits of any system ; the moral interest he gave them took no set form or predetermined pattern ; its manifestations wore the diversity of that creation from which they were drawn.

Let me ask those who hear me to accompany me in a brief review of his life and his principal works.

Thomas Cole was born in the year 1802, at Bolton, in Lancashire, England. He came to this country with his family when sixteen years of age. He regarded himself, however, as an American, and claimed the United States as the country of his relatives. His father passed his youth here, and his grandfather, I have heard him say, lived the greater part of his life in the United States.

After a short stay in Philadelphia, the family removed to Steubenville, in Ohio. Cole was early in the habit of amusing himself with drawing, observant of the aspect of nature and fond of remarking the varieties of scenery. An invincible diffidence led him to avoid society and to wander alone in woods and solitudes, where he found that serenity which forsook him in the company of his fellows. He took long rambles in the forests along the banks of the Ohio, on which Steubenville is situated, and acquired that love of walking which continued through life. His first drawings were imitated from the designs on English chinaware; he then copied engravings, and tried engraving, in a very rude way we must presume, both on wood and copper. In 1820, when the artist was eighteen years of age, a portrait painter named Stein, came to Steubenville, who lent him an English work on drawing, treating of design, composition and color. The study of this work seems not only to have given him an idea of the principles of the art, but to have revealed to him in some sort the extraordinary powers that were slumbering within him. He read it again and again with the greatest eagerness; it became his constant companion, and he resolved to be a painter. He provided himself with a palette, pencils and colors, and after one or two experiments in portrait painting, which were pronounced satisfactory, left his father's house on foot one February morning, on a tour through some of the principal villages of Ohio. From St. Clairsville, which he first reached, he wandered to Zanesville, from Zanesville to Chillicothe, and finally, after an absence of several months, during which he painted but few pictures, and experienced many hardships and discouragements, returned to Steubenville no richer than when he left it. In one of these journeys, that from Zanesville to Chillicothe, he walked sixty miles in a single day.

The family afterwards removed to Pittsburgh, and here, on the banks of the Monongahela, in the year 1823, he first struck into the path which led him to excellence and renown. The country about Pittsburgh is uncommonly beautiful, a region of hills and glens, rich meadows and noble forests, and charming combinations of wood and water, and great luxuriance and variety of vegetation. After the hour of nine in the morning, he was engaged in a manufactory established by his father, but until that time he was abroad, studying the aspect of the country, and for the first time making sketches from nature. Before the buds began to open, he drew the leafless trees, imitated the disposition of the boughs and twigs, and as the leaves came forth, studied and copied the various characters of foliage. I may date from this period the birth of his practical skill as a landscape painter, though I have little doubt that in his earlier wanderings on the banks of the Ohio, and perhaps in his still earlier rambles in the fields of Lancashire, he had cherished the close inspection of nature, and unconsciously laid up in his memory treasures of observation, from which he afterwards drew liberally, when long practice had given him the ready hand and the power of throwing upon the canvas at pleasure the images that rose and lived in his mind. In no part of the world where painting is practised as an art, does the forest vegetation present so great a variety as here; and of that variety Cole seemed a perfect master. I see in his delineations of trees a robust vigor of hand which leaves nothing to desire, and a diversity of character which seems to me almost boundless. Of this mastery and variety the picture which bears the name of the Mountain Home, one of his later works, is a remarkable example.

The business in which his father had engaged proved unsuccessful; it was abandoned, and late in the autumn of 1823 Cole took his departure for Philadelphia, with the design of trying his fortune in that city. The winter which followed was a winter of hardship and suffering, the particulars of which are related with some minuteness in Dunlap's book on American Artists. But he had youth on his side, and the hopes of youth, and a good constitution, and an unconquerable determination to excel, without which no artist ever became great. Between that determination and his acute sensiveness there must have been many a hard conflict, but it prevailed. He

obtained permission to draw at the Pennsylvania
Academy of the Fine Arts, received some trifling
commissions, struggled through that winter and the
next, and in the spring of 1824 joined his family,
who had now removed to New York.

It was here that the public were first made acquainted with his merits, and that the day of his fame
first dawned upon him. He had painted several
landscapes, which were placed in a shop for sale.
One of them was purchased by Mr. Bruen, an hon-
orary member of this Academy, for a small sum, but
the purchaser was so much delighted with it, that he
immediately sought the acquaintance of the artist, and
furnished him with the means of studying and copying the scenery of the Hudson. Three pictures
were produced by him in the summer of 1824, which
were exposed for sale at the price of twenty-five
dollars each. They were purchased by three artists,
—I mention the fact with great pleasure,—three
artists who generously and cordially acknowledged
their merit, and continued ever after his friends—
Trumbull, Dunlap, and Durand. "This youth,"
said Trumbull, when he saw them, "has done what
I have all my life attempted in vain."

Two of the pictures of which I am speaking are
in the exhibition opened for the benefit of his family.

since his death. They are not equal to his later works, but they are skilful, faithful and original, and these qualities, once pointed out, made them the subject of general admiration.

In one of the earlier editions of his poem entitled The Vanity of Human Wishes, Johnson thus enumerates the calamities incident to the life of a scholar :

> Toil, envy, want, the garret and the jail.

Afterwards, when he had experienced what it was to possess a patron, he changed the line to

> Toil, envy, want, the *patron* and the jail.

Men of letters in the present age have luckily little to do with patrons; the community is their patron; the more general diffusion of education and of the habit of reading enables the man of decided literary talent to obtain from the people surer and more constant rewards than he formerly received from the bounty of the. great. The painter, however, addresses himself to a taste much less generally cultivated than that of reading, and the works of his art are. not, like books, in the power of every man to purchase and possess. He is therefore by no means secure from the misfortune of patronage.

It was the fate of Cole, at this period of his life,

1*

to meet with a patron. When his pictures first attracted the public attention, as I have already related, a dashing Englishman, since known as the author of a wretched book about the United States, who had married the heiress of an opulent American family, professed to take a warm interest in the young painter, and charged himself with the task of advancing his fortunes. He invited him to pass the winter at his house, on his estate in the country, and engaged him to paint a number of landscapes, for which he was to pay him twenty or thirty dollars each, a trifling compensation for such works as Cole could even then produce, but which I have no doubt, seemed to him at that time munificent. It would hardly become the place or the occasion were I to relate the particulars of the treatment which the artist received from his patron, the miserable and cheerless apartments he assigned him, the supercilious manner by which he endeavored to drive him from his table to take his meals with the children of the family, and the general disrespect of his demeanor. These would have been a sufficient motive with Cole to leave the place immediately, but for the apprehension that his kind friends in New York, who had taken so strong an interest in his success, might ascribe this step to an inconstant temper, or to a character morbidly jealous of its dignity. He imposed upon himself, therefore, though deeply hurt and offended, the penance of remaining, labored assiduously at his easel, and executed several pictures which justified the high opinion his New York friends entertained of his genius. Fortunately, for a considerable part of the winter, he was relieved of the presence of his patron, who went to pass his time in the amusements of a neighboring city.

As early as he could finish the pictures on which he was engaged, he quitted the roof of the Englishman, and returned to New York without payment for what he had done. Some time afterwards he compromised with this encourager of youthful genius, accepted half the compensation originally stipulated, and relinquished his claim to the remainder.

The works executed by Cole during this winter were sent by his generous patron as presents to his friends; they were samples of the talent which he had discovered, cherished and rewarded. One of the paintings in the present exhibition, is said to belong to this period of the artist's life. It is numbered 81 in the collection—a wild mountain scene, where a bridge of two planks crosses a chasm, through which flows a mountain stream. It has not the boldness and frankness, the assured touch, of his later productions, but it is full of beauty. There are the mountain summits, unmistakably American, with their infinity of tree-tops, a beautiful management of light, striking forms of trees and rocks in the foreground, and a certain lucid darkness in the waters below. The whole shows that Cole, amidst the discomfort and vexations which surrounded him, suffered no depression of his faculties, and that the vision of what he had observed in external nature came to him, in all its beauty, and remained with him until his pencil had transferred it to the canvas.

There had been no necessity of providing Cole with a patron. The public had already learned to admire his works under the guidance of those who were esteemed the best judges, and their attention being once gained, his success was certain. From that time he had a fixed reputation, and was numbered among the men of whom 'our country had reason to be proud. I well remember what an enthusiasm was awakened by these early works of his, inferior as I must deem them to his maturer productions,—the delight which was expressed at the opportunity of contemplating pictures which carried the eye over scenes of wild grandeur peculiar to our country, over our aërial mountain-tops with their mighty growth of forest never touched by the axe, along the banks of streams never deformed by culture, and into the depth of skies bright with the hues of our own climate ; skies such as few but Cole could ever paint, and through the transparent abysses of which it seemed that you might send an arrow out of sight.

In 1825 the National Academy of the Arts of Design was founded. This great enterprise, for such I must call it, was principally effected by the exertions of one who has since been lost to art, though translated perhaps, so far as the mere material interests of society are concerned, to a sphere of greater usefulness. I may speak of him, therefore, as an academician, as freely as if he had departed this life. In establishing the Academy he met with many obstacles and discouragements, but they gave way before his ingenuity and perseverance. "Do you know," said a friend of mine, scarce less highly endowed as a connoisseur than as a man of letters ; " do you know what Morse is doing among the artists ? He has made them lay aside their jealousies, and forget their quarrels ; he has inspired them with a desire to raise their profession to its proper dignity, and has united them into an association for the purpose."

At that time the New York Academy of the Fine Arts was in existence ; it had Colonel Trumbull with his great reputation at its head, and numbered among its members nearly all the men of wealth in New York, who desired to be regarded as friends of the fine arts. The new association of artists, not satisfied with the manner in which it was conducted, nor with the opportunities it afforded to pupils, asked that a certain number of artists should be placed in the board of its directors. This demand, after some negotiation, was refused, and Morse led his band of artists boldly to the conflict with the old Academy and its opulent patrons. They founded the Academy of the Arts of Design, governed solely by artists ; appealed from the patronage of the few to the general judgment of the community, and triumphed. The barren exhibitions of the old Academy, with their large proportion of casts and pictures which had been seen again and again, were deserted for the brilliant novelties offered by the new, and finally the elder of the two rivals expired by a death so easy and unnoticed, that few, I suspect, now recollect the date of its dissolution.

The Academy of Design meanwhile has gone on with a constant increase of prosperity, presenting from year to year richer and more creditable exhibitions, though some, who have been rendered fastidious by what they have learned from these very exhibitions, absurdly maintain the contrary ; it has gone on with an increasing revenue, till it is able not only to support an excellent school for the instruction of pupils of both sexes, but to pension the widows of the academicians.

Let me say a word or two concerning the artist I have just named, for many years the president of this institution, and worthy to stand at the head of an association of which Cole was a member. He possessed in a high degree all the learning and knowledge of his art. The bent of his genius was towards historical painting, in which various circumstances—want of encouragement was the principal —prevented him from taking that rank to which he might otherwise have raised himself. He was embarrassed somewhat by another obstacle ; the turn of his mind was experimental, a quality more fortunate for a scientific discoverer than an artist, and he boldly trusted himself to new paths, in which perhaps he sometimes lost his way. Yet from time to time he would astonish the world with glimpses of the great powers which he possessed, and which only needed opportunity and steady exercise to mature them into their due strength and excellence. "I know what is in him," said the great Allston, in a letter to Dunlap, "better, perhaps, than any one else. If he will only bring out all that is there, he will show powers that many now do not dream of."

In that fraternity of artists which founded the Academy, was another man of genius who began his career almost at the same moment with Cole, and who closed it in death two or three years earlier. Inman, the first vice-president of the institution, was a portrait painter of extraordinary merit, great facility of pencil, a pleasing style of color, and a power of happy selection from the various expressions of countenance which a sitter brings to the artist. The versatility of his powers was surprising: he has left behind him specimens of landscape, of figures in groups, in repose or in action, which show that he might have excelled in any branch of the art. His view of Rydal Water, painted for one of our number, from a spot near the dwelling of the poet Wordsworth, is a picture of extreme beauty; a soft aerial scene, like a dream of Paradise; the little sheet of water seems one of the lakes of the Happy Valley, and the mountains are like hills of fairy land. He was not a man like Cole, to linger long in contemplation of the objects he would delineate, to study them till he had exhausted all they could offer to his observation, and till their image became incorporated with his mind. What he saw, he saw at a glance, and transferred it to the canvass with the same rapidity, and with surprising precision. His works owe nothing to revision, and possess a certain unlabored grace which makes us delight in reverting to them.

With such men, and others worthy to be their colleagues, Cole was associated in the early days of the Academy. At its first exhibition, in 1826, he contributed a snow-piece, not one of his most remarkable works, perhaps, but bearing the characteristics of his manner. He now received frequent commissions, and somewhat more than two years later, near the close of 1828, was enabled to gratify a desire which all artists feel with more or less strength, to visit Europe. He went first to England, where our countryman Cooper received him with kindness, and introduced him to the poet Rogers, who took much interest in him, and gave him a commission for a picture. The great portrait painter, Lawrence, behaved to him in a most friendly manner, but he died not long after his arrival. His residence in England does not seem to have been favorable to his serenity of mind. He complained of the gloom of the climate, accustomed as he had been, ever since he became an artist, to our brilliant skies, and the almost superabundant light of our atmosphere ; and he was much affected by the coldness of the English artists, who saw nothing in his pictures to commend. Turner, with his splendid faults, his undeniable mastery in some respects, and his egregious defiance of nature in others, had taken possession of the public taste, and it was no easy matter for so true a painter as Cole, unsupported by the favorable testimony of those who were recognized by the public as judges of art, to obtain for his works an impartial consideration. He sent pictures to the public exhibitions in London for two successive seasons, and, though the subjects were American, they were hung in such situations that even his friends, familiar with his manner, could not distinguish them for his.

In May, 1831, he left England for Paris, hoping to be able to study awhile at the Louvre ; but at that time its walls were covered with an exhibition of modern French paintings, of which he liked neither the subjects nor the treatment, and he proceeded immediately to Italy. It appears from a letter of his to Dunlap, that even after his arrival in that country, he found it hard to shake off the depression of spirits which kept possession of him during his residence in England. It left him, however, and he speaks with delight of his sojourn in Florence, which he calls the painter's paradise. He studied the noble collections of art which it contains, drew sedulously from life, and executed his Sunset on the Arno, and several other works. Many of those who hear me will probbly recollect this picture, a fine painting, with the river gleaming in the middle ground, the dark woods of the Cascine on the right, and above, in the distance, the mountain summits half dissolved in the vapory splendor which belongs to an Italian sunset.

From Florence he went to Rome, where he had his studio in a house once occupied by Claude. He seems to have studied the remarkable and beautiful country in the neighborhood of the eternal city, scattered with ruins, and the fine effects of the Roman climate, even more than the objects contained in its magnificent repositories of art. Here he made sketches from which he afterwards painted some of his best pictures. Naples attracted him further south, and from Naples he made an excursion to Paestum. He used to relate that as he was preparing for a visit to the solitary temples, which are all that is left of that ancient city, he happened to speak of his design in presence of an Englishman who had just returned from them. "Why do you go to Paestum?" said the Englishman; "you will see nothing there but a few old buildings." He went, however, saw the old buildings, the grandest and most perfect remains of the architecture of Greece, standing

" ———between the mountains and the sea,"

in a spot where, in the beautiful words of the same poet,

" The air is sweet with violets running wild,"

but which the pestilential climate has made a desert; he saw and painted a view of them for an American lady.

While in Italy, the manner of Cole underwent a considerable change ; a certain timid softness of manner—in comparison I mean with his later style—was laid aside for that free and robust boldness in imitating the effects of nature, which has ever since characterized his works. I recollect that when his picture of the Fountain of Egeria, painted abroad, appeared in our exhibition, this change was generally remarked and was regretted by many, who preferred the gentle beauty of his earlier style, attained by repeated and careful touches, and who were half-disposed to wish that the artist had never seen the galleries of Europe.

It seems to me, however, that the transition to this bolder manner was the natural consequence of his advance in art and of confidence in his own powers, and that it would have taken place if he had never seen a picture by the European masters. It is not unusual with men of powerful genius in any of the fine arts, that their earlier essays are marked with a certain graceful indecision, a stopping short of the highest effect, on account of some hesitation as to the means of producing it, or some fear of the manner in which it will be received. From this if they had never departed they could never have become great. With riper powers, higher skill and a knowledge of their own strength, they become impatient of commonplace beauty, and rise by a necessity of their nature to a more masculine method of treatment. Connoisseurs trace this change in the paintings of Raphael; critics in the poetry of Byron.

That Cole would have been a great painter if he had never studied abroad, scarcely less great on that account, no man can doubt. But would he have been able to paint some of these pictures which we most value and most affectionately admire; that fine one, for example, of the Ruins of Aqueducts in the Campagna of Rome, with its broad masses of shadow dividing the sunshine, that bathes the solitary plain strown with ruins, its glorious mountains in the distance and its silence made visible to the eye? Would he have ever given us a picture like that which bears the name of The Present, a scene of loneliness, populous with the reminiscences of days gone by; or a picture like that great final one, the Course of Empire? Cole owed much to the study of nature in the Old World, but very little, I think, to its artists. He speaks in his letter of the delight with which he regarded the works of the older painters of Italy, on account of their love for the truth of nature, the simplicity and single-heartedness with which they imitated it, and their freedom from the constraint of system; but I see slight traces of anything which he could have caught from their manner. He had a better teacher, and copied the works of a greater artist.

Cole came back to America in 1832, recalled somewhat sooner than he wished by the ill health of his parents and their desire for his return. Within a year or two afterwards, he began the series of large pictures, so well known to the public under the name of the Course of Empire. I shall not weary those who hear me with any particular description of these paintings, which are among the most remarkable and characteristic of his works. The subject is finely conceived, and though the execution of each is not equal, they have all some peculiar excellence. The second, representing the pastoral state of mankind, ranks among his most pleasing landscapes; the fifth and last, placing before us the remains of a great city crumbling into earth, reclaimed by nature to nourish her vegetation and to furnish herbage for the flock, is one of those pictures which Cole only could paint. The third is an architectural piece of great splendor, with an imposing arrangement of stately structures; the fourth, though the subject was not of that kind which he delighted to paint, is full of invention and energy, and the struggle between the host of the besiegers and the crowd of the besieged, is given in such a manner as to blend simplicity of effect with variety of detail. "I have been engaged ever since I saw you," said he in a letter to one of his friends, "in sacking and burning a city, and I am well nigh tired of such horrid work. I *did* believe it was my best picture, but I took it down stairs to-day and got rid of the notion."

The Course of Empire, I find on looking over some of his letters, was not completed till 1836. It was painted for one of the most generous and judicious friends of art whom the country ever had, Luman Reed, who died before the artist had finished the series.

It was while he was thus engaged that he married and fixed his residence at Catskill, in a region singular for its romantic beauty, where the remainder of his life was as happy as domestic harmony, his own gentle and genial temper, and the love of those by whom he was surrounded, could make it. His genius had grown prolific as it ripened ; and in this charming retreat he executed some of his noblest works. Among these I must class the Departure and Return, produced in 1837. There could not be a finer choice of circumstances nor a more exquisite treatment of them than is found in these pictures. In the first, a spring morning, breezy and sparkling, the mists starting and soaring from the hills; the chieftain in gallant array at the head of his retainers, issuing from the castle—in the second, an autumnal evening, calm, solemn, a church illuminated by the beams of the setting sun, and the corpse of the chief borne in silence towards the consecrated place—these are but a meagre epitome of what is contained in these two pictures. In both, the figures are extremely well managed, though in this respect he was not always so fortunate, nor did his strength lie in that direction. The two works which he named the Past and Present, produced in the year following, have scarcely less merit as a whole ; the latter of them is one of those pictures, rich, solemn, full of matter for study and reflection, in producing which Cole had no rival.

In 1840 he completed another series of large paintings, called the Voyage of Life, of simpler and less elaborate design than the Course of Empire, but more purely imaginative. The conception of the series is a perfect poem. The child, under the care of its guardian angel, in a boat heaped with buds and flowers, floating down a stream which issues from the shadowy cavern of the past and flows between banks bright with flowers and the beams of the rising sun ; the youth, with hope in his gesture and aspect, taking command of the helm, while his winged guardian watches him anxiously from the shore; the mature man, hurried onward by the perilous rapids and eddies of the river; the aged navigator, who has reached, in his frail and now idle bark, the mouth of the stream, and is just entering the great ocean which lies before him in mysterious shadow, set before us the different stages of human life under images of which every beholder admits the beauty and deep significance. The second of this series, with the rich luxuriance of its foreground, its pleasant declivities in the distance, and its gorgeous but shadowy structures in the piled clouds, is one of the most popular of Cole's compositions.

About this time Cole thought of painting Medora watching for the return of the Corsair, as related in

Byron's poem, for a gentleman who had commission-
ed a picture, but who, after some reflection and discussion with his friends, abandoned the subject and
adopted in its place one suggested by this stanza
in Coleridge's admirable little poem of Love :—

> "She leaned against the armed man,
> The statue of the armed knight ;
> She stood and listened to my harp
> Amid the lingering light."

This picture remains, I am told, among the things
which he left unfinished at his death. Another work
produced in 1840 was the Architect's Dream, an as-
semblage of structures, Egyptian, Grecian, Gothic,
Moorish, such as might present itself to the imagination of one who had fallen asleep after reading a
work on the different styles of architecture. The
subject was in a measure forced upon him by the im-
portunity of an architect, who seems to have imagined that he was able to give Cole some important
hints in his art, and desired a work which should
combine " history and landscape and the architecture of different styles and ages." The painter, good-
naturedly, attempted to accommodate his genius to
this caprice, but the picture produced did not satisfy
the architect, who probably had no distinct idea of

what he wanted, and who intimated his wish that Cole should try again. Cole wrote back in some displeasure, offering to return such compensation as he had received and to consider the commission as at an end. This I suppose, was done, as the picture is in the possession of one of the painter's relatives.

In July, 1841, Cole sailed on a second visit to Europe. On this occasion he travelled much in Switzerland, which he had never before seen, lingering as long as the limits of the time he had prescribed to himself would allow him in that remarkable country, and filling his mind with its wonders of beauty and grandeur. From Switzerland he passed to Italy, whence he made an excursion to the island of Sicily, with the scenery of which he was greatly delighted. On its bold rocky summits and in its charming valleys he found everywhere scattered the remains of a superb architecture, and gazed without satiety upon the luxuriance of its vegetation in which the plants of the tropics spring intermingled with those of temperate climes. In his letters, written from this island, he speaks with an enthusiastic delight of the abundance of flowers with which the waste places were enlivened : flowers which here we cultivate assiduously in our gardens, but which are shed profusely over the wildernesses of ancient but almost depopulated Sicily.

One of his pictures—I might place it among his earlier works, for it was painted before his first visit to Europe—strikingly illustrates the great delight he took in flowers. Some of those who hear me will doubtless recollect his picture of the Garden of Eden. In this work he attempted what was almost beyond the power of the pencil, a representation of the bloom and brightness which poets attribute to the abode of man in a state of innocence. In the distance were gleaming waters, and winding valleys, and bowers on the gentle slopes of the hills ; but nearer, in the foreground, the painter has lavished upon the garden a profusion of bloom, and hidden the banks and oppressed the shrubs with a weight of " flowers of all hues," as Milton calls these ornaments of his Paradise. A single flower, or a group of several, may be very well managed by the artist, but when he attempts to portray an expanse of bloom, a whole landscape, or any large portion of it, overspread and colored by them, we feel the imperfection of the instruments he is obliged to use, and are disappointed by the want of vividness in the impression he strives to create. The Eden of Cole has great merits as a scene of tranquil beauty, but there

was that in its design to which the power of the pencil was not adequate.

He saw other things, however, in Sicily. The
aspect of Mount Etna seemed to have taken a strong
hold on his imagination. Several views of it have
been given by his pencil, one of which is in the exhibition of his works now open. A still larger one
was painted by him some time after his return, which
presented a nearer view of the mountain filling the
greater part of the canvas with its huge cone. It
was completed in a very few days, and was a miracle
of rapid and powerful execution. It was not so generally admired as many of his works, and no doubt
had in it some of the imperfections of haste; but for
my part I never stood before it without feeling that
sense of elevation and enlargement with which we
look upon huge and lofty mountains in nature. With
me, at least, the artist had succeeded in producing
the effect at which he aimed. I have no doubt that
he painted it with a mind full of the greatness of the
subject, with a feeling of sublime awe produced by
the image of that mighty mountain, the summit of
which is white with perpetual snow, while the slopes
around its base are basking in perpetual summer,
and on whose peak the sunshine yet lingers, while
the valleys at its foot lie in the evening twilight.

Of course he passed some time at Rome in his second visit to Europe. In this old capital he produced a duplicate of the Voyage of Life. Thorwaldsen came to visit him. "These pictures," said the illustrious Dane, "are something wholly new in art. They are highly poetical in conception, and admirable in their execution."

In August, 1842, Cole returned to his family in Catskill

In 1844 died Verbryck, one of the younger members of the Academy. He sleeps among the forest trees of Greenwood Cemetery, in a lowly spot chosen by himself, before his death, which would not attract your attention if you were not looking for it. There the grave of the modest and amiable artist is decked with flowering plants, set and tended by hands which perform the pious office when no one observes them. He was a painter of much promise, with a strong enthusiasm for his art and earnest meditation on its principles, but he was withheld by a feebleness of constitution from doing what his genius, if seconded by a more robust physical nature, would have given him the power to do. His productions, for the most part, have in them a shadow of sadness, as if darkened by the contemplation of that early fate which he knew to impend over him, and which took him away from a life that seemed to give him everything worth living for.

It was not long before his death that in landing at Brooklyn from one of the ferry-boats, I met Cole, who said to me, "I have just paid a visit to Verbryck and looked over his sketches with him, in order that he might select one from which I am to paint a picture for a friend of his." On further conversation I found that a picture had been ordered of Verbryck, and the money advanced for it by the gentleman who is now president of the New York Gallery, and who knows how to be munificent without ostentation. At the time the commission was given, Verbryck hesitated at taking it, on account of the precarious state of his health, but Cole, who took great interest both in his personal character and his genius, advised him to accept it, and promised that if what he feared should come to pass, he would paint the picture in his stead. The dying artist we may suppose, was uneasy that he could not perform his engagement, and Cole had delicately renewed his offer. Verbryck selected a sketch of a quiet rural scene, such as might naturally be preferred by one in whose veins the powers of life were feebly struggling against disease, whose frame was languid while his blood was fevered, and to whom a serene and healthful repose would appear the most desirable of all conditions. This picture was afterwards executed, and forms the seventh in the collection now open to the public. It has no particular advantage of subject;—a winding river, the Thames, flows tranquilly between sloping banks of green, and groups of trees overlook the waters. Yet it is painted with great care, for Cole was not a man to perform this act of piety in a slight and hurried manner; and the admirable disposition of objects and the perfect truth with which they are rendered, make it a work on which the eye dwells long without being weary. It is much prized by the owner, by whom it is regarded, I presume, as a memorial, not only of Cole's genius but of his goodness, and of that friendship between the two artists, which, interrupted for a brief space, is now doubtless renewed in another life.

Cole had never wrought with greater vigor nor after nobler conceptions than in the years which immediately preceded the close of his life. The admiration for his works, which I think had somewhat declined after his second visit to Europe, had revived. Such pictures as the Mountain Home, the Mountain Ford, the Arch of Nero, and many others, had recalled it in all its original fervor. A certain negligence of detail has been objected to some of Cole's works, produced in the maturity of his genius, but I have seen an artist, a painter of American landscapes, whose name will rank among those of the first landscape painters of the age, stand before the Arch of Nero, unable to find words for the full expression of that admiration with which he regarded the perfection of its parts, and the easy and happy dexterity with which they were rendered to the eye.

His last great work was the unfinished series of the Cross and the World, in which, as in many of his previous works, he sought to exemplify his favorite position that landscape painting was capable of the deepest moral interest and deserved to stand second to no other department of the art. Three only of the five pictures of which it was to be composed are finished, and in these we know not what changes in design or execution might have been made, had he lived to complete and harmonize every part of the design ; but that design is one of singular grandeur, and was capable, in his hands, of a noble execution.

To the second picture in this series I might object that it makes the life of the good man too much a life of pain, difficulty and danger. The path of his Pilgrim of the Cross is over steeps and precipices, interrupted by fearful chasms, amidst darkness and tempest, and torrents that threaten to sweep him from his footing, with no resting places of innocent re-

2*

freshment nor intervals of secure and easy passage after the first asperities of the way are overcome. The most ascetic of those who have written on the Christian life hardly go this length. Even Bunyan provides for his Pilgrim the Delectable Mountains, and the fruitful and pleasant land of Beulah, and the hospitable entertainments of the House of the Interpreter. But in the third of the series I acknowledge a power of genius which makes me, for the moment, fully assent to Cole's idea of the dignity of his department of the art. That Pilgrim arrived at the end of his journey on the summit of the mountain; that ineffable glory in the heavens before which he kneels, the luminous path over the enkindled clouds leading upward to it, the mountain height shooting with verdure under the beams of that celestial day, the darkness sullenly recoiling on either side, the ethereal messengers sent to conduct the wayfarer to his rest, form altogether a picture which could only have been produced by a mind of vast creative power quickened by a fervid poetic inspiration. The idea is Miltonic, said a friend when he first beheld it. It *is* Miltonic; it is worthy to be ranked with the noblest conceptions of the great religious epic poet of the world.

It was while he was engaged in painting this series that the summons of death came. An inflammation of the lungs, a sudden and brief illness, closed his life on the 13th of February. On the third day after the attack he despaired of recovery and began to make preparations for death. The close of his life was like the rest of it, serene and peaceful, and he passed into that next stage of existence, from which we are separated by such slight and frail barriers, with unfaltering confidence in the divine goodness, like a docile child guided by the kindly hand of a parent, suffering itself to be led without fear into the darkest places.

His death was widely lamented. How we were startled by the first news of it, which we refused to believe—it came so suddenly, when we knew that a few days before he was in his highest vigor of body and mind, resolutely laboring on great projects of art, and we looked forward to a long array of years for one who lived so wisely, and for whom so splendid a destiny on earth seemed to be ordained! On the little community in which he lived, the calamity fell with a peculiar weight. The day of his funeral was a solemn day and a sad one in Catskill; the shops were closed and business was suspended in obedience to a common feeling of sorrow.

For that sorrow there was good cause; for in Cole there was no disproportion between the cultiva-

tion of his moral and that of his intellectual character. He was unspotted by worldly vices, gentle, just,
beneficent, true, kind to the unfortunate, quick to in-
terfere when wrong or suffering were inflicted on the
helpless, whether on his fellow-man or the brute
creation. His religion, fervently as it was cherished,
was without ostentation or austerity, not a thing by
itself, but a sentiment blended and interwoven with
all the actions of his daily life. His manners were
cheerful, even playful, and his ready ingenuity was
employed in various ways to promote the innocent
amusements of the neighborhood in which he lived.
I remember asking one of his relatives for some examples of his goodness of heart. "His whole life,"
was the reply, "seemed made up of such examples;
he never appeared to be in the wrong; he never did
anything which gave us offence or caused us regret.
We delighted to have him always with us ; we were
sorry whenever he left us and glad when he returned." He is now gone forth forever ; gone forth to
gladden his friends no more with his return; the
home which was brightened by his presence is desolate ; the sorrow for his absence is perpetual.

Of his merits as an artist I ought to express an
opinion with diffidence, standing before you as I do,
a stammerer among those who speak the true dialect

of art. Let me say, however, that to me it seems that he is certain to take a higher rank after his death than was yielded to him in his life. When I visit the collection of his pictures lately made for exhibition; when I see how many great works are before me, and think of the many which could not be brought into the collection; when I consider with what mastery, yet with what reverence he copied the forms of nature, and how he blended with them the profoundest human sympathies, and made them the vehicle, as God has made them, of great truths and great lessons, when I see how directly he learned his art from the creation around him, and how resolutely he took his own way to greatness, I say within myself, this man will be reverenced in future years as a great master in art? he has opened a way in which only men endued with rare strength of genius can follow him. One of the very peculiarities which has been objected to him as a fault, a certain crudeness, as it has been called, in the coloring, appears to me a proof of his exquisite art. He did not paint for this year or for the next, but for centuries to come; his tints were so chosen and applied that he knew they would be harmonized by time, and already in several of his paintings that hoary artist has nearly completed the work which the painter left him to do.

Reverencing his profession as the instrument of good to mankind, Cole pursued it with an assiduity which knew no remission. I have heard him say that he never willingly allowed a day to pass without some touch of the pencil. He delighted in hearing old ballads sung or books read while he was occupied in painting, seeming to derive, from the ballad or the book, a healthful excitement in the task which employed his hand. So accustomed had he grown to this double occupation that he would sometimes desire his female friends to read to him while he was writing letters. In the contemplation of nature, however, for the purposes of his art, I remember to have heard him say that the presence of those who were not his familiar friends, disturbed him. To that task he surrendered all his faculties, and no man, I suppose, ever took into his mind a more vivid image of what he beheld. His sketches were sometimes but the slightest notes of his subject, often unintelligible to others, but to him luminous remembrancers from which he would afterwards reconstruct the landscape with surprising fidelity. He carried to his painting room the impressions received by the eye and there gave them to the canvas; he even complained of the distinctness with which they haunted him. "Have you not found," said he, writing to a distinguished friend—" I have—that you never succeed in painting scenes, however beautiful, immediately on returning. from them ?   I must wait for time to draw a veil over the common details, the unessential parts, which shall leave the great features whether the beautiful or the sublime, dominant in the mind."

He could not endure a town life ; he must live in the continual presence of rural scenes and objects. A country life he believed essential to the cheerfulness of the artist and to a healthful judgment of his own works ; in the throng of men he thought that the artist was apt to lean too much on the judgment of others, and to find their immediate approbation necessary to his labors.   In the retirement of ti country, he held that the simple desire of excellence was likely to act with more strength and less disturbance, and that its products would be worthier and nobler.   He could not bear that his art should be degraded by inferior motives. " I do not mean," said he, not long before his death, " to paint any more pictures with a direct view to profit."

There are few, I suppose, who do not recollect the lines of Walter Scott, beginning thus :

> " Call it not vain ; they do not err
> Who say, that when the poet dies,
> Mute nature mourns her worshipper,
> And celebrates his obsequies."

This is said of the poet ; but the landscape painter is admitted to a closer familiarity with nature than the poet. He studies her aspect more minutely and watches with a more affectionate.attention its varied expressions. Not one of her forms is lost upon him ; not a gleam of sunshine penetrates her green recesses ; not a cloud casts its shadow unobserved by him ; every tint of the morning or the evening, of the gray or the golden noon, of the near or the remote object is noted by his eye and copied by his pencil. All her boundless variety of outlines and shades become almost a part of his being and are blended with his mind.

We might imagine, therefore, a sound of lament for him whom we have lost in the voices of the streams and in the sighs of the wind among the groves, and an aspect of sorrow in earth's solitary places ; we might dream that the conscious valleys miss his accustomed visits, and that the autumnal glories of the woods are paler because of his departure. But the sorrow of this occasion is too grave for such fancies. Let me say, however, that we feel that much is taken away from the charm of nature when such a man departs. To us who remain, the region of the Catskills, where he wandered and studied and sketched, and wrought his sketches into such glorious creations, is saddened by a certain desolate feeling when we behold it or think of it. The mind that we knew was abroad in those scenes of grandeur and beauty, and which gave them a higher interest in our eyes, has passed from the earth, and we see that something of power and greatness is withdrawn from the sublime mountain tops and the broad forests and the rushing waterfalls.

Withdrawn I have said—not extinguished, translated to a state of larger light, and nobler beauty and higher employments of the intellect. It is when I contemplate the death of such a man as Cole under such circumstances as attended his, that I feel most certain of the spirit's immortality. In his case the painful problem of old age was not presented, in which the mind sometimes seems to expire before the body, and often to wither with the same decline. He left us in the mid-strength of his intellect, and his great soul, unharmed and unweakened by the disease which brought low his frame, amidst the bitter anguish of the loved ones who stood around him, when the hour of its divorce from the material organs had come, calmly retired behind the veil which hides from us the world of disembodied spirits.

JAMES FENIMORE COOPER.

JAMES FENIMORE COOPER.

A DISCOURSE ON HIS LIFE, GENIUS AND WRITINGS, DELIVERED AT METROPOLITAN HALL, NEW YORK, FEBRUARY 25, 1852.

It is now somewhat more than a year, since the friends of James Fenimore Cooper, in this city, were planning to give a public dinner to his honor. It was intended as an expression both of the regard they bore him personally, and of the pride they took in the glory his writings had reflected on the American name. We thought of what we should say in his hearing; in what terms, worthy of him and of us, we should speak of the esteem in which we held him, and of the interest we felt in a fame which had already penetrated to the remotest nook of the earth inhabited by civilized man.

To-day we assemble for a sadder purpose: to pay to the dead some part of the honors then intended for the living. We bring our offering, but he is not here who should receive it; in his stead are vacancy and silence; there is no eye to brighten at our words, and no voice to answer. " It is an empty office that we perform," said Virgil, in his melodious verses, when commemorating the virtues of the young Marcellus, and bidding flowers be strewn, with full hands, over his early grave. We might apply the expression to the present occasion, but it would be true in part only. We can no longer do anything for him who is departed, but we may do what will not be without fruit to those who remain. It is good to occupy our thoughts with the example of eminent talents in conjunction with great virtues. His genius has passed away with him ; but we may learn, from the history of his life, to employ the faculties we possess with useful activity and noble aims ; we may copy his magnanimous frankness, his disdain of everything that wears the faintest semblance of deceit, his refusal to comply with current abuses, and the courage with which, on all occasions, he asserted what he deemed truth, and combated what he thought error.

The circumstances of Cooper's early life were remarkably suited to confirm the natural hardihood and manliness of his character, and to call forth and exercise that extraordinary power of observation, which accumulated the materials afterwards wielded and shaped by his genius. His father, while an inhabitant of Burlington, in New Jersey, on the pleasant banks of the Delaware, was the owner of large possessions on the borders of the Otsego Lake in our own State, and here, in the newly-cleared fields, he built, in 1786, the first house in Cooperstown. To this home, Cooper, who was born in Burlington, in the year 1789, was conveyed in his infancy, and here, as he informs us in his preface to the *Pioneers*, his first impressions of the external world were obtained. Here he passed his childhood, with the vast forest around him, stretching up the mountains that overlook the lake, and far beyond, in a region where the Indian yet roamed, and the white hunter, half Indian in his dress and mode of life, sought his game,—a region in which the bear and the wolf were yet hunted, and the panther, more formidable than either, lurked in the thickets, and tales of wanderings in the wilderness, and encounters with these fierce animals, beguiled the length of the winter nights. Of this place, Cooper, although early removed from it to pursue his studies, was an occasional resident throughout his life, and here his last years were wholly passed.

At the age of thirteen he was sent to Yale College, where, notwithstanding his extreme youth,—for, with the exception of the poet Hillhouse, he was the youngest of his class, and Hillhouse was afterwards withdrawn,—his progress in his studies is said to have been honorable to his talents. He left the college, after a residence of three years, and became a midshipman in the United States navy. Six years he followed the sea, and there yet wanders, among those who are fond of literary anecdote, a story of the young sailor who, in the streets of one of the English ports, attracted the curiosity of the crowd by explaining to his companions a Latin motto in some public place. That during this period he made himself master of the knowledge and the imagery which he afterwards employed to so much advantage in his romances of the sea, the finest ever written, is a common and obvious remark; but it has not been, so far as I know, observed that from the discipline of a seaman's life he may have derived much of his readiness and fertility of invention, much of his skill in surrounding the personages of his novels with imaginary perils, and rescuing them by probable expedients. Of all pursuits, the life of a sailor is that which familiarizes men to danger in its most fearful shapes, most cultivates presence of mind, and most effectually calls forth the resources of a prompt and fearless dexterity by which imminent evil is avoided.

In 1811, Cooper having resigned his post as midshipman, began the year by marrying Miss Delancy, sister of the present bishop of the diocese of Western

New York, and entered upon a domestic life happily passed to its close. He went to live at Mamaroneck, in the county of Westchester, and while here he wrote and published the first of his novels, entitled *Precaution.* Concerning the occasion of writing this work, it is related, that once as he was reading an English novel to Mrs. Cooper, who has, within a short time past, been laid in the grave beside her illustrious husband, and of whom we may now say, that her goodness was no less eminent than his genius, he suddenly laid down the book, and said, " I believe I could write a better myself." Almost immediately he composed a chapter of a projected work of fiction, and read it to the same friendly judge, who encouraged him to finish it, and when it was completed, suggested its publication. Of this he had at the time no intention, but he was at length induced to submit the manuscript to the examination of the late Charles Wilkes, of this city, in whose literary opinions he had great confidence. Mr. Wilkes advised that it should be published, and to these circumstances we owe it that Cooper became an author.

I confess I have merely dipped into this work. The experiment was made with the first edition, deformed by a strange punctuation—a profusion of commas, and other pauses, which puzzled and repel-

3

led me. Its author, many years afterwards, revised and republished it, correcting this fault, and some faults of style also, so that to a casual inspection it appeared almost another work. It was a professed delineation of English manners, though the author had then seen nothing of English society. It had, however, the honor of being adopted by the country whose manners it described, and, being early republished in Great Britain, passed from the first for an English novel. I am not unwilling to believe what is said of it, that it contained a promise of the powers which its author afterwards put forth.

Thirty years ago, in the year 1821, and in the thirty-second of his life, Cooper published the first of the works by which he will be known to posterity, the *Spy*. It took the reading world by a kind of surprise; its merit was acknowledged by a rapid sale; the public read with eagerness and the critics wondered. Many withheld their commendations on account of defects in the plot or blemishes in the composition, arising from want of practice, and some waited till they could hear the judgment of European readers. Yet there were not wanting critics in this country, of whose good opinion any author in any part of the world might be proud, who spoke of it in terms it deserved. " Are you not delighted," wrote a literary friend to me, who has since risen to high distinction as a writer, both in verse and in prose, " are you not delighted with the *Spy*, as a work of infinite spirit and genius?" In that word genius lay the explanation of the hold which the work had taken on the minds of men. What it had of excellence was peculiar and unborrowed; its pictures of life, whether in repose or activity, were drawn, with broad lights and shadows, immediately from living originals in nature or in his own imagination. To him whatever he described was true; it was made a reality to him by the strength with which he conceived it. His power in the delineation of character was shown in the principal personage of his story, Harvey Birch, on whom, though he has chosen to employ him in the ignoble office of a spy, and endowed him with the qualities necessary to his profession,—extreme circumspection, fertility in stratagem, and the art of concealing his real character—qualities which, in conjunction with selfishness and greediness, make the scoundrel, he has bestowed the virtues of generosity, magnanimity, an intense love of country, a fidelity not to be corrupted, and a disinterestedness beyond temptation. Out of this combination of qualities he has wrought a character which is a favorite in all nations, and with all classes of mankind.

It is said that if you cast a pebble into the ocean, at the mouth of our harbor, the vibration made in the water passes gradually on till it strikes the icy barriers of the deep at the south pole. The spread of Cooper's reputation is not confined within narrower limits. The *Spy* is read in all the written dialects of Europe, and in some of those of Asia. The French, immediately after its first appearance, gave it to the multitudes who read their far-diffused language, and placed it among the first works of its class. It was rendered into Castilian, and passed into the hands of those who dwell under the beams of the Southern Cross. At length it crossed the eastern frontier of Europe, and the latest record I have seen of its progress towards absolute universality, is contained in a statement of the *International Magazine*, derived, I presume, from its author, that in 1847 it was published in a Persian translation at Ispahan. Before this time, I doubt not, they are reading it in some of the languages of Hindostan, and, if the Chinese ever translated anything, it would be in the hands of the many millions who inhabit the far Cathay.

I have spoken of the hesitation which American critics felt in admitting the merits of the *Spy*, on account of crudities in the plot or the composition, some of which, no doubt, really existed. An excep-

tion must be made in favor of the *Port Folio* which
in a notice writen by Mrs. Sarah Hall, mother of the
editor of that periodical, and author of *Conversations
on the Bible*, gave the work a cordial welcome ; and
Cooper, as I am informed, never forgot this act of
timely and ready kindness.

It was perhaps favorable to the immediate success of the *Spy*, that Cooper had few American authors to divide with him the public attention.   That
crowd of clever men and women who now write for
the magazines, who send out volumes of essays,
sketches, and poems, and who supply the press with
novels, biographies, and historical works, were then,
for the most part, either stammering their lessons in
the schools, or yet unborn.   Yet it is worthy of note,
that just about the time that the *Spy* made its appearance, the dawn of what we now call our literature
was just breaking.   The concluding number of
Dana's *Idle Man*, a work neglected at first, but now
numbered among the best things of the kind in our
language, was issued in the same month.   The
Sketch Book was then just completed ; the world was
admiring it, and its author was meditating *Bracebridge Hall*.   Miss Sedgwick, about the same time,
made her first essay in that charming series of novels
of domestic life in New England, which have gained

her so high a reputation. Percival, now unhappily silent, had just put to press a volume of poems. I have a copy of an edition of Halleck's *Fanny*, published in the same year ; the poem of *Yamoyden*, by Eastburn and Sands, appeared almost simultaneously with it. Livingston was putting the finishing hand to his *Report on the Penal Code of Louisiana*, a work written with such grave, persuasive eloquence, that it belongs as much to our literature as to our jurisprudence. Other contemporaneous American works there were, now less read. Paul Allen's poem of *Noah* was just laid on the counters of the booksellers. Arden published, at the same time, in this city, a translation of Ovid's *Tristia*, in heroic verse, in which the complaints of the effeminate Roman poet were rendered with great fidelity to the original, and sometimes not without beauty. If I may speak of myself, it was in that year that I timidly intrusted to the winds and waves of public opinion a small cargo of my own—a poem entitled *The Ages*, and half a dozen shorter ones, in a thin duodecimo volume, printed at Cambridge.

We had, at the same time, works of elegant literature, fresh from the press of Great Britain, which are still read and admired. Barry Cornwall, then a young suitor for fame, published in the same year his *Mar-*

cia Colonna ; Byron, in the full strength and fertility of his genius, gave the readers of English his tragedy of *Marino Falicro,* and was in the midst of his spirited controversy with Bowles concerning the poetry of Pope. The *Spy* had to sustain a comparison with Scott's *Antiquary,* published simultaneously with it, and with Lockhart's *Valerius,* which seems to me one of the most remarkable works of fiction ever composed.

In 1823, and in his thirty-fourth year, Cooper brought out his novel of the *Pioneers,* the scene of which was laid on the borders of his own beautiful lake. In a recent survey of Mr. Cooper's works, by one of his admirers, it is intimated that the reputation of this work may have been in some degree factitious. I cannot think so; I cannot see how such a work could fail of becoming, sooner or later, a favorite. It was several years after its first appearance that I read the *Pioneers,* and I read it with a delighted astonishment. Here, said I to myself, is the poet of rural life in this country—our Hesiod, our Theocritus, except that he writes without the restraint of numbers, and is a greater poet than they. In the *Pioneers,* as in a moving picture, are made to pass before us the hardy occupations and spirited amusements of a prosperous settlement, in a fertile region, encompassed for leagues around with the primeval wilderness of woods. The seasons in their different aspects, bringing with them their different employments ; forests falling before the axe ; the cheerful population, with the first mild day of spring, engaged in the sugar orchards ; the chase of the deer through the deep woods, and into the lake ; turkey-shooting, during the Christmas holidays, in which the Indian marksman vied for the prize of skill with the white man ; swift sleigh rides under the bright winter sun, and perilous encounters with wild animals in the forests ; these, and other scenes of rural life, drawn, as Cooper knew how to draw them, in the bright and healthful coloring of which he was master, are interwoven with a regular narrative of human fortunes, not unskilfully constructed ; and how could such a work be otherwise than popular ?

In the *Pioneers*, Leatherstocking is first introduced—a philosopher of the woods, ignorant of books, but instructed in all that nature, without the aid of science, could reveal to the man of quick senses and inquiring intellect, whose life has been passed under the open sky, and in companionship with a race whose animal perceptions are the acutest and most cultivated of which there is any example. But Leatherstocking has higher qualities ; in him there is a genial blending of the gentlest virtues of the civilized man with the better nature of the aboriginal tribes ; all that in them is noble, generous, and ideal, is adopted into his own kindly character, and all that is evil is rejected. But why should I attempt to analyze a character so familiar ? Leatherstocking is acknowledged, on all hands, to be one of the noblest, as well as most striking and original creations of fiction. In some of his subsequent novels, Cooper—for he had not yet attained to the full maturity of his powers—heightened and ennobled his first conception of the character, but in the *Pioneers* it dazzled the world with the splendor of novelty.

His next work was the *Pilot*, in which he showed how, from the vicissitudes of a life at sea, its perils and escapes, from the beauty and terrors of the great deep, from the working of a vessel on a long voyage, and from the frank, brave, and generous, but peculiar character of the seamen, may be drawn materials of romance by which the minds of men may be as deeply moved as by anything in the power of romance to present. In this walk, Cooper has had many disciples, but no rival. All who have since written romances of the sea have been but travellers in a country of which he was the great discoverer; and none of them all seemed to have loved a ship as

3*

Cooper loved it, or have heen able so strongly to interest all classes of readers in its fortunes. Among other personages drawn with great strength in the *Pilot*, is the general favorite, Tom Coffin, the thorough seaman, with all the virtues and one or two of the infirmities of his profession, superstitious, as seamen are apt to be, yet whose superstitions strike us as but an irregular growth of his devout recognition of the Power who holds the ocean in the hollow of his hand ; true hearted, gentle, full of resources, collected in danger, and at last calmly perishing at the post of duty, with the vessel he has long guided, by what I may call a great and magnanimous death. His rougher and coarser companion, Boltrope, is drawn with scarcely less skill, and with a no less vigorous hand.

The *Pioneers* is not Cooper's best tale of the American forest, nor the *Pilot*, perhaps, in all respects, his best tale of the sea ; yet, if he had ceased to write here, the measure of his fame would possibly have been scarcely less ample than it now is. Neither of them is far below the best of his productions, and in them appear the two most remarkable creations of his imagination—two of the most remarkable characters in all fiction.

It was about this time that my acquaintance with Cooper began, an acquaintance of more than a quarter of a century, in which his deportment towards me was that of unvaried kindness. He then resided a considerable part of the year in this city, and here he had founded a weekly club, to which many of the most distinguished men of the place belonged. Of the members who have since passed away, were Chancellor Kent, the jurist; Wiley, the intelligent and liberal bookseller; Henry D. Sedgwick, always active in schemes of benevolence; Jarvis, the painter, a man of infinite humor, whose jests awoke inextinguishable laughter; De Kay, the naturalist; Sands, the poet; Jacob Harvey, whose genial memory is cherished by many friends. Of those who are yet living was Morse, the inventor of the electric telegraph; Durand, then one of the first of engravers, and now no less illustrious as a painter; Henry James Anderson, whose acquirements might awaken the envy of the ripest scholars of the old world; Halleck, the poet and wit; Verplanck, who has given the world the best edition of Shakspeare for general readers; Dr. King, now at the head of Columbia College, and his two immediate predecessors in that office. I might enlarge the list with many other names of no less distinction. The army and navy contributed their proportion of members, whose names are on record in our national history. Cooper when in town was always present, and I remember being struck with the inexhaustible vivacity of his conversation and the minuteness of his knowledge, in everything which depended upon acuteness of observation and exactness of recollection. I remember, too, being somewhat startled, coming as I did from the seclusion of a country life, with a certain emphatic frankness in his manner, which, however, I came at last to like and to admire. The club met in the hotel called Washington Hall, the site of which is now occupied by part of the circuit of Stewart's marble building.

Lionel Lincoln, which cannot be ranked among the successful productions of Cooper, was published in 1825; and in the year following appeared the *Last of the Mohicans*, which more than recovered the ground lost by its predecessor. In this work, the construction of the narrative has signal defects, but it is one of the triumphs of the author's genius that he makes us unconscious of them while we read. It is only when we have had time to awake from the intense interest in which he has held us by the vivid reality of his narrative, and have begun to search for faults in cold blood, that we are able to find them.

In the *Last of the Mohicans*, we have a bolder portraiture of Leatherstocking than in the *Pioneers*.

This work was published in 1826, and in the same year Cooper sailed with his family for Europe. He left New York as one of the vessels of war, described in his romances of the sea, goes out of port, amidst the thunder of a parting salute from the big guns on the batteries. A dinner was given him just before his departure, attended by most of the distinguished men of the city, at which Peter A. Jay presided, and Dr. King addressed him in terms which some then thought too glowing, but which would now seem sufficiently temperate, expressing the good wishes of his friends, and dwelling on the satisfaction they promised themselves in possessing so illustrious a representative of American literature in the old world. Cooper was scarcely in France when he remembered his friends of the weekly club, and sent frequent missives to be read at its meetings; but the club missed its founder, went into a decline, and not long afterwards quietly expired.

The first of Cooper's novels published after leaving America was the *Prairie*, which appeared early in 1827, a work with the admirers of which I wholly agree. I read it with a certain awe, an undefined sense of sublimity, such as one experiences on entering for the first time, upon those immense grassy deserts from which the work takes its name. The squatter and his family—that brawny old man and his large-limbed sons, living in a sort of primitive and patriarchal barbarism, sluggish on ordinary occasions, but terrible when roused, like the hurricane that sweeps the grand but monotonous wilderness in which they dwell—seem a natural growth of the ancient fields of the West. Leatherstocking, a hunter in the *Pioneers*, a warrior in the *Last of the Mohicans*, and now in his extreme old age, a trapper on the prairie, declined in strength but undecayed in intellect, and looking to the near close of his life and a grave under the long grass, as calmly as the laborer at sunset looks to his evening slumber, is no less in harmony with the silent desert in which he wanders. Equally so, are the Indians, still his companions, copies of the American savage somewhat idealized but not the less a part of the wild nature in which they have their haunts.

Before the year closed, Cooper had given the world another nautical tale, the *Red Rover*, which with many, is a greater favorite than the *Pilot*, and with reason, perhaps, if we consider principally the incidents, which are conducted and described with a greater mastery over the springs of pity and terror.

It happened to Cooper while he was abroad, as it not unfrequently happens to our countrymen, to hear the United States disadvantageously compared with Europe. He had himself been a close observer of things both here and in the old world, and was conscious of being able to refute the detractors of his country in regard to many points. He published, in 1828, after he had been two years in Europe, a series of letters, entitled *Notions of the Americans by a travelling Bachelor*, in which he gave a favorable account of the working of our institutions and vindicated his country from various flippant and ill-natured misrepresentations of foreigners. It is rather too measured in style, but is written from a mind full of the subject, and from a memory wonderfully stored with particulars. Although twenty-four years have elapsed since its publication, but little of the vindication has become obsolete.

Cooper loved his country and was proud of her history and her institutions, but it puzzles many that he should have appeared, at different times, as her eulogist and her censor. My friends, she is worthy both of praise and of blame, and Cooper was not the man to shrink from bestowing either, at what seemed to him the proper time. He defended her from detractors abroad; he sought to save her from flatterers at

home. I will not say that he was in as good-humor
with his country when he wrote *Home as Found*, as
when he wrote his *Notions of the Americans*, but
this I will say, that whether he commended or censured, he did it in the sincerity of his heart, as a true
American, and in the belief that it would do good.
His *Notions of the Americans* were more likely to
lessen than to increase his popularity in Europe,
inasmuch as they were put forth without the slightest
regard to European prejudices.

In 1829, he brought out the novel entitled *The
Wept of Wishton-Wish*, one of the few of his works
which we now rarely hear mentioned. He was engaged in the composition of a third nautical tale,
which he afterwards published under the name of the
Water-Witch, when the memorable revolution of the
Three Days of July broke out. He saw a government, ruling by fear and in defiance of public opinion,
overthrown in a few hours, with little bloodshed ; he
saw the French nation, far from being intoxicated
with their new liberty, peacefully addressing themselves to the discussion of the institutions under
which they were to live. A work which Cooper
afterwards published, his *Residence in Europe*, gives
the outline of a plan of government for France furnished by him at that time to La Fayette, with

whom he was in habits of close and daily intimacy. It was his idea to give permanence to the new order of things by associating two strong parties in its support, the friends of legitimacy and the republicans. He suggested that Henry V. should be called to the hereditary throne of France, a youth yet to be educated as the head of a free people, that the peerage should be abolished, and a legislature of two chambers established, with a constituency of at least a million and a half of electors; the senate to be chosen by the general vote, as the representative of the entire nation, and the members of the other house to be chosen by districts, as the representatives of the local interests. To the middle ground of politics so ostentatiously occupied by Louis Philippe at the beginning of his reign, he predicted a brief duration, believing that it would speedily be merged in despotism, or supplanted by the popular rule. His prophecy has been fulfilled more amply than he could have imagined—fulfilled in both its alternatives.

In one of the controversies of that time, Cooper bore a distinguished part. The *Revue Britannique,* a periodical published in Paris, boldly affirmed the government of the United States to be one of the most expensive in the world, and its people among the most heavily taxed of mankind. This assertion was supported with a certain show of proof, and the writer affected to have established the conclusion that a republic must necessarily be more expensive than a monarchy. The partisans of the court were delighted with the reasoning of the article, and claimed a triumph over our ancient friend La Fayette, who, during forty years, had not ceased to hold up the government of the United States as the cheapest in the world. At the suggestion of La Fayette, Cooper replied to this attack upon his country in a letter which was translated into French, and, together with another from General Bertrand, for many years a resident in America, was laid before the people of France.

These two letters provoked a shower of rejoiners, in which, according to Cooper, misstatements were mingled with scurrility. He commenced a series of letters on the question in dispute, which were published in the *National,* a daily sheet, and gave the first evidence of that extraordinary acuteness in controversy which was no 'ess characteristic of his mind than the vigor of his imagination. The enemies of La Fayette pressed into their service Mr. Leavitt Harris, of New Jersey, afterwards our *chargé d'affaires* at the court of France, but Cooper replied to Mr. Harris in the *National* of May 2d, 1832, closing a discussion in which he had effectually silenced those who objected to our institutions on the score of economy. Of these letters, which would form an important chapter in political science, no entire copy, I have been told, is to be found in this country.

One of the consequences of earnest controversy is almost invariably personal ill-will. Cooper was told by one who held an official station under the French government, that the part he had taken in this dispute concerning taxation would neither be forgotten nor forgiven. The dislike he had incurred in that quarter was strengthened by his novel of the *Bravo*, published in the year 1831, while he was in the midst of his quarrel with the aristocratic party. In that work, of which he has himself justly said that it was thoroughly American in all that belonged to it, his object was to show how institutions, professedly created to prevent violence and wrong, become, when perverted from their natural destination, the instruments of injustice; and how, in every system which makes power the exclusive property of the strong, the weak are sure to be oppressed. The work is written with all the vigor and spirit of his best novels; the magnificent city of Venice, in which the scene of the story is laid, stands continually before the imagination; and from time to time the gorgcous ceremonies of the Venetian republic pass under our eyes, such as the marriage of the Doge with the Adriatic, and the contest of the gondolas for the prize of speed. The Bravo himself and several of the other characters are strongly conceived and distinguished, but the most remarkable of them all is the spirited and generous-hearted daughter of the jailer.

It has been said by some critics, who judge of Cooper by his failures, that he had no skill in drawing female characters. By the same process, it might, I suppose, be shown that Raphael was but an ordinary painter. It must be admitted that when Cooper drew a lady of high breeding, he was apt to pay too much attention to the formal part of her character, and to make her a mere bundle of cold proprieties. But when he places his heroines in some situations in life which leaves him nothing to do but to make them natural and true, I know of nothing finer, nothing more attractive or more individual than the portraitures he has given us.

Figaro, the wittiest of the French periodicals, and at that time on the liberal side, commended the *Bravo*, the journals on the side of the government censured it. *Figaro* afterwards passed into the hands of the aristocratic party, and Cooper became the object of its attacks : he was not, however, a man to be driven from any purpose which he had formed, either by flattery or abuse, and both were tried with equal ill success. In 1832 he published his *Heidenmauer*, and in 1833 his *Headsman of Berne*, both with a political design similar to that of the *Bravo*, though neither of them takes the same high rank among his works.

In 1833, after a residence of seven years in different parts of Europe, but mostly in France, Cooper returned to his native country. The welcome which met him here was somewhat chilled by the effect of the attacks made upon him in France, and remembering with what zeal, and at what sacrifice of the universal acceptance which his works would otherwise have met, he had maintained the cause of his country against the wits and orators of the court party in France, we cannot wonder that he should have felt this coldness as undeserved. He published, shortly after his arrival in this country, *A letter to his Countrymen* in which he complained of the censures cast upon him in the American newspapers, gave a history of the part he had taken in exposing the misstatements of the *Revue Britannique*, and warned his countrymen against the too common error of resorting, with a blind deference, to foreign authorities, often swayed by national or political prejudices, for our opinions of American authors. Going beyond this topic, he examined and reprehended the habit of applying to the interpretation of our own constitution maxims derived from the practice of other governments, particularly that of Great Britain. The importance of construing that instrument by its own principles, he illustrated by considering several points in dispute between parties of the day, on which he gave very decided opinions.

The principal effect of this pamphlet, as it seemed to me, was to awaken in certain quarters a kind of resentment that a successful writer of fiction should presume to give lessons in politics. I meddle not here with the conclusions to which he arrived, though must be allowed to say that they were stated and argued with great ability. In 1835 Cooper published The *Monnikins*, a satirical work, partly with a political aim ; and in the same year appeared the *American Democrat*, a view of the civil and social relations of the United States, discussing more gravely various topics touched upon in the former work, and pointing out in what respects he deemed the American people in their practice to have fallen short of the excellence of their institutions.

He found time, however, for a more genial task— that of giving to the world his observations on foreign countries. In 1836 appeared his *Sketches of Swit-zerland*, a series of letters in four volumes, the second part published about two months after the first, a delightful work, written in a more fluent and flexible style than his *Notions of the Americans*. The first part of *Gleanings in Europe*, giving an account of his residence in France, followed in the same year; and the second part of the same work, containing his observations on England, was published in April, 1837. In these works, forming a series of eight volumes, he relates and describes with much of the same distinctness as in his novels; and his remarks on the manners and institutions of the different countries, often sagacious, and always peculiarly his own, derive, from their frequent reference to contemporary events, an historical interest.

In 1838 appeared *Homeward Bound* and *Home as Found*, two satirical novels, in which Cooper held up to ridicule a certain class of conductors of the newspaper press in America. These works had not the good fortune to become popular. Cooper did not, and, because he was too deeply in earnest, perhaps would not, infuse into his satirical works that gayety without which satire becomes wearisome. I believe, however, that if they had been written by anybody else, they would have met with more favor; but the

world knew that Cooper was able to give them something better, and would not be satisfied with anything
short of his best.   Some childishly imagined that because, in the two works I have just mentioned, a
newspaper editor is introduced, in whose character
almost every possible vice of his profession is made
to find a place, Cooper intended an indiscriminate attack upon the whole body of writers for the newspaper press, forgetting that such a portraiture was a
satire only on those to whom it bore a likeness.   We
have become less sensitive and more reasonable of
late, and the monthly periodicals make sport for their
readers of the follies and ignorance of the newspaper
editors, without awakening the slightest resentment ;
but Cooper led the way into this sort of discipline, and
I remember some instances of towering indignation
at his audacity expressed in the journals of that time.

The next year Cooper made his appearance before the public in a new department of writing ; his
Naval History of the United States was brought out
in two octavo volumes at Philadelphia, by Carey and
Lea.   In writing his stories of the sea, his attention
had been much turned to this subject, and his mind
filled with striking incidents from expeditions and
battles in which our naval commanders had been engaged.   This made his task the lighter ; but he

gathered his materials with great industry, and with a conscientious attention to exactness, for he was not a man to take a fact for granted, or allow imagination to usurp the place of inquiry. He digested our naval annals into a narrative, written with spirit it is true, but with that air of sincere dealing which the reader willingly takes as a pledge of its authenticity.

An abridgment of the work was afterwards prepared and published by the author. The *Edinburgh Review*, in an article professing to examine the statements both of Cooper's work and of *The History of the English Navy*, written by Mr. James, a surgeon by profession, made a violent attack upon the American historian. Unfortunately, it took James's narrative as its sole guide, and followed it implicitly, Cooper replied in the *Democratic Review* for January, 1840, and by a masterly analysis of his statements, convicting James of self-contradiction in almost every particular in which he differed from himself, refuted both James and the reviewer. It was a refutation which admitted of no rejoinder.

Scarce anything in Cooper's life was so remarkable, or so strikingly illustrated his character, as his contest with the newspaper press. He engaged in it after provocations, many and long-endured, and prosecuted it through years with great energy, perseverance, and practical dexterity, till he was left master of the field. In what I am about to say of it, I hope I shall not give offence to any one, as I shall speak without the slightest malevolence towards those with whom he waged this controversy. Over some of them, as over their renowned adversary, the grave has now closed. Yet where shall the truth be spoken, if not beside the grave?

I have already alluded to the principal causes which provoked the newspaper attacks upon Cooper. If he had never meddled with questions of government on either side of the Atlantic, and never satirized the newspaper press, I have little doubt that he would have been spared these attacks. I cannot, however, ascribe them all, or even the greater part of them, to personal malignity. One journal followed the example of another, with little reflection, I think, in most cases, till it became a sort of fashion, not merely to decry his works, but to arraign his motives.

It is related that, in 1832, while he was at Paris, an article was shown him in an American newspaper, purporting to be a criticism on one of his works, but reflecting with much asperity on his personal character. "I care nothing," he is reported to have said, "for the criticism, but I am not indifferent to the slander. If these attacks on my character should be kept up five years after my return to America, I shall resort to the New York courts for protection." He gave the newspaper press of this State the full period of forbearance on which he had fixed, but finding that forbearance seemed to encourage assault, he sought redress in the courts of law.

When these litigations were first begun, I recollect it seemed to me that Cooper had taken a step which would give him a great deal of trouble, and effect but little good. I said to myself—

" Alas! Leviathan is not so tamed ! "

As he proceeded, however, I saw that he had understood the matter better than I. He put a hook into the nose of this huge monster, wallowing in his inky pool and bespattering the passers-by : he dragged him to the land and made him tractable. One suit followed another ; one editor was sued, I think, half-a-dozen times ; some of them found themselves under a second indictment before the first was tried. In vindicating himself to his reader, against the charge of publishing one libel, the angry journalist often floundered into another. The occasions of these prosecutions seem to have been always carefully considered, for Cooper was almost uniformly successful in obtaining verdicts. In a letter of his, written in

February, 1843, about five years, I think, from the commencement of the first prosecutions, he says, " I have beaten every man I have sued, who has not retracted his libels."

In one of these suits, commenced against the late William L. Stone of the *Commercial Advertiser*, and referred to the arbitration of three distinguished lawyers, he argued himself the question of the authenticity of his account of the battle of Lake Erie, which was the matter in dispute. I listened to his opening ; it was clear, skilful, and persuasive, but his closing argument was said to be splendidly eloquent. " I have heard nothing like it," said a barrister to me, " since the days of Emmet."

Cooper behaved liberally towards his antagonists, so far as pecuniary damages were concerned, though some of them wholly escaped their payment by bankruptcy. After, I believe, about six years of litigation, the newspaper press gradually subsided into a pacific disposition towards its adversary, and the contest closed with the account of pecuniary profit and loss, so far as he was concerned, nearly balanced. The occasion of these suits was far from honorable to those who provoked them, but the result was, I had almost said, creditable to all parties ; to him, as the courageous prosecutor, to the administration of justice in this country, and to the docility of the news-paper press, which he had disciplined into good man-ners.

It was while he was in the midst of these litiga-tions, that he published, in 1840, the *Pathfinder.* People had begun to think of him as a controver-sialist, acute, keen, and persevering, occupied with his personal wrongs and schemes of attack and defence. They were startled from this estimate of his character by the moral duty of that glorious work—I must so call it; by the vividness and force of its delineations, by the unspoiled love of nature apparent in every page, and by the fresh and warm emotions which everywhere gave life to the narrative and the dia-logue. Cooper was now in his fifty-first year, but nothing which he had produced in the earlier part of his literary life was written with so much of what might seem the generous fervor of youth, or showed the faculty of invention in higher vigor. I recollect that near the time of its appearance I was informed of an observation made upon it by one highly distin-guished in the literature of our country and of the age, between whom and the author an unhappy cool-ness had for some years existed. As he finished the reading of the Pathfinder, he exclaimed, " They may say what they will of Cooper; the man who wrote this book is not only a great man, but a good man."

The readers of the *Pathfinder* were quickly reconciled to the fourth appearance of Leatherstocking, when they saw him made to act a different part from any which the author had hitherto assigned him—when they saw him shown as a lover, and placed in the midst of associations which invested his character with a higher and more affecting heroism. In this work are two female characters, portrayed in a masterly manner,—the corporal's daughter, Mabel Dunham, generous, resolute, yet womanly, and the young Indian woman, called by her tribe the Dew of June, a personification of female truth, affection, and sympathy, with a strong aboriginal cast, yet a product of nature as bright and pure as that from which she is named.

Mercedes of Castile, published near the close of the same year, has none of the stronger characteristics of Cooper's genius ; but in the *Deerslayer*, which appeared in 1841, another of his Leatherstocking tales, he gave us a work rivalling the Pathfinder. Leatherstocking is brought before us in his early youth, in the first exercise of that keen sagacity which is blended so harmoniously with a simple and ingenuous goodness. The two daughters of the retired freebooter dwelling on the Otsego lake, inspire scarcely less interest than the principal personage ; Judith, in the pride of her beauty and intellect, her good impulses contending with a fatal love of admiration, holding us fascinated with a constant interest in her fate, which, with consummate skill, we are permitted rather to conjecture than to know ; and Hetty, scarcely less beautiful in person, weak-minded, but wise in the midst of that weakness beyond the wisdom of the loftiest intellect, through the power of conscience and religion. The character of Hetty would have been a hazardous experiment in feebler hands, but in his it was admirably successful.

The *Two Admirals* and *Wing-and-Wing* were given to the public in 1842, both of them taking a high rank among Cooper's sea-tales. The first of these is a sort of naval epic in prose ; the flight and chase of armed vessels hold us in breathless suspense, the sea-fights are described with a terrible power. In the later sea-tales of Cooper, it seems to me that the mastery with which he makes his grand processions of events pass before the mind's eye is even greater than in his earlier. The next year he published the *Wyandotte or Hutted Knoll*, one of his beautiful romances of the woods, and in 1844 two more of his sea-stories, *Afloat and Ashore* and *Miles*

Wallingford its sequel. The long series of his nautical tales was closed by *Jack Tier or the Florida
Reef*, published in 1848, when Cooper was in his
sixtieth year, and it is as full of spirit, energy, invention, life-like presentation of objects and events—

The vision and the faculty divine—

as anything he has written.

Let me pause here to say that Cooper, though not
a manufacturer of verse, was in the highest sense of
the word a poet ; his imagination wrought nobly and
grandly, and imposed its creations on the mind of the
reader for realities. With him there was no wither-
ing, or decline, or disuse of the poetic faculty : as he
stepped downwards from the zenith of life, no shadow or chill came over it ; it was like the year of some
genial climates, a perpetual season of verdure, bloom,
and fruitfulness. As these works came out, I was
rejoiced to see that he was unspoiled by the controversies in which he had allowed himself to become
engaged ; that they had not given, to these better
expressions of his genius, any tinge of misanthropy,
or appearance of contracting and closing sympathies,
any trace of an interest in his fellow-beings less large
and free than in his earlier works.

Before the appearance of his *Jack Tier*, Cooper

published, in 1845 and the following year, a series of novels relating to the Anti-rent question, in which he took great interest. He thought that the disposition manifested in certain quarters to make concessions to what he deemed a denial of the rights of property was a first step in a most dangerous path. To discourage this disposition, he wrote *Satanstoe*, *The Chainbearer*, and *The Red-skins*. They are didactic in their design, and want the freedom of invention which belongs to Cooper's best novels; but if they had been written by anybody but Cooper,—by a member of Congress, for example, or an eminent politician of any class,—they would have made his reputation. It was said, I am told, by a distinguished jurist of our state, that they entitled the author to as high a place in law as his other works had won for him in literature.

I had thought, in meditating the plan of this discourse, to mention all the works of Mr. Cooper, but the length to which I have found it extending has induced me to pass over several written in the last ten years of his life, and to confine myself to those which best illustrate his literary character. The last of his novels was *The Ways of the Hour*, a work in which the objections he entertained to the trial by jury in civil causes were stated in the form of a narrative.

4*

It is a voluminous catalogue—that of Cooper's published works—but it comprises not all he wrote. He committed to the fire, without remorse, many of the fruits of his literary industry. It was understood, some years since, that he had a work ready for the press on the *Middle States of the Union*, principally illustrative of their social history; but it has not been found among his manuscripts, and the presumption is that he must have destroyed it. He had planned a work on the *Towns of Manhattan*, for the publication of which he made arrangements with Mr. Putman of this city, and a part of which, already written, was in press at the time of his death. The printed part has since been destroyed by fire, but a portion of the manuscript was recovered. The work, I learn, will be completed by one of the family, who, within a few years past, has earned an honorable name among the authors of our country. Great as was the number of his works, and great as was the favor with which they were received, the pecuniary rewards of his success were far less than has been generally supposed—scarcely, as I am informed, a tenth part of what the common rumor made them. His fame was infinitely the largest acknowledgment which this most successful of American authors received for his labors.

The Ways of the Hour appeared in 1850. At this time his personal appearance was remarkable. He seemed in perfect health, and in the highest energy and activity of his faculties. I have scarcely seen any man at that period of life on whom his years sat more lightly. His conversation had lost none of its liveliness, though it seemed somewhat more genial and forbearing in tone, and his spirits none of their elasticity. He was contemplating, I have since been told, another Leatherstocking tale, deeming that he had not yet exhausted the character; and those who consider what new resources it yielded him in the *Pathfinder* and the *Deerslayer*, will readily conclude that he was not mistaken.

The disease, however, by which he was removed, was even then impending over him, and not long afterwards his friends here were grieved to learn that his health was declining. He came to New York so changed that they looked at him with sorrow, and after a stay of some weeks, partly for the benefit of medical advice, returned to Cooperstown, to leave it no more. His complaint gradually gained strength, subdued a constitution originally robust, and finally passed into a confirmed dropsy. In August, 1851, he was visited by his excellent and learned friend, Dr. Francis, a member of the weekly club which he had founded in the early part of his literary career. He found him bearing the sufferings of his disease with manly firmness, gave him such medical counsels as the malady appeared to require, prepared him delicately for its fatal termination, and returned to New York with the most melancholy anticipations. In a few days afterwards, Cooper expired, amid the deep affliction of his family, on the 14th of September, the day before that on which he should have completed his sixty-second year. He died, apparently without pain, in peace and religious hope. The relations of man to his Maker, and to that state of being for which the present is but a preparation, had occupied much of his thoughts during his whole lifetime, and he crossed, with a serene composure, the mysterious. boundary which divides this life from the next.

The departure of such a man, in the full strength of his faculties,—on whom the country had for thirty years looked as one of the permanent ornaments of its literature, and whose name had been so often associated with praise, with renown, with controversy, with blame, but never with death,—diffused a universal awe. It was as if an earthquake had shaken the ground on which we stood, and showed the grave opening by our path. In the general grief for his

loss, his virtues only were remembered, and his failings forgotten.

Of his failings I have said little ; such as he had
were obvious to all the world ; they lay on the surface of his character ; those who knew him least made
the most account of them. With a character so made
up of positive qualities—a character so independent
and uncompromising, and with a sensitiveness far
more acute than he was willing to acknowledge, it is
not surprising that occasions frequently arose to bring
him, sometimes into friendly collision, and sometimes
into graver disagreements and misunderstandings
with his fellow-men. For his infirmities, his friends
found an ample counterpoise in the generous sincerity of his nature. He never thought of disguising his
opinions, and he abhorred all disguise in others ; he
did not even deign to use that show of regard towards
those of whom he did not think well, which the world
tolerates, and almost demands. A manly expression
of opinion, however different from his own, command-
ed his respect./ Of his own works, he spoke with the
same freedom as of the works of others ; and never
hesitated to express his judgment of a book for the
reason that it was written by himself ; yet he could
bear with gentleness any dissent from the estimate
he placed on his own writings. His character was

like the bark of the cinnamon, a rough and astringent rind without, and an intense sweetness within. Those who penetrated below the surface found a genial temper, warm affections, and a heart with ample place for his friends, their pursuits, their good name, their welfare. They found him a philanthropist, though not precisely after the fashion of the day; a religious man, most devout where devotion is most apt to be a feeling rather than a custom, in the household circle; hospitable, and to the extent of his means liberal-handed in acts of charity. They found, also, that though in general he would as soon have thought of giving up an old friend as of giving up an opinion, he was not proof against testimony, and could part with a mistaken opinion as one parts with an old friend who has been proved faithless and unworthy. In short, Cooper was one of those who, to be loved, must be intimately known.

Of his literary character I have spoken largely in the narrative of his life, but there are yet one or two remarks which must be made to do it justice. In that way of writing in which he excelled, it seems to me that he united in a pre-eminent degree, those qualities which enabled him to interest the largest number of readers. He wrote not for the fastidious, the over-refined, the morbidly delicate; for these find in his

genius something too robust for their liking—something by which their sensibilities are too rudely
shaken ; but he wrote for mankind at large—for men
and women in the ordinary healthful state of feeling—and in their admiration he found his reward. It
is for this class that public libraries are obliged to
provide themselves with an extraordinary number of
copies of his works : the number in the Mercantile
Library in this city, I am told, is forty. Hence it is,
that he has earned a fame, wider, I think, than any
author of modern times—wider, certainly, than any
author, of any age, ever enjoyed in his lifetime. All
his excellences are translatable—they pass readily
into languages the least allied in their genius to that
in which he wrote, and in them he touches the heart
and kindles the imagination with the same power as
in the original English.

Cooper was not wholly without humor; it is
sometimes found lurking in the dialogue of Harvey
Birch, and of Leatherstocking ; but it forms no considerable element in his works ; and if it did, it would
have stood in the way of his universal popularity,
since of all qualities, it is the most difficult to trans-
fuse into a foreign language. Nor did the effect he
produced upon the reader depend on any grace of
style which would escape a translator of ordinary

skill. With his style, it is true, he took great pains, and in his earlier works, I am told, sometimes altered the proofs sent from the printer so largely that they might be said to be written over. Yet he attained no special felicity, variety, or compass of expression. His style, however, answered his purpose; it has defects, but it is manly and clear, and stamps on the mind of the reader the impression he intended to convey. I am not sure that some of the very defects of Cooper's novels do not add, by a certain force of contrast, to their power over the mind. He is long in getting at the interest of his narrative. The progress of the plot, at first, is like that of one of his own vessels of war, slowly, heavily, and even awkwardly working out of a harbor. We are impatient and weary, but when the vessel is once in the open sea, and feels the free breath of heaven in her full sheets, our delight and admiration is all the greater at the grace, the majesty, and power with which she divides and bears down the waves, and pursues her course, at will, over the great waste of waters.

Such are the works so widely read, and so universally admired, in all the zones of the globe, and by men of every kindred and every tongue; works which have made of those who dwell in remote latitudes, wanderers in our forests, and observers of our manners, and have inspired them with an interest in our history. A gentleman who had returned from Europe just before the death of Cooper, was asked what he found the people of the Continent doing. " They all are reading Cooper," he answered; "in the little kingdom of Holland, with its three millions of inhabitants, I looked into four different translations of Cooper in the language of the country." A traveller, who has seen much of the middle classes of Italy, lately said to me, " I found that all they knew of America, and that was not little, they had learned from Cooper's novels; from him they had learned the story of American liberty, and through him they had been introduced to our Washington; they had read his works till the shores of the Hudson, and the valleys of Westchester, and the banks of Otsego lake, had become to them familiar ground."

Over all the countries into whose speech this great man's works have been rendered by the labors of their scholars, the sorrow of that loss which we deplore is now diffusing itself. Here we lament the ornament of our country, there they mourn the death of him who delighted the human race. Even now, while I speak, the pulse of grief which is passing through the nations has haply just reached some remote neighborhood ; the news of his death has been brought to some dwelling on the slopes of the Andes, or amidst the snowy wastes of the North, and the dark-eyed damsel of Chile, or the fair-haired maid of Norway, is sad to think that he whose stories of heroism and true love have so often kept her for hours from her pillow, lives no more.

He is gone! but the creations of his genius, fixed in living words, survive the frail material organs by which the words were first traced. They partake of a middle nature, between the deathless mind and the decaying body of which they are the common offspring, and are, therefore, destined to a duration, if not eternal, yet indefinite. The examples he has given in his glorious fictions, of heroism, honor, and truth, of large sympathies between man and man, of all that is good, great, and excellent, embodied in personages marked with so strong an individuality that we place them among our friends and favorites; his frank and generous men, his gentle and noble women, shall live through centuries to come, and only perish with our language. I have said with our language; but who shall say when it may be the fate of the English language to be numbered with the extinct forms of human speech? Who shall declare which of the present tongues of the civilized world will survive its fellows? It may be that some one of them, more fortunate than the rest, will long outlast them, in some undisturbed quarter of the globe, and in the midst of a new civilization. The creations of Cooper's genius, even now transferred to that language, may remain to be the delight of the nations through another great cycle of centuries, beginning after the English language and its contemporaneous form of civilization shall have passed away.

WASHINGTON IRVING.

WASHINGTON IRVING.

A DISCOURSE ON HIS LIFE, CHARACTER AND GENIUS, DELIV-
ERED BEFORE THE NEW YORK HISTORICAL SOCIETY, AT
THE ACADEMY OF MUSIC, IN NEW YORK, APRIL 3, 1860.

We have come together, my friends, on the birthday of an illustrious citizen of our republic, but so recent is his departure from among us, that our assembling is rather an expression of sorrow for his death
than of congratulation that such a man was born into
the world. His admirable writings, the beautiful products of his peculiar genius, remain to be the enjoyment of the present and future generations. We
keep the recollection of his amiable and blameless
life and his kindly manners, and for these we give
thanks ; but the thought will force itself upon us that
the light of his friendly eye is quenched, that we
must no more hear his beloved voice nor take his
welcome hand. It is as if some genial year had just
closed and left us in frost and gloom ; its flowery
spring, its leafy summer, its plenteous autumn, flown,
never to return. Its gifts are strewn around us ; its
harvests are in our garners ; but its season of bloom,

and warmth, and fruitfulness is past. We look around us and see that the sunshine, which filled the the golden ear and tinged the reddening apple, brightens the earth no more.

Twelve years since, the task was assigned me to deliver the funeral eulogy of Thomas Cole, the great father of landscape painting in America, the artist who first taught the pencil to portray, with the boldness of nature, our wild forests and lake shores, our mountain regions and the borders of our majestic rivers. Four years later I was bidden to express, in such terms as I could command, the general sorrow which was felt for the death of Fenimore Cooper, equally great and equally the leader of his countrymen in a different walk of creative genius. Another grave has been opened, and he who has gone down to it, earlier than they in his labors and his fame, was, like them, foremost in the peculiar walk to which his genius attracted him. Cole was taken from us in the zenith of his manhood; Cooper, when the sun of life had stooped from its meridian. In both instances the day was darkened by the cloud of death before the natural hour of its close; but Irving was permitted to behold its light until, in the fulness of time and by the ordinary appointment of nature, it was carried below the horizon.

Washington Irving was born in New York, on the third of April, 1783, but a few days after the news of the treaty with Great Britain, acknowledging our independence, had been received, to the great contentment of the people. He opened his eyes to the light, therefore, just in the dawn of that Sabbath of peace which brought rest to the land after a weary seven years' war—just as the city of which he was a native, and the republic of which he was yet to be the ornament, were entering upon a career of greatness and prosperity of which those who inhabited them could scarce have dreamed. It seems fitting that one of the first births of the new peace, so welcome to the country, should be that of a genius as kindly and fruitful as peace itself, and destined to make the world better and happier by its gentle influences. In one respect, those who were born at that time had the advantage of those who are educated under the more vulgar influences of the present age. Before their eyes, were placed, in the public actions of the men who achieved our revolution, noble examples of steady rectitude, magnanimous self-denial, and cheerful self-sacrifice for the sake of their country. Irving came into the world when these great and virtuous men were in the prime of their manhood, and passed his youth in the midst of

5

that general reverence which gathered round them as they grew old.

William Irving, the father of the great author, was a native of Scotland—one of a race in which the instinct of veneration is strong—and a Scottish woman was employed as a nurse in his household. It is related that one day while she was walking in the street with her little charge, then five years old, she saw General Washington in a shop, and entering, led up the boy, whom she presented as one to whom his name had been given. The general turned, laid his hand on the child's head, and gave him his smile and his blessing, little thinking that they were bestowed upon his future biographer. The gentle pressure of that hand Irving always remembered, and that blessing, he believed, attended him through life. Who shall say what power that recollection may have had in keeping him true to high and generous aims?

At the time that Washington Irving was born, the city of New York contained scarcely more than twenty thousand inhabitants. During the war its population had probably diminished. The town was scarcely built up to Warren street; Broadway, a little beyond, was lost among grassy pastures and tilled fields; the Park, in which now stands our City Hall, was an open common, and beyond it gleamed, in a hollow among the meadows, a little sheet of fresh water, the Kolch, from which a sluggish rivulet stole through the low grounds called Lispenard's Meadows. and, following the course of what is now Canal street, entered the Hudson. With the exception of the little corner of the island below the present City Hall, the rural character of the whole region was unchanged, and the fresh air of the country entered New York at every street. The town at that time contained a mingled population, drawn from different countries; but the descendants of the old Dutch settlers formed a large proportion of the inhabitants, and these preserved many of their peculiar customs, and had not ceased to use the speech of their ancestors at their fireside. Many of them lived in the quaint old houses, built of small yellow bricks from Holland, with their notched gable-ends on the street, which have since been swept away with the language of those who built them.

In the surrounding country, along its rivers and beside its harbors, and in many parts far inland, the original character of the Dutch settlements was still less changed. Here they read their Bibles and said their prayers and listened to sermons in the ancestral tongue. Remains of this language yet linger in a few neighborhoods; but in most, the common schools, and the irruptions of the Yankee race, and the growth of a population newly derived from Europe, have stifled the ancient utterances of New Amsterdam. I remember that, twenty years since, the market people of Bergen chattered Dutch in the steamers which brought them in the early morning to New York. I remember also that, about ten years before, there were families in the westernmost towns of Massachusetts where Dutch was still the household tongue, and matrons of the English stock, marrying into them, were laughed at for speaking it so badly.

It will be readily inferred that the isolation in which the use of a language, strange to the rest of the country, placed these people, would form them in a character of peculiar simplicity, in which there was a great deal that was quaint and not a little that would appear comic to their neighbors of the Anglo-Saxon stock. It was in the midst of such a population, friendly and hospitable, wearing their faults on the outside, and living in homely comfort on their fertile and ample acres, that the boyhood and early youth of Irving were passed. He began, while yet a stripling, to wander about the surrounding country, for the love of rambling was the most remarkable peculiarity of that period of his life. He became, as he himself writes, familiar with all the neighboring places famous in history or fable ; knew every spot where a murder or a robbery had been committed or a ghost seen ; strolled into the villages, noted their customs and talked with their sages, a welcome guest doubtless, with his kindly and ingenuous manners and the natural playful turn of his conversation.

I dwell upon these particulars because they help to show how the mind of Irving was trained, and by what process he made himself master of the materials afterward wrought into the forms we so much admire.   It was in these rambles that his strong love of nature was awakened and nourished.   Those who only know the island of New York as it now is, see few traces of the beauty it wore before it was levelled and smoothed from side to side for the builder.   Immediately without the little town, it was charmingly diversified with heights and hollows, groves alternating with sunny openings, shining tracks of rivulets, quiet country-seats with trim gardens, broad avenues of trees, and lines of pleached hawthorn hedges.   I came to New York in 1825, and I well recollect how much I admired the shores of the Hudson above Canal street, where the dark rocks jutted far out in the water, with little bays between, above which drooped forest trees overrun with wild vines. No less beautiful were the shores of the East River, where the orchards of the Stuyvesant estate reached to cliffs beetling over the water, and still further on were inlets between rocky banks bristling with red cedars. Some idea of this beauty may be formed from looking at what remains of the natural shore of New York island, where the tides of the East River rush to and fro by the rocky verge of Jones' Wood.

Here wandered Irving in his youth, and allowed the aspect of that nature which he afterward portrayed so well to engrave itself on his heart; but his excursions were not confined to this island. He became familiar with the banks of the Hudson, the extraordinary beauty of which he was the first to describe. He made acquaintance with the Dutch neighborhoods sheltered by its hills, Nyack, Haverstraw, Sing Sing, and Sleepy Hollow, and with the majestic Highlands beyond. His rambles in another direction led him to ancient Communipaw, lying in its quiet recess by New York bay; to the then peaceful Gowanus, now noisy with the passage of visitors to Greenwood and thronged with funerals; to Hoboken, Horsimus and Paulus Hook, which has since become a city. A ferry-boat dancing on the rapid tides took him over to Brooklyn, now our flourishing and beautiful neighbor city; then a cluster of Dutch farms, whose possessors lived in broad, low houses, with stoops in front, over-shadowed by trees.

The generation with whom Irving grew up read the *Spectator* and the *Rambler*, the essays and tales of Mackenzie and those of Goldsmith; the novels of the day were those of Richardson, Fielding and Smollett; the religious world were occupied with the pages of Hannah More, fresh from the press, and with the writings of Doddridge; politicians sought their models of style and reasoning in the speeches of Burke and the writings of Mackintosh and Junius. These were certainly masters of whom no pupil needed to be ashamed, but it can hardly be said that the style of Irving was formed in the school of any of them. His father's library was enriched with authors of the Elizabethan age, and he delighted, we are told, in reading Chaucer and Spenser. The elder of these great poets might have taught him the art of heightening his genial humor with poetic graces, and from both he might have learned a freer mastery over his native English than the somewhat formal taste of that day encouraged. Cowper's poems, at that time, were in everybody's hands, and if his father had not those of Burns, we must believe that he was no Scotchman. I think we may fairly infer that if the style of Irving took a bolder range than was allowed in the way of writing which prevailed when he was a youth, it was owing, in a great degree, to his studies in the poets, and especially in those of the earlier English literature.

He owed little to the schools, though he began to attend them early. His first instructions were given when he was between four and six years old, by Mrs. Ann Kilmaster, at her school in Ann street, who seems to have had some difficulty in getting him through the alphabet. In 1789, he was transferred to a school in Fulton street, then called Partition street, kept by Benjamin Romaine, who had been a soldier in the Revolution—a sensible man and a good disciplinarian, but probably an indifferent scholar—and here he continued till he was fourteen years of age. He was a favorite with the master, but preferred reading to regular study. At ten years of age he delighted in the wild tales of Ariosto, as translated by Hoole; at eleven, he was deep in books of voyages and travels which he took to school and read by stealth. At that time he composed with remarkable ease and fluency, and exchanged tasks with the other boys, writing their compositions, while they solved his problems in arithmetic, which he detested. At the age of thirteen he tried his hand at composing a play, which was performed by children at a friend's house, and of which he afterward forgot every part, even the title.

Romaine gave up teaching in 1797, and in that year Irving entered a school kept in Beekman street, by Jonathan Irish, probably the most accomplished of his instructors. He left this school in March, 1798, but continued for a time to receive private lessons from the same teacher, at home. Dr. Francis, in his pleasant reminiscences of Irving's early life, speaks of him as preparing to enter Columbia College, and as being prevented by the state of his health; but it is certain that an indifference to the acquisition of learning had taken possession of him at that age, which he afterward greatly regretted.

At the age of sixteen he entered his name as a student at law in the office of Josiah Ogden Hoffman, an eminent advocate, who, in later life, became a judge in one of our principal tribunals. It was while engaged in his professional studies that he made his first appearance as an author. I should have mentioned, among the circumstances that favored the unfolding of his literary capacities, that two of his elder brothers were men of decided literary tastes, William Irving, some seventeen years his senior, and Dr. Peter Irving, who, in the year 1802,

5*

founded a daily paper in New York, at a time when a daily paper was not, as now, an enterprise requiring a large outlay of capital, but an experiment that might be tried and abandoned with little' risk. Dr. Irving established the *Morning Chronicle*, and his younger brother contributed a series of essays, bearing the signature of Jonathan Oldstyle, of which Mr. Duyckinck, whose judgment I willingly accept, says that they show how early he acquired the style which so much charms us in his later writings.

In 1804, having reached the age of twenty-one, Irving, alarmed by an increasing weakness of the chest, visited Europe for the sake of his health. He sailed directly to the south of France, landed at Bordeaux in May, and passed two months in Genoa, where he embarked for Messina, in search of a softer climate than any to be found on the Italian peninsula. While at Messina, he saw the fleet of Nelson sweeping by that port on its way to fight the great naval battle of Trafalgar. He made the tour of Sicily, and crossing from Palermo to Naples, proceeded to Rome. Here he formed the acquaintance of Washington Allston, who was then entering on a career of art as extraordinary as that of Irving in literature. With Allston he made long rambles in the picturesque neighborhood of that old city, visited the galleries of its palaces and villas, and studied their works of art with a delight that rose to enthusiasm. He thought of the dry pursuit of the law which awaited his return to America, and for which he had no inclination, and almost determined to be a painter. Allston encouraged him in this disposition, and together they planned the scheme of a life devoted to the pursuit of art. It was fortunate for the world that, as Irving reflected on the matter, doubts arose in his mind which tempered his enthusiasm, and led him to a different destiny. The two friends separated, each to take his own way to renown—Allston to become one of the greatest of painters, and Irving to take his place among the greatest of authors. Leaving Italy, Irving passed through Switzerland to France, resided in Paris several months, travelled through Flanders and Holland, went to England, and returned to his native country in 1806, after an absence of two years.

At the close of the year he was admitted to practice as an attorney-at-law. He opened an office, but it could not be said that he ever became a practitioner. He began the year 1807 with the earliest of those literary labors which have won him the admiration of the world. On the twenty-fourth of January appeared, in the form of a small pamphlet, the first number of a periodical entitled *Salmagundi*, the joint production of himself, his brother William, and James K. Paulding. The elder brother contributed the poetry, with hints and outlines for some of the essays, but nearly all the prose was written by the two younger associates.

William Irving, however, had talent enough to have taken a more important part in the work. He was a man of wit, well educated, well informed, and author of many clever things written for the press, in a vein of good-natured satire, and published without his name. He was held in great esteem on account of his personal character, and had great weight in Congress, of which he was for some years a member.*

When *Salmagundi* appeared, the quaint old Dutch town in which Irving was born had become transformed to a comparatively gay metropolis. Its population of twenty thousand souls had enlarged to more than eighty thousand, although its aristocratic class had yet their residences in what now seems to us the narrow space between the Battery and Wall street. The modes and fashions of Europe were imported fresh and fresh. *Salmagundi* speaks of leather

* See a brief but well written memoir of William Irving, by Dr. Berrian.

breeches as all the rage for a morning dress, and flesh-colored smalls for an evening party. Gay equipages dashed through the streets. A new theatre had risen in Park Row, on the boards of which Cooper, one of the finest of declaimers, was performing to crowded houses. The churches had multiplied faster than the places of amusement; other public buildings of a magnificence hitherto unknown, including our present City Hall, had been erected; Tammany Hall, fresh from the hands of the builder, overlooked the Park. We began to affect a taste for pictures, and the rooms of Michael Paff, the famous German picture dealer in Broadway, were a favorite lounge for such connoisseurs as we then had, who amused themselves with making him talk of Michael Angelo. Ballston Springs were the great fashionable watering-place of the country, to which resorted the planters of the South with splendid equipages and troops of shining blacks in livery.

Salmagundi satirized the follies and ridiculed the humors of the time with great prodigality of wit and no less exuberance of good nature. In form it resembles the *Tatler*, and that numerous brood of periodical papers to which the success of the *Tatler* and *Spectator* gave birth; but it is in no sense an imitation. Its gayety is its own; its style of humor is

not that of Addison nor Goldsmith, though it has all
the genial spirit of theirs; nor is it borrowed from any
other writer.   It is far more frolicsome and joyous,
yet tempered by a native gracefulness. *Salmagundi*
was manifestly written without the fear of criticism
before the eyes of the authors, and to this sense of
perfect freedom in the exercise of their genius is
probably owing the charm and delight with which
we still read it.   Irving never seemed to place
much value on the part he contributed to this work,
yet I doubt whether he ever excelled some of those
papers in *Salmagundi* which bear the most evident
marks of his style ; and Paulding, though he has since
acquired a reputation by his other writings, can hardly be said to have written anything better than the
best of those which are ascribed to his pen.

Just before *Salmagundi* appeared, several of the
authors who gave the literature of England its present character had begun to write. For five years the
quarterly issues of the *Edinburgh Review*, then in
the most brilliant period of its existence, had been
before the public. Hazlitt had taken his place among
the authors, and John Foster had published his essays. Of the poets, Rogers, Campbell and Moore
were beginning to be popular ; Wordsworth had published his *Lyrical Ballads ;* Scott, his *Lay of the Last*

Minstrel; Southey, his *Madoc;* and Joanna Baillie two volumes of her plays. In this revival of the creative power in literature it is pleasant to see that our own country took part, contributing a work of a character as fresh and original as any they produced on the other side of the Atlantic.

Nearly two years afterward, in the autumn of 1809, appeared in the *Evening Post*, addressed to the humane, an advertisement requesting information concerning a small elderly gentleman named Knickerbocker, dressed in a black coat and cocked hat, who had suddenly left his lodgings at the Columbian Hotel in Mulberry street, and had not been heard of afterward. In the beginning of November, a *Traveller* communicated to the same journal the information that he had seen a person answering to this description, apparently fatigued with his journey, resting by the road-side a little north of Kingsbridge. Ten days later, Seth Handaside, the landlord of the Columbian Hotel, gave notice, through the same journal, that he had found in the missing gentleman's chamber "a curious kind of written book," which he should print by way of reimbursing himself for what his lodger owed him. In December following, Inskeep and Bradford, booksellers, published *Diedrich Knickerbocker's History of New York.*

Salmagundi had prepared the public to receive this work with favor, and Seth Handaside had no reason to regret having undertaken its publication. I recollect well its early and immediate popularity. I was then a youth in college, and having committed to memory a portion of it to repeat as a declamation before my class, I was so overcome with laughter, when I appeared on the floor, that I was unable to proceed, and drew upon myself the rebuke of the tutor.

I have just read this *History of New York* over again, and I found myself no less delighted than when I first turned its pages in my early youth. When I compare it with other works of wit and humor of a similar length, I find that, unlike most of them, it carries forward the reader to the conclusion without weariness or satiety, so unsought, spontaneous, self-suggested are the wit and the humor. The author makes us laugh, because he can no more help it than we can help laughing. Scott, in one of his letters, compared the humor of this work to that of Swift. The rich vein of Irving's mirth is of a quality quite distinct from the dry drollery of Swift, but they have this in common, that they charm by the utter absence of effort, and this was probably the ground of Scott's remark. A critic in the *London Quarterly*, some years after its appearance, spoke of it as a " tantalizing book," on account of his inability to understand what he called " the point of many of the allusions in this political satire." I fear he must have been one of those respectable persons who find it difficult to understand a joke unless it be accompanied with a commentary opening and explaining it to the humblest capacity. Scott found no such difficulty. " Our sides," he says, in a letter to Mr. Brevoort, a friend of Irving, written just after he had read the book, " are absolutely sore with laughing." The mirth of the " History of New York" is of the most transparent sort, and the author, even in the later editions, judiciously abstained from any attempt to make it more intelligible by notes.

I find in this work more manifest traces than in his other writings of what Irving owed to the earlier authors in our language. The quaint poetic coloring, and often the phraseology, betray the disciple of Chaucer and Spenser. We are conscious of a flavor of the olden time, as of a racy wine of some rich vintage—

> " Cooled a long age in the deep-delvèd earth."

I will not say that there are no passages in this work which are not worthy of their context ; that we do not sometimes meet with phraseology which we

could wish changed, that the wit does not sometimes run wild and drop here and there a jest which
we could willingly spare. We forgive, we overlook,
we forget all this as we read, in consideration of the
entertainment we have enjoyed, and of that which
beckons us onward in the next page. Of all mock-
heroic works, *Knickerbocker's History of New York*
is the gayest, the airiest, and the least tiresome.

In 1848 Mr. Irving issued an edition of this work,
to which he prefixed what he called an " Apology,"
intended in part as an answer to those who thought
he had made too free with the names of our old
Dutch families. To speak frankly, I do not much
wonder that the descendants of the original founders
of New Amsterdam should have hardly known
whether to laugh or look grave on finding the names
of their ancestors, of whom they never thought but
with respect, now connected with ludicrous associations, by a wit of another race. In one of his excellent historical discourses Mr. Verplanck had gently
complained of this freedom, expressing himself, as he
said, more in sorrow than in anger. Even the sorrow, I believe, must have long since wholly passed
away, when it is seen how little Irving's pleasant-
ries have detracted from the honor paid to the early
history of our city—at all events, I do not see how

it could survive Irving's good-humored and graceful
Apology.

It was not long after the publication of the *History of New York* that Irving abandoned the profession of law, for which he had so decided a distaste as
never to have fully tried his capacity for pursuing it.
Two of his brothers were engaged in commerce, and
they received him as a silent partner. He did not,
however, renounce his literary occupations. He
wrote, in 1810, a memoir of Campbell, the poet, prefixed to an edition of the writings of that author,
which appeared in Philadelphia; and in 1813 and the
following year, employed himself as editor of the *Analectic Magazine*, published in the same city; making
the experiment of his talent for a vocation to which
men of decided literary tastes in this country are
strongly inclined to betake themselves. Those who
remember this magazine cannot have forgotten that
it was a most entertaining miscellany, partly compiled from English publications, mostly periodicals,
and partly made up of contributions of some of our
own best writers. Paulding wrote for it a series of
biographical accounts of the naval commanders of the
United States, which added greatly to its popularity; and Verplanck contributed memoirs of Commodore Stewart and General Scott, Barlow, the poet,

and other distinguished Americans, which were re-ceived with favor. *The Life of Campbell*, with the exception perhaps of some less important contributions to the magazine, is the only published work of Irving between the appearance of the *History of New York*, in 1809, and that of the *Sketch Book*, in 1819.

It was during this interval that an event took place which had a marked influence on Irving's future life, affected the character of his writings, and, now that the death of both parties allows it to be spoken of without reserve, gives a peculiar interest to his personal history. He became attached to a young lady whom he was to have married. She died unwedded, in the flower of her age ; there was a sorrowful leave-taking between her and her lover, as the grave was about to separate them on the eve of what should have been her bridal ; and Irving, ever after, to the close of his life, tenderly and faithfully cherished her memory. In one of the biographical notices published immediately after Irving's death, an old, well-worn copy of the Bible is spoken of, which was kept lying on the table in his chamber, within reach of his bedside, bearing her name on the title page in a delicate female hand—a relic which we may presume to have been his constant companion. Those who are fond of searching, in the biographies of eminent men, for the circumstances which determined the bent of their genius, find in this sad event, and the cloud it threw over the hopeful and cheerful period of early manhood, an explanation of the transition from the unbounded playfulness of the *History of New York* to the serious, tender and meditative vein of the *Sketch Book*.

In 1815, soon after our second peace with Great Britain, Irving again sailed for Europe, and fixed himself at Liverpool, where a branch of the large commercial house to which he belonged was established. His old love of rambling returned upon him; he wandered first into Wales, and over some of the finest counties of England, and then northward to the sterner region of the Scottish Highlands. His memoir of Campbell had procured him the acquaintance and friendship of that poet. Campbell gave him, more than a year after his arrival in England, a letter of introduction to Scott, who, already acquainted with him by his writings, welcomed him warmly to Abbotsford, and made him his friend for life. Scott sent a special message to Campbell, thanking him for having made him known to Irving. " He is one of the best and pleasantest acquaintances," said Scott, " that I have made this many a day."

In the same year that he visited Abbotsford his brothers failed. The changes which followed the peace of 1815, swept away their fortunes and his together, and he was now to begin the world anew.

In 1819, he began to publish the *Sketch Book.* It was written in England and sent over to New York, where it was issued by Van Winkle, in octavo numbers containing from seventy to a hundred pages. In the preface he remarked that he was " unsettled in his abode," that he had "his cares and vicissitudes," and could not, therefore, give these papers the " tranquil attention necessary to finished composition." Several of them were copied with praise in the London *Literary Gazette*, and an intimation was conveyed to the author, that some person in London was about to publish them entire. He preferred to do this himself, and accordingly offered the work to the famous bookseller, Murray. Murray was slow in giving the matter his attention, and Irving, after a reasonable delay, wrote to ask that the copy which he had left with him might be returned. It was sent back with a note, pleading excess of occupation, the great cross of all eminent booksellers, and alleging the " want of scope in the nature of the work," as a reason for declining it. This was discouraging, but Irving had the enterprise to print the first volume in

London, at his own risk. It was issued by John Miller, and was well received, but a month afterward the publisher failed. Immediately Sir Walter Scott came to London and saw Murray, who allowed himself to be persuaded, the more easily, doubtless on account of the partial success of the first volume, that the work had more "scope" than he supposed, and purchased the copyright of both volumes for two hundred pounds, which he afterward liberally raised to four hundred.

Whoever compares the *Sketch Book* with the *History of New York* might at first, perhaps, fail to recognize it as the work of the same hand, so much graver and more thoughful is the strain in which it is written. A more attentive examination, however, shows that the humor in the lighter parts is of the same peculiar and original cast, wholly unlike that of any author who ever wrote, a humor which Mr. Dana happily characterized as "a fanciful playing with common things, and here and there beautiful touches, till the ludicrous becomes half picturesque." Yet one cannot help perceiving that the author's spirit had been sobered since he last appeared before the public, as if the shadow of a great sorrow had fallen upon it. The greater number of the papers are addressed to our deeper sympathies and some of them, as, for example, the *Broken Heart, The Widow and Her Son*, and *Rural Funerals*, dwell upon the saddest themes. Only in two of them—*Rip Van Winkle* and the *Legend of Sleepy Hollow*—does he lay the reins loose on the neck of his frolicsome fancy, and allow it to dash forward without restraint; and these rank among the most delightful and popular tales ever written. In our country they have been read, I believe, by nearly everybody who can read at all.

The *Sketch Book*, and the two succeeding works of Irving, *Bracebridge Hall* and the *Tales of a Traveller*, abound with agreeable pictures of English life, seen under favorable lights and sketched with a friendly pencil. Let me say here, that it was not to pay court to the English that he thus described them and their country; it was because he could not describe them otherwise. It was the instinct of his mind to attach itself to the contemplation of the good and the beautiful, wherever he found them, and to turn away from the sight of what was evil, misshapen and hateful. His was not a nature to pry for faults, or disabuse the world of good-natured mistakes; he looked for virtue, love and truth among men, and thanked God that he found them in such large measure. If there are touches of satire in his writings, he is the best-natured and most amiable of satirists, amiable beyond Horace; and in his irony—for there is a vein of playful irony running through many of his works—there is no tinge of bitterness.

I rejoice, for my part, that we have had such a writer as Irving to bridge over the chasm between the two great nations—that an illustrious American lived so long in England, and was so much beloved there, and sought so earnestly to bring the people of the two countries to a better understanding with each other, and to wean them from the animosities of narrow minds. I am sure that there is not a large-minded and large-hearted man in all our country who can read over the *Sketch Book* and the other writings of Irving, and disown one of the magnanimous sentiments they express with regard to England, or desire to abate the glow of one of his warm and cheerful pictures of English life. Occasions will arise, no doubt, for saying some things in a less accommodating spirit, and there are men enough on both sides of the Atlantic who can say them; but Irving was not sent into the world on that errand. A different work was assigned him in the very structure of his mind, and the endowments of his heart—a work of peace and brotherhood, and I will say for him that he nobly performed it.

6

Let me pause here to speak of what I believe to have been the influence of the *Sketch Book* upon American literature. At the time it appeared, the periodical lists of new American publications were extremely meagre, and consisted, to a great extent, of occasional pamphlets and dissertations on the questions of the day. The works of greater pretension were, for the most part, crudely and languidly made up, and destined to be little read. A work like the *Sketch Book*, welcomed on both sides of the Atlantic, showed the possibility of an American author acquiring a fame bounded only by the limits of his own language, and gave an example of the qualities by which it might be won. Within two years afterward, we had Cooper's *Spy* and Dana's *Idle Man;* the press of our country began, by degrees, to teem with works composed with a literary skill and a spirited activity of intellect until then little known among us. Every year the assertion that we had no literature of our own became less and less true ; and now, when we look over a list of new works by native authors, we find, with an astonishment amounting almost to alarm, that the most voracious devourer of books must despair of being able to read half those which make a fair claim upon his attention. It was since 1819 that the great historians of our country, whose praise is in the mouths of all the nations, began to write. One of them built up the fabric of his fame long after Irving appeared as an author, and slept with Herodotus two years before Irving's death; another of the band lives yet to be the ornament of the association before which I am called to speak, and is framing the annals of his country into a work for future ages. Within that period has arisen among us the class who hold vast multitudes spellbound in motionless attention by public discourses, the most perfect of their kind, such as make the fame of Everett. Within that period our theologians have learned to write with the elegance and vivacity of the essayists. We had but one novelist before the era of the *Sketch Book;* their number is now beyond enumeration by any but a professed catalogue-maker, and many of them are read in every cultivated form of human speech. Those whom we acknowledge as our poets—one of whom is the special favorite of our brothers in language, who dwell beyond the sea—appeared in the world of letters and won its attention after Irving had become famous. We have wits, and humorists, and amusing essayists, authors of some of the airiest and most graceful compositions of the present century, and we owe them to the new impulse given to our literature in 1819. I look abroad on these stars of our literary firmament—some crowded together with their minute points of light in a galaxy—some standing apart in glorious constellations; I recognize Arcturus, and Orion, and Perseus, and the glittering jewels of the Southern Crown, and the Pleiades shedding sweet influences; but the Evening Star, the soft and serene light that glowed in their van, the precursor of them all, has sunk below the horizon. The spheres, meantime, perform their appointed courses; the same motion which lifted them up to the mid-sky bears them onward to their setting; and they, too, like their bright leader, must soon be carried by it below the earth.

Irving went to Paris in 1820, where he passed the remainder of the year and part of the next, and where he became acquainted with the poet Moore, who frequently mentions him in his Diary. Moore and he were much in each other's company; and the poet has left on record an expression of his amazement at the rapidity with which *Bracebridge Hall*, was composed— one hundred and thirty pages in ten days. The winter of 1822 found him in Dresden. In that year was published *Bracebridge Hall*, the groundwork of which is a charming description of country life in England, interspersed with narratives, the scene of which is laid in other countries. Of these, the Norman tale of

Annette Delarbre seems to me the most beautiful and affecting thing of its kind in all his works; so beautiful, indeed, that I can hardly see how he who has once read it can resist the desire to read it again. In *Bracebridge Hall* we have the Stout Gentleman, full of certain minute paintings of familiar objects, where not a single touch is thrown in that does not heighten the comic effect of the narrative. If I am not greatly mistaken, the most popular novelists of the day have learned from this pattern the skill with which they have wrought up some of their most striking passages, both grave and gay. In composing *Bracebridge Hall*, Irving showed that he had not forgotten his native country; and in the pleasant tale of Dolph Heyliger he went back to the banks of that glorious river beside which he was born.

In 1823, Irving, still a wanderer, returned to Paris, and, in the year following, gave the world his *Tales of a Traveller*. Murray, in the mean time, had become fully weaned from the notion that Irving's writings lacked the quality which he called "scope," for he had paid a thousand guineas for the copyright of *Bracebridge Hall*, and now offered fifteen hundred pounds for the *Tales of a Traveller*, which Irving accepted. "He might have had two thousand," says Moore, but this assembly will not, I hope, think the worse of him, if it be acknowledged that the world contained men who were sharper than he at driving a bargain. The *Tales of a Traveller* are most remarkable for their second part, entitled *Buckthorne and his Friends*, in which the author introduces us to literary life in its various aspects, as he had observed it in London, and to the relations in which authors at that time stood to the booksellers.   His sketches of the different personages are individual, characteristic and diverting, yet with what a kindly pencil they are all drawn ! His good nature overspreads and harmonizes everything, like the warm atmosphere which so much delights us in a painting.

Irving, still "unsettled in his abode," passed the winter of 1825 in the south of France. When you are in that region you see the snowy summits of the Spanish Pyrenees looking down upon you ; Spanish visitors frequent the watering-places ; Spanish peddlers, in their handsome costume, offer you the fabrics of Barcelona and Valencia ; Spanish peasants come to the fairs ; the traveller feels himself almost in Spain already, and is haunted by the desire of visiting that remarkable country. To Spain, Irving went in the latter part of the year, invited by our Minister at Madrid, Alexander H. Everett, at the suggestion of Mr. Rich, the American Consul, an industrious and intelligent collector of Spanish works relating to America. His errand was to translate into English the documents relating to the discovery and early history of our Continent, collected by the research of Navarrete. He passed the winter of 1826 at the Spanish capital, as the guest of Mr. Rich; the following season took him to Granada, and he lingered awhile in that beautiful region, profusely watered by the streams that break from the Snowy Ridge. In 1827, he again visited the south of Spain, gathering materials for his *Life of Columbus,* which, immediately after his arrival in Spain, he had determined to write, instead of translating the documents of Navarrete. In Spain he began and finished that work, after having visited the places associated with the principal events in the life of his hero. Murray was so well satisfied with its "scope" that he gave him three thousand guineas for the copyright, and laid it before the public in 1828. Like the other works of Irving, it was published here at the same time as in London.

The *Life and Voyages of Christopher Columbus* placed Irving among the historians, for the biography of that great discoverer is a part, and a remarkable part, of the history of the world. Of what was strictly and simply personal in his adventures, much, of course, has passed into irremediable oblivion; what was both personal and historical is yet outstanding above the shadow that has settled upon the rest. The work of Irving was at once in everybody's hands and eagerly read. Navarrete vouched for its historical accuracy and completeness. Jeffrey declared that no work could ever take its place. It was written with a strong love of the subject, and to this it owes much of its power over the reader. Columbus was one of those who, with all their faculties occupied by one great idea, and bent on making it a practical reality, are looked upon as crazed, and pitied and forgotten if they fail; but if they succeed, are venerated as the glory of their age. The poetic elements of his character and history, the grandeur and mystery of his design, his prophetic sagacity, his hopeful and devout courage, and his disregard of the ridicule of meaner intellects took a strong hold on the mind of Irving, and formed the inspiration of the work.

Mr. Duyckinck gives, on the authority of one who knew Irving intimately, an instructive anecdote relating to the *Life of Columbus*. When the work was nearly finished it was put into the hands of Lieutenant Slidell Mackenzie, himself an agreeable writer, then on a visit to Spain, who read it with a view of giving a critical opinion of its merits. "It is quite perfect," said he, on returning the manuscript, "except the style, and that is unequal." The remark made such an impression on the mind of the author that he wrote over the whole narrative with the view of making the style more uniform, but he afterward thought that he had not improved it.

In this I have no doubt that Irving was quite right, and that it would have been better if he had never touched the work after he had brought it to the state which satisfied his individual judgment. An author can scarce commit a greater error than to alter what he writes, except when he has a clear perception that the alteration is for the better, and can make it with as hearty a confidence in himself as he felt in giving the work its first shape. What strikes me as an occasional defect in the *Life of Columbus* is this elaborate uniformity of style—a certain prismatic coloring in passages where absolute simplicity would have satisfied us better. It may well be supposed that Irving originally wrote some parts of the work with the quiet plainness of a calm relater of facts, and others, with the spirit and fire of one who had become warmed with his subject, and this probably gave occasion to what was said of the inequality of the style. The attempt to elevate the diction of the simpler por-

6*

tions, we may suppose, marred what Irving afterward perceived had really been one of the merits of the work.

In the spring of 1829, Irving made another visit to the south of Spain collecting materials from which he afterward composed some of his most popular works. When the traveller now visits Granada and is taken to the Alhambra, his guide will say, " Here is one of the curiosities of the place ; this is the chamber occupied by Washington Irving," and he will show an apartment, from the windows of which you have a view of the Genil, with the mountain peaks overlooking it, and hear the murmur of many mountain brooks at once, as they hurry to the plain. In July of the same year, he repaired to London, where he was to act as Secretary of the American Legation. We had at that time certain controversies with the British government which were the subject of negotiation. Irving took great interest in these, and in some letters which I saw at the time, stated the points in dispute at considerable length and with admirable method and perspicuity. In London he published his *Chronicles of the Conquest of Granada*, one of the most delightful of his works, an exact history,—for such it is admitted to be by those who have searched most carefully the ancient records of Spain,—yet so full of personal incident, so diversified with surprising turns of fortune, and these wrought up with such picturesque effect, that, to use an expression of Pope, a young lady might read it by mistake for a romance. In 1831, he gave the world another work on Spanish history, the *Voyages of the Companions of Columbus*, and in the year following, the *Alhambra*, which is another *Sketch Book*, with the scenes laid in Spain.

While in Spain, Irving had planned a Life of Cortez, the Conqueror of Mexico, and collected the facts from which it was to be written. When, afterward, he had actually begun the composition of the work, he happened to learn that Prescott designed to write the *History of the Mexican Conquest*, and immediately he desisted. It was his intention to interweave with the narrative, descriptions of the ancient customs of the aborigines, such as their modes of warfare and their gorgeous pageants, by way of relief to the sanguinary barbarities of the Conquest. He saw what rich materials of the picturesque these opened to him, and if he had accomplished his plan, he would probably have produced one of his most popular works.

In 1832, Irving returned to New York. He returned, after an absence of seventeen years, to find his native city doubled in population; its once quiet waters alive with sails and furrowed by steamers passing to and fro; its wharves crowded with masts; the heights which surround it, and which he remembered wild and solitary and lying in forest, now crowned with stately country seats, or with dwellings clustered in villages, and everywhere the activity and bustle of a prosperous and hopeful people. And he, too, how had he returned? The young and comparatively obscure author, whose works had only found here and there a reader in England, had achieved a fame as wide as the civilized world. All the trophies he had won in this field he brought home to lay at the feet of his country. Meanwhile all the country was moved to meet him; the rejoicing was universal that one who had represented us so illustriously abroad was henceforth to live among us.

Irving hated public dinners, but he was forced to accept one pressed upon him by his enthusiastic countrymen. It was given at the City Hotel on the 30th of May, Chancellor Kent presiding, and the most eminent citizens of New York assembling at the table. I remember the accounts of this festivity reaching me as I was wandering in Illinois hovering on the skirts of the Indian war, in a region now populous, but then untilled and waste, and I could only write to Irving and ask leave to add my voice to the

general acclamation.   In his address at the dinner,
Chancellor Kent welcomed the historian of New Amsterdam back to his native city ; and Irving, in reply,
poured forth his heart in the warmest expressions of
delight at finding himself again among his countrymen and kindred, in a land of sunshine and freedom
and hope.   " I am asked," he said, "how long I
mean to remain here.   They know little of my heart
who can ask me this question.   I answer, as long as
I live."

The instinct of rambling had not, however, for-
saken him.   In the summer after his return he made
a journey to the country west of the Mississippi, in
company with Mr. Ellsworth, a commissioner intrusted with the removal of certain Indian tribes, and
roamed over wild regions, then the hunting-grounds
of the savage, but into which the white man has since
brought his plough and his herds.   He did not publish his account of this journey until 1835, when it
appeared as the first volume of the *Crayon Miscellany*, under the title of a *Tour on the Prairies*.   In
this work the original West is described as Irving
knew how to describe it, and the narrative is in that
vein of easy gayety peculiar to his writings.   *Abbotsford and Newstead Abbey* formed the second volume
of the *Crayon Miscellany*, and to these he afterward

added another, entitled *Legends of the Conquest of Spain.*

In 1836, he published *Astoria ; or, Anecdotes of an Enterprise beyond the Rocky Mountains ;* a somewhat curious example of literary skill. A voluminous commercial correspondence was the dull ore of the earth which he refined and wrought into symmetry and splendor. Irving reduced to a regular narrative the events to which it referred, bringing out the picturesque whenever he found it, and enlivening the whole with touches of his native humor. His nephew, Pierre M. Irving, lightened his labor materially by examining and collating the letters and making memoranda of their contents. In 1837, he prepared for the press the *Adventures of Captain Bonneville, of the United States Army, in the Rocky Mountains and the Far West.* He had the manuscript journal of Bonneville before him, but the hand of Irving is apparent in every sentence.

About the time that this work appeared, Irving was drawn into the only public controversy in which, so far as I know, he ever engaged. William Leggett then conducted a weekly periodical entitled the *Plaindealer,* remarkable both for its ability and its love of disputation. It attacked Mr. Irving for altering a line or two in one of my poems, with a view of making it less offensive to English readers, and for writing a preface to the American edition of his *Tour on the Prairies*, full of professions of love for his country, which were studiously omitted from the English edition. From these circumstances the *Plain-dealer* drew an inference unfavorable to Irving's sincerity.

I should here mention, and I hope I may do it without much egotism, that when a volume of my poems was published here in the year 1832, Mr. Verplanck had the kindness to send a copy of it to Irving, desiring him to find a publisher for it in England. This he readily engaged to do, though wholly unacquainted with me, and offered the volume to Murray. "Poetry does not sell at present," said Murray, and declined it. A bookseller in Bond street, named Andrews, undertook its publication, but required that Irving should introduce it with a preface of his own. He did so, speaking of my verses in such terms as would naturally command for them the attention of the public, and allowing his name to be placed in the title-page as the editor. The edition, in consequence, found a sale. It happened, however, that the publisher objected to two lines in a poem called the *Song of Marion's Men.* One of them was

"The British soldier trembles,"

and Irving good-naturedly consented it should be altered to

"The foeman trembles in his camp."

The other alteration was of a similar character.

To the accusations of the *Plaindealer*, Irving replied with a mingled spirit and dignity which almost makes us regret that his faculties were not oftener roused into energy by such collisions, or, at least, that he did not sometimes employ his pen on controverted points. He fully vindicated himself in both instances, showing that he had made the alterations in my poem from a simple desire to do me service, and that with regard to the *Tour on the Prairies*, he had sent a manuscript copy of it to England for publication, at the same time that he sent another to the printer here ; and that it would have been an absurdity to address the English edition to the American public. But as this was the first time that he had appeared before his countrymen as an author since his return from Europe, it was but proper that he should express to them the feelings awakened by their generous welcome. "These feelings," he said, "were genuine, and were not expressed with half the warmth with which they were entertained ;" an assertion which every reader, I believe, was disposed to receive literally.

In his answer to the *Plaindealer*, some allusions were made to me which seemed to imply that I had taken part in this attack upon him. To remove the impression, I had sent a note to the *Plaindealer*, for publication, in which I declared in substance that I never had complained of the alterations of my poem— that though they were not such as I should have made, I was certain they were made with the kindest intentions, and that I had no feeling toward Mr. Irving but gratitude for the service he had rendered me. The explanation was graciously accepted, and in a brief note, printed in the *Plaindealer*, Irving pronounced my acquittal.

Several papers were written by Irving, in 1839 and the following year, for the *Knickerbocker*, a monthly periodical conducted by his friend, Lewis Gaylord Clark, all of them such as he only could write. They were afterward collected into a volume, entitled *Wolfert's Roost*, from the ancient name of that beautiful residence of his on the banks of the Hudson, in which they were mostly written. They were, perhaps, read with more interest in the volume than in the magazine, just as some paintings of the highest merit are seen with more pleasure in the artist's room than on the walls of an exhibition.

In 1842, he went to Spain as the American min-

ister, and remained in that country for four years.   I
have never understood that anything occurred during
that time to put his talents as a negotiator to any rig-
orous test.   He was a sagacious and intelligent observer; his connection with the American Legation
in London had given him diplomatic experience, and
I have heard that he sent home to his government
some valuable despatches on the subject of our relations with Spain.   In other respects, he did, at least,
what all American ministers at the European courts
are doing, and I suppose my hearers understand very
well what that is; but if there had been any question
of importance to be settled, I think he might have ac-
quitted himself as well as many who have had a higher reputation for dexterity in business.   When I was
at Madrid in 1857, a distinguished Spaniard said
to me: " Why does not your government send out
Washington Irving to this court? Why do you not
take as your agent the man whom all Spain admires,
venerates, loves? I assure you, it would be difficult
for our government to refuse anything which Irving
should ask, and his signature would make almost any
treaty acceptable to our people."

Returning in 1846, Irving went back to Sunnyside, on the Hudson, and continued to make it his
abode for the rest of his life.   Those who passed up

and down the river before the year 1835, may remember a neglected cottage on a green bank, with a few locust-trees before it, close to where a little brook brings in its tribute to the mightier stream. In that year Irving became its possessor; he gave it the name it now wears, planted its pleasant slopes with trees and shrubs, laid it out in walks, built outhouses, and converted the cottage into a more spacious dwelling, in the old Dutch style of architecture, with crow-steps on the gables; a quaint, picturesque building, with "as many angles and corners, "to use his own words, "as a cocked hat." He caused creeping plants and climbing roses to be trained up its walls; the trees he planted prospered in that sheltered situation, and were filled with birds, which would not leave their nests at the approach of the kind master of the place. The house became almost hidden from sight by their lofty summits, the perpetual rustlings of which, to those who sat within, were blended with the murmurs of the water. Van Tassel would have had some difficulty in recognizing his old abode in this little paradise, with the beauty of which one of Irving's friends* has made the public familiar in prose and verse.

At Sunnyside, Irving wrote his *Life of Oliver*

* H. T. Tuckerman.

Goldsmith. Putnam, the bookseller, had said to him one day: "Here is Foster's *Life of Goldsmith;* I think of republishing it." "I once wrote a Memoir of Goldsmith," answered Irving, "which was prefixed to an edition of his works printed at Paris ; and I have thought of enlarging it and making it more perfect." "If you will do that," was the reply of the bookseller, "I shall not republish the Life by Foster." Within three months afterward, Irving's *Life of Goldsmith,* was finished and in press. It was so much superior to the original sketch in the exactness of the particulars, the entertainment of the anecdotes, and the beauty of the style, that it was really a new work. For my part, I know of nothing like it. I have read no biographical memoir which carries forward the reader so delightfully and with so little tediousness of recital or reflection. I never take it up without being tempted to wish that Irving had written more works of the kind; but this could hardly be ; for where could he have found another Goldsmith ?

In 1850, appeared his *Lives of Mahomet and his Successors,* composed principally from memoranda made by him during his residence in Spain ; and in the same year he completed the revisal of his works for a new edition, which was brought out by Putnam, a bookseller of whose obliging and honorable conduct he delighted to speak. Irving was a man with whom it was not easy to have a misunderstanding; but, even if he had been of a different temper, these commendations would have been none the less deserved.

When Cooper died, toward the close of the year 1850, Irving, who had not long before met him, apparently in the full vigor of his excellent constitution, was much shocked by the event, and took part in the meetings held for the purpose of collecting funds to erect a monument to his memory in this city—a design which, I am sorry to say, has wholly failed. He wrote a letter advising that the monument should be a statue, and attended the great memorial meeting held in Metropolitan Hall, in February of the next year, at which Webster presided. He was then near the end of his sixty-eighth year, and was remarked as one over whom the last twenty years had passed lightly. He, whom Dr. Francis describes as in early life a slender and delicate youth, preserving his health by habitual daily exercise, appeared before that vast assembly a fresh, well-preserved gentleman scarcely more than elderly, with firm but benevolent features, well-knit and muscular limbs, and an elastic step, the sign of undiminished physical vigor.

In his retirement at Sunnyside, Irving planned and executed his last great work, the *Life of Wash-*

ington, to which he says he had long looked forward as his crowning literary effort. Constable, the Edinburgh bookseller, had proposed it to him thirty years before, and he then resolved to undertake it as soon as he should return to the United States. It was postponed in favor of other projects, but never abandoned. At length the expected time seemed to have arrived; his other tasks had been successfully performed; the world was waiting for new works from his pen; his mind and body were yet in their vigor; the habit and the love of literary production yet remained, and he addressed himself to this greatest of his labors.

Yet he had his misgivings, though they could not divert him from his purpose. "They expect too much—too much," he said to a friend of mine, to whom he was speaking of the magnitude of the task and the difficulty of satisfying the public. We cannot wonder at these doubts. At the time when he began to employ himself steadily on this work, he was near the age of threescore and ten, when with most men the season of hope and confidence is past. He was like one who should begin the great labor of the day when the sun was shedding his latest beams, and what if the shadows of night should descend upon him before his task was ended? A vast labor had been

thrown upon him by the almost numberless documents
and papers recently brought to light relating to the
events in which Washington was concerned—such as
were amassed and digested by the research of Sparks,
and accompanied by the commentary of his excellent
biography. These were all to be carefully examined
and their spirit extracted. Historians had in the mean
time arisen in our country, of a world-wide fame,
with whose works his own must be compared, and he
was to be judged by a public whom he, more than almost any other man, had taught to be impatient of
mediocrity.

I do not believe, however, that Irving's task
would have been performed so ably if it had been
undertaken when it was suggested by Constable ; the
narrative could not have been so complete in its
facts ; it might not have been written with the same
becoming simplicity. It was fortunate that the work
was delayed till it could be written from the largest
store of materials, till its plan was fully matured in
all its fair proportions, and till the author's mind had
become filled with the profoundest veneration for his
subject.

The simplicity already mentioned is the first quality of this work which impresses the reader. Here
is a man of genius, a poet by temperament, writing

the life of a man of transcendent wisdom and virtue—
a life passed amidst great events, and marked by in-
estimable public services. There is a constant temptation to eulogy, but the temptation is resisted; the
actions of his hero are left to speak their own praise.
He records events reverently, as one might have recorded them before the art of rhetoric was invented,
with no exaggeration, with no parade of reflection;
the lessons of the narrative are made to impress
themselves on the mind by the earnest and conscientious relation of facts. Meantime the narrator
keeps himself in the background, solely occupied with
the due presentation of his subject. Our eyes are
upon the actors whom he sets before us—we never
think of Mr. Irving.

A closer examination reveals another great merit
of the work, the admirable proportion in which the
author keeps the characters and events of his story.
I suppose he could hardly have been conscious of
this merit, and that it was attained without a direct
effort. Long meditation had probably so shaped and
matured the plan in his mind, and so arranged its
parts in their just symmetry, that, executing it consci-
entiously as he did, he could not have made it a
different thing from what we have it. There is nothing distorted, nothing placed in too broad a light or

thrown too far in the shade. The incidents of our Revolutionary War, the great event of Washington's life, pass before us as they passed before the eyes of the commander-in-chief himself, and from time to time varied his designs. Washington is kept always in sight, and the office of the biographer is never allowed to become merged in that of the historian.

The men who were the companions of Washington in the field or in civil life, are shown only in their association with him, yet are their characters drawn, not only with skill and spirit, but with a hand that delighted to do them justice. Nothing, I believe, could be more abhorrent to Irving's ideas of the province of a biographer, than the slightest detraction from the merits of others, that his hero might appear the more eminent. So remarkable is his work in this respect, that an accomplished member of the Historical Society,* who has analyzed the merits of the *Life of Washington* with a critical skill which makes me ashamed to speak of the work after him, has declared that no writer, within the circle of his reading, " has so successfully established his claim to the rare and difficult virtue of impartiality."

I confess, my admiration of this work becomes the greater the more I examine it. In the other

* G. W. Greene. " Biographical Studies."

writings of Irving are beauties which strike the reader at once. In this I recognize qualities which lie deeper, and which I was not sure of finding—a rare equity of judgment; a large grasp of the subject; a profound philosophy, independent of philosophical forms, and even instinctively rejecting them; the power of reducing an immense crowd of loose materials to clear and orderly arrangement ; and forming them into one grand whole, as a skilful commander, from a rabble of raw recruits, forms a disciplined army, animated and moved by a single will.

The greater part of this last work of Irving was composed while he was in the enjoyment of what might be called a happy old age. This period of his life was not without its infirmities, but his frame was yet unwasted, his intellect bright and active, and the hour of decay seemed distant. He had become more than ever the object of public veneration, and in his beautiful retreat enjoyed all the advantages with few of the molestations of acknowledged greatness ; a little too much visited, perhaps, but submitting to the intrusion of his admirers with his characteristic patience and kindness. That retreat had now become more charming than ever, and the domestic life within was as beautiful as the nature without. A surviving brother, older than himself, shared it with

him, and several affectionate nephews and nieces
stood to him in the relation of sons and daughters.
He was surrounded by neighbors who saw him daily,
and honored and loved him the more for knowing
him so well.

While he was engaged in writing the last pages
of his *Life of Washington,* his countrymen heard
with pain that his health was failing and his strength
ebbing away. He completed the work, however,
though he was not able to revise the last sheets, and
we then heard that his nights had become altogether
sleepless. He was himself of opinion that his labors
had been too severe for his time of life, and had
sometimes feared that the power to continue them
would desert him before his work could be finished.
A catarrh, to which he had been subject, had by
some injudicious prescription, been converted into an
asthma; and the asthma, according to the testimony
of his physician, Dr. Peters, one of the most attentive and assiduous of his profession, was at length
accompanied by an enlargement of the heart. This
disease ended in the usual way by a sudden dissolution. On the 28th of November last, in the
evening, he had withdrawn to his room, attended
by one of his nieces carrying his medicines, when
he complained of a sudden feeling of intense sad-

ness, sank immediately into her arms, and died without a struggle.

Although he had reached an age beyond which life is rarely prolonged, the news of his death was everywhere received with profound sorrow. The whole country mourned, but the grief was most deeply felt in his immediate neighborhood; the little children wept for the loss of their good friend. When the day of his funeral arrived, the people gathered from far and near to attend it; this capital poured forth its citizens; the trains on the railway were crowded, and a multitude, like a mass meeting, but reverentially silent, moved through the streets of the neighboring village which had been dressed in the emblems of mourning, and clustered about the church and the burial ground. It was the first day of December; the pleasant Indian summer of our climate had been prolonged far beyond its usual date; the sun shone with his softest splendor, and the elements were hushed into a perfect calm; it was like one of the blandest days of October. The hills and forests, the meadows and waters which Irving had loved, seemed listening, in that quiet atmosphere, as the solemn funeral service was read.

It was read over the remains of one whose life had well prepared his spirit for its new stage of being. Irving did not aspire to be a theologian, but his heart was deeply penetrated with the better part of religion, and he had sought humbly to imitate the example of the Great Teacher of our faith.

That amiable character which makes itself so manifest in the writings of Irving was seen in all his daily actions. He was ever ready to do kind offices; tender of the feelings of others; carefully just, but ever leaning to the merciful side of justice; averse to strife; and so modest that the world never ceased to wonder how it should have happened that one so much praised should have gained so little assurance. He envied no man's success, he sought to detract from no man's merits, but he was acutely sensitive both to praise and to blame—sensitive to such a degree that an unfavorable criticism of any of his works would almost persuade him that they were as worthless as the critic represented them. He thought so little of himself that he could never comprehend why it was that he should be the object of curiosity or reverence.

From the time that he began the composition of his *Sketch Book*, his whole life was the life of an author. His habits of composition were, however, by no means regular. When he was in the vein, the periods would literally stream from his pen; at other times he would scarcely write anything. For two years after the failure of his brothers at Liverpool, he found it almost impossible to write a line. He was throughout life an early riser, and when in the mood, would write all the morning and till late in the day, wholly engrossed with his subject. In the evening he was ready for any cheerful pastime, in which he took part with an animation almost amounting to high spirits. These intervals of excitement and intense labor, sometimes lasting for weeks, were succeeded by languor, and at times by depression of spirits, and for months the pen would lie untouched; even to answer a letter at these times was an irksome task.

In the evening he wrote but very rarely, knowing —so at least, I infer—that no habit makes severer demands upon the nervous system than this. It was owing, I doubt not, to this prudent husbanding of his powers, along with his somewhat abstinent habits and the exercise which he took every day, that he was able to preserve unimpaired to so late a period the faculties employed in original composition. He had been a vigorous walker and a fearless rider, and in his declining years he drove out daily, not only for the sake of the open air and motion, but to refresh his mind with the aspect of nature. One of his favorite recreations was listening to music, of which he was an indulgent critic, and he contrived to be pleased and soothed by strains less artfully modulated than fastidious ears are apt to require.

His facility in writing and the charm of his style were owing to very early practice, the reading of good authors, and the native elegance of his mind; and not, in my opinion, to any special study of the graces of manner or any anxious care in the use of terms and phrases. Words and combinations of words are sometimes found in his writings to which a fastidious taste might object; but these do not prevent his style from being one of the most agreeable in the whole range of our literature. It is transparent as the light, sweetly modulated, unaffected, the native expression of a fertile fancy, a benignant temper, and a mind which, delighting in the noble and the beautiful, turned involuntarily away from their opposites. His peculiar humor was, in a great measure, the offspring of this constitution of his mind. This "fanciful playing with common things," as Mr. Dana calls it, is never coarse, never tainted with grossness, and always in harmony with our better sympathies. It not only tinged his writings, but overflowed in his delightful conversation.

I have thus set before you, my friends, with such

measure of ability as I possess, a rapid and imperfect sketch of the life, character and genius of Washington Irving. Other hands will yet give the world a bolder, more vivid and more exact portraiture. In the mean time, when I consider for how many years he stood before the world as an author, with a still increasing fame—half a century in this most changeful of centuries—I cannot hesitate to predict for him a deathless renown. Since he began to write, empires have risen and passed away ; mighty captains have appeared on the stage of the world, performed their part, and been called to their account ; wars have been fought and ended, which have changed the destinies of the human race. New arts have been invented and adopted, and have pushed the old out of use ; the household economy of half mankind has undergone a revolution. Science has learned a new dialect and forgotten the old ; the chemist of 1807 would be a vain babbler among his brethren of the present day, and would in turn become bewildered in the attempt to understand them. Nation utters speech to nation in words that pass from realm to realm with the speed of light. Distant countries have been made neighbors ; the Atlantic Ocean has become a narrow frith, and the Old World and the New shake hands across it ; the East and the West look in at each other's windows. The new inventions bring new calamities, and men perish in crowds by the recoil of their own devices. War has learned more frightful modes of havoc, and armed himself with deadlier weapons; armies are borne to the battle-field on the wings of the wind, and dashed against each other and destroyed with infinite bloodshed. We grow giddy with this perpetual whirl of strange events, these rapid and ceaseless mutations; the earth seems to reel under our feet, and we turn to those who write like Irving, for some assurance that we are still in the same world into which we were born; we read and are quieted and consoled. In his pages we see that the language of the heart never becomes obsolete; that Truth and Good and Beauty, the offspring of God, are not subject to the changes which beset the inventions of men. We become satisfied that he whose works were the delight of our fathers, and are still ours, will be read with the same pleasure by those who come after us.

If it were becoming, at this time and in this assembly, to address our departed friend as if in his immediate presence, I would say : " Farewell! thou who hast entered into the rest prepared, from the foundation of the world, for serene and gentle spirits like thine :   Farewell! happy in thy life, happy in thy

7*

death, happier in the reward to which that death was the assured passage ; fortunate in attracting the admiration of the world to thy beautiful writings, still more fortunate in having written nothing which did not tend to promote the reign of magnanimous forbearance and generous sympathies among thy fellow-men. The brightness of that enduring fame which thou hast won on earth is but a shadowy symbol of the glory to which thou art admitted in the world beyond the grave. Thy errand upon earth was an errand of peace and good-will to men, and thou art in a region where hatred and strife never enter, and where the harmonious activity of those who inhabit it acknowledges no impulse less noble or less holy than that of love."

FITZ-GREENE HALLECK.

FITZ-GREENE HALLECK.

NOTICES OF HIS LIFE AND WRITINGS, READ BEFORE THE NEW YORK HISTORICAL SOCIETY, FEBRUARY, 3, 1869.

I have yielded with some hesitation to the request that I should read before the Historical Society a paper on the Life and Writings of Fitz-Greene Halleck. I hesitated, because the subject had been most ably treated by others. I consented, because it seemed to be expected, by his friends and admirers, that one who like myself was so nearly his contemporary, who read his poems as they appeared, and through whom several of the finest of them were given to the world, ought not to let a personal friend, a genial companion and an admirable poet pass from us without some words setting forth his merits and our sorrow. It is, besides, a relief under such a loss to dwell upon the characteristic qualities of the departed. It seems in an imperfect manner to prolong his existence among us ; as we repeat his words we seem to behold the friendly brightness of his eye ; we hear the familiar tones of his voice. It is as when, in looking upon the quivering surface of a river, we see the image of an object on the bank which is itself hidden from our eyes.

The southern shore of Connecticut, bordering on the Long Island Sound, is a beautiful region. I have never passed along this shore, extending from Byron river to the Naugatuck, without admiring it. Here the somewhat severe climate of New England is softened by the sea air and the shelter of the hills. Such charming combinations of rock and valley, of forest and stream, of smooth meadows, quiet inlets and green promontories are rarely to be found. A multitude of clear and rapid rivers, the king of which is the majestic Connecticut, here wind their way to the Sound among picturesque hills, cliffs and woods.

It was at Guilford, in this pleasant region, before which the Sound expands into a sea, that Halleck, on the 8th of July, 1790, was born. Poets, it is true, and poets of great genius, have been born in cities or in countries of the tamest aspect; yet I think it may be truly said that the sense of diversified beauty or solemn grandeur is awakened and nourished in the young mind by those qualities in the scenery which surround the poet's childhood. I do not find, however, in Halleck's verses, any particular recognition of the uncommon beauty of the region to which he owed his birth. In the well-known lines on Connecticut, he says:

> " And still her gray rocks tower above the sea,
> That crouches at their feet a conquered wave ;
> "Tis a rough land of earth, and stone, and tree," etc.

In another passage of the same poem, where he celebrates the charms of the region, he speaks solely of the tints of the atmosphere and the autumnal glory of its forests :

> " ———in the autumn time
> Earth has no purer and no lovelier clime."

> " Her clear warm heaven at noon, the mist that shrouds
> Her twilight hills, her cool and starry eves,
> The glorious splendor of her sunset clouds,
> The rainbow beauty of her forest leaves," etc.

Yet that this omission did not arise from any insensibility to the beauty of form in landscape is sufficiently manifested by the enthusiastic apostrophe to Weehawken, which escapes from him, as if in spite of himself, in his Fanny, amidst the satirical reflections which form the staple of the poem. He gave a higher proof of his affection for his birth-place, withdrawing in the evening of life from the bustling city where the greater part of his years had been spent, and where he had acquired his fame, to the pleasant haunts of his childhood, to dwell where his parents dwelt, to die where they died, and to be buried beside them. His end was like that of the rivers of his native State, which after dashing and sparkling over their stony beds, lay themselves down between quiet meadows and glide softly to the Sound.

Halleck had a worthy parentage. His father, Israel Halleck, according to Mr. Duyckinck, was a man of extensive reading, a tenacious memory, pithy conversation and courteous manners. His mother was of the Eliot family, a descendant of John Eliot, one of the noblest of the New England worthies, the translator of the Bible into the Indian language, the religious teacher, friend, and protector, of the Indians, the rigid non-conformist, the charitable pastor who distributed his salary among his needy neighbors, who preached and prayed against wigs and tobacco, without being able to triumph over the power of fashion or the force of habit, and of whom it is said that his sermons were remarkable for their simplicity of expression and freedom from the false taste of the age. Halleck inherited his ancestor's spirit of non-conformity. He would argue in favor of an established church among people with whom the dissociation of Church and State was an article of political faith, and astonished his republican neighbors by declaring himself a partisan of monarchy. He was not easily diverted from any course of conduct by deference to public opinion. Mr. Cozzens relates, that when Jacob Barker had fallen under the public censure, Halleck, then his clerk, was told that he ought to leave his service. He answered that he would not desert the sinking ship, and that the time to stand by his friends was when they were unfortunate. He had a certain persistency of temper which was transmitted, I think, from the old Puritan stock. It was some fifteen or twenty years after he came to live in New York that he said to me, " I like to go on with the people whom I begin with. I have the same boarding-house now that I had when I first came to town ; my clothes are made by the same tailor, and I employ the same shoemaker."

I do not find that Halleck began to write verses prematurely. Poetry, with most men, is one of the sins of their youth, and a great deal of it is written before the authors can be justly said to have reached years of discretion. With the greater number it runs its course and passes off like the measles or the chicken pox : with a few it takes the chronic form and lasts a lifetime ; and I have known cases of persons attacked by it in old age. A very small number who begin, like Milton, Cowley and Pope, to write verses when scarce out of childhood, afterwards become eminent as poets ; but as a rule, precocity in this department of letters is no sign of genius. In the verses of Halleck which General Wilson has collected, written in 1809 and 1810 and earlier, I discern but slight traces of his peculiar genius, and none of the grace and spirit which afterwards became so marked. They are better, it is true, than the juvenile poems which encumber the later collections of the poetry of Thomson, but they are not characteristic. Between the time when they were written, and that in which he produced the poems which are commonly called the Croakers, his poetic faculty ripened rapidly, and as remarkably as that of Byron between the publication of his *Hours of Idleness*, and that of his *Childe Harold*. His fancy had been quickened into new life ; he had learned to wield his native language like a master; he had discovered that he was a wit as well as a poet; and his verse had acquired that sweetness and variety of modulation which afterwards distinguished it. The poems which bear the signature of Croaker and Croaker and Co., written by him in conjunction with his friend, Joseph Rodman Drake, began in 1819 to appear in the *Evening Post*, then conducted by Mr. Coleman. That gentleman observed their merit with surprise, commended them in his daily sheet, and was gratified to learn that the whole town was talking of them. It was several years after this that Mr. Coleman said to me, " I was curious to see the young men whose witty verses, published in my journal, made so much noise, and desired an interview with them. They came before me and I was greatly struck by their appearance. Drake looked the poet ; you saw the stamp of genius in every feature. Halleck had the aspect of a satirist."

There is a certain manner common to both authors in these poems. They both wrote with playfulness and gayety, and although with the freedom of men who never expected to be known, yet without malignity ; but it seems to me that Halleck drove home his jests with the sharpest percussion, and there are some flashes of that fire which blazed out in his *Marco Bozzaris*.

The poem entitled *Fanny* was published about that time. It is, in the main, a satire upon those who, finding themselves in the possession of wealth suddenly acquired, rush into extravagant habits of living, give expensive entertainments, and as a natural consequence sink suddenly into the obscurity from which they rose. But the satire takes a wider range. The poet jests at everything that comes in his way ; authors, politicians, men of science, each is booked for a pleasantry; all are made to contribute to the expense of the entertainment set before the reader. The sting of his witticisms was not unfelt, and I think was in some cases resented. People do not like to be laughed at, however pleasant it may be to those who laugh. At a later period Halleck saw the truth of what Pope says of ridicule—

" The muse may give thee but the gods must guide—"

and he published an edition of his *Fanny*, with notes, in which he took care to make a generous reparation to those whom he had offended. But *Fanny* is not all satire, and here and there in the poem are bursts of true lyrical enthusiasm.

Some comparison has been made between the *Fanny* of Halleck and the satirical poems of Byron. But Halleck was never cynical in his satire, and Byron was. I remember reading a remark made by Voltaire, on the *Dunciad* of Pope. "It wants gayety," said the French critic. Gayety is the predominating quality of Halleck's satire as hatred is that of the satire of Pope and Byron. Byron delighted in thinking how his victim would writhe under the blows he gave him. Halleck's satire is the overflow of a mirthful temperament. He sees things in a ludicrous light, and laughs without reflecting that the object of his ridicule might not like the sport as well as himself.

In 1822 Halleck visited England and the continent of Europe. Of what he saw there I do not know that there is any record remaining except his noble poem entitled *Burns*, and the spirited and playful verses on Alnwick Castle.

It was in 1825, before Halleck's reputation as a poet had reached its full growth, that I took up my residence in New York. I first met him at the hospitable board of Robert Sedgwick, Esq., and remember being struck with the brightness of his eye, which every now and then glittered with mirth, and with the graceful courtesy of his manners. Something was said of the length of time that he had lived in New York—"You are not from New England?" said our host. "I certainly am," was Halleck's reply. "I am from Connecticut." "Is it possible?" exclaimed Mr. Sedgwick. "Well, you are the only New Englander that I ever saw in whom the tokens of his origin were not as plain as the mark set upon the forehead of Cain."

I was at that time one of the editors of a monthly magazine, the *New York Review*, which was soon gathered to the limbo of extinct periodicals. Halleck brought to it his poem of *Marco Bozzaris*, and in 1826 the lines entitled *Connecticut*. The first of these poems became immediately a favorite, and was read by everybody who cared to read verses. I remember that at an evening party, at the house, I think, of Mr. Henry D. Sedgwick, it was recited by Mrs. Nichols, the same who not long afterward gave the public an English translation of Manzoni's *Promessi Sposi*. She had a voice of great sweetness and power, capable of expressing every variety of emotion. She was in the midst of the poem, her thrilling voice the only sound in the room, and every ear intently listening to her accents, when suddenly she faltered; her memory had lost one of the lines. At that instant a clear and distinct voice, supplying the forgotten passage, was heard from a group in a corner of the room; it was the voice of the poet. With this aid she took up the recitation and went on triumphantly to the close, surrounded by an audience almost too deeply interested to applaud.

The poem entitled *Burns*, of which let me say I am not sure that the verses are not the finest in which one poet ever celebrated another, was contributed by Halleck, in 1827, to the *United States Review*, which I bore a part in conducting. Halleck had been led by his admiration of the poetry of Campbell to pay a visit to the charming valley, celebrated by

that poet in his *Gertrude of Wyoming*. In memory
of this he wrote the lines entitled *Wyoming*, which
he handed me for publication in the same magazine.
Before the *United States Review* shared the fate of
its predecessor, there appeared the first printed collection of Halleck's poetical writings with the title of
Alnwick Castle and other Poems, published by G.
Carvill & Company, in 1827. I had the pleasure of
saying to the readers of the Review how greatly I admired it.

At that time the Recorder of our city was appointed by the governor of the State. Those who
are not familiar with the judicial system of this State,
need, perhaps, to be told that the Recorder is not the
keeper of the city archives, but the judge of an important criminal court. In 1828, and for some years
before and afterward, the office was held by Mr.
Richard Riker, a man of great practical shrewdness
and the blandest manners, who was accused by some
of adjusting his political opinions to the humors of
the day, and was, therefore, deemed a proper subject
of satire. One day I met Halleck, who said to me :
" I have an epistle in verse from an old gentleman to
the Recorder which, if you please, I will send to you
for the *Evening Post*. It is all in my head and you
shall have it as soon as I have written it out." I

should mention here that Halleck was in the habit of composing verses without the aid of pen and ink, keeping them in his memory, and retouching them at his leisure.   In due time the *Epistle to the Recorder, by Thomas Castaly, Esq.*, came to hand, was published in the *Evening Post*, and was immediately read by the whole town.   It seems to me one of the happiest of Halleck's satirical poems.   The man in office, who was the subject of it, must have hardly known whether to laugh or be angry, and it was impossible, one would think, to be perfectly at ease when thus made the plaything of a poet and pelted with all manner of gibes, sly allusions and ironical compliments, for the amusement of the public. Among its strokes of satire the epistle has passages of graceful poetry.   Halleck, after the manner of the ancients, in leading his victim to the sacrifice, had hung its horns with garlands of flowers.   The Recorder, however, is said to have borne this somewhat disrespectful, but by no means ill-natured assault, with the same apparent composure as he endured the coarser attacks of the newspapers.

In 1827 and the two following years, Dr. Bliss, a liberal-minded bookseller of this city, published annually, at the season of the winter holidays, a small volume of miscellanies entitled the *Talisman*.   They

were written almost exclusively by three authors:
Mr. Verplanck, eminent in our literature and still
fortunately spared to perform important public services ; Robert C. Sands, a man of abounding wit, prematurely lost to the world of letters, and myself as
the third contributor. For the volume which appeared in 1828, Halleck offered us one of his most remarkable poems, *Red Jacket*, and I need not say
how delighted we were to grace our collection by
anything so vigorous, spirited and original. It was illustrated by an engraving from a striking full length
portrait of the old Indian chief, by the elder Wier,
then in the early maturity of his powers as an artist.

After the publication of these poems there follows an interval of thirty-five years which is almost a
blank in Halleck's literary history. Between 1828
and 1863 he seems to have produced nothing worthy
of note except the additions which he made to his
poem of *Connecticut*, in an edition published by Red-
field, in 1852, and these are fully worthy of his reputation. It is almost unaccountable that an author,
still in the highest strength of his faculties, who had
written to such acceptance, should not have been
tempted to write more for a public which he knew
was eager to read whatever came from his pen.
" When an author begins to be quoted," said Hal-

leck once to me, "he is already famous." Halleck
found that he was quoted, but he was not a man to
go on writing because the world seemed to expect it.
It was only in 1863, when he was already seventy-
three years of age, that he wrote for the *New York
Ledger* his *Young America*, a poem, which, though
not by any means to be placed among his best, contains, as Mr. Cozzens, in a paper read before this Society, justly remarks, passages which remind us of his
earlier vigor and grace.

Yet, if in that interval he did not occupy himself
with poetic composition, he gave much of his leisure
to the poetry of others. I have never known any
one, I think, who seemed to take so deep a delight in
the poetry that perfectly suited his taste. He tran-
scribed it; he read it over and over; he dwelt upon
it until every word of it became engraven upon his
memory; he recited it with glistening eyes and a
voice and frame tremulous with emotion. Mr. F. S.
Cozzens has sent me a scrap of paper on which he
had copied a passage of eight lines of verse, and under them had written these sentences: " I find these
verses in an album. Do you know the writer? I
would give a hundred pounds sterling, payable out of
any money in my treasury not otherwise appropri-
ated, to be capable of writing the two last lines."

I was most agreeably surprised as well as flatter-
ed, the other day, to receive from General Wilson,
who has collected the poetical writings of Halleck,
and is engaged in preparing his Life and Letters for
the press, a copy, in the poet's handwriting of some
verses of mine entitled *The Planting of the Apple
Tree*, which he had taken the pains to transcribe,
and which General Wilson had heard him repeat
from memory in his own fine manner.

Halleck loved to ramble in the country, for the
most part, I believe, alone. Once he did me the favor to make me his companion. It was while the region from Hoboken to Fort Lee was yet but thinly
sprinkled with habitations, and the cliffs which overlook the river on its western bank had lain in forest
from the time that Hendrick Hudson entered the
great stream which bears his name. We were on a
slow-going steamer, which we left at the landing of
Bull's Ferry. "Do you not go on with us, Mr. Halleck?" asked the Captain. "No," was the answer;
"I am in a hurry." We walked on to Fort Lee,
where we made a short stop at the house of a publi-
can named Reynolds, who is mentioned in Duyckinck's memoir, an English radical, a man of no little mother wit, and a deep strong voice, which he
greatly loved to hear. Halleck had known him when

he exercised his vocation in town, and took pleasure, I think, in hearing his ready rejoinders to the poet's praises of a monarchy and an established church; and Reynolds, proud of the acquaintance of so eminent a man as Halleck, received him with demonstrations of delight. We returned over the heights of Weehawken to look at the magnificent view so finely celebrated by Halleck in his *Fanny*, with its glorious bay, its beautiful isles, its grand headlands and its busy cities, the murmur of which was heard blending with the dash of waves at the foot of the cliff.

I have mentioned that Halleck was early a clerk in the office of Mr. Barker. He was afterwards employed in the same capacity by John Jacob Astor, the richest man of his day in New York, and exceedingly sagacious and fortunate in his enterprises. His term of employment by Mr. Astor came, however, to an end; and I think that he was then compelled by the narrowness of his means to practise a rigid economy. He was of too independent a spirit to allow himself to be drawn into a situation which would incline him to keep out of the way of a creditor. He was an excellent accountant; I have a letter from one of his friends, speaking of his skill in difficult and intricate computations, in which Mr. Astor employed him with confidence. Perhaps the habit of exactness in this vocation led to exactness in his dealings with all men. His example is an encouraging one for poets and wits, since it teaches that a lively fancy and practical good sense do not necessarily stand in each other's way. Somebody has called prudence a rascally virtue, and I have heard Halleck himself rail at it, and refer to Benjamin Franklin as a man who had acquired a false reputation by his dexterity in taking care of his own interests. But Halleck did not disdain to practise the virtue which he decried, and he knew, as well as Franklin himself, that prudence, in the proper sense of the term, is wisdom applied to the ordinary affairs of life ; that it includes forecast, one of the highest operations of the intellect, and the due adjustment of means to ends, without which a man is useless both to himself and to society, except as a blunderer by whose example others may be warned.

I think it was some time after he had given up his clerkship that Mr. Astor left him a small legacy, to which the son, Mr. William B. Astor, made a liberal addition. Halleck then withdrew from the city in which he had passed forty years of his life, to Guilford, his native place, in which the Eliots, his ancestors on the mother's side, had dwelt for nearly two centuties. Here, in the houschold of an unmarried sister, older than himself and now living, he passed his later years among his books, with some infirmities of body, but with intellectual faculties still vigorous, his wit as keen and lively as when he wrote his *Epistle to the Recorder*, and his delight in the verses of his favorite poets and in the happy expression of generous sentiments as deeply felt and as easily awakened as when he wrote his noble poem on *Woman.*

It was not far from the time of which I speak that some of Halleck's personal and literary friends gave him a dinner at the rooms of the Club called the Century. It fell to me to preside, and in toasting our guest I first spoke, in such terms as I was able to command, of the merits of his poetry, as occupying a place in our literature like the poetry of Horace in the literature of ancient Rome. I dwelt upon the playfulness and grace of his satire and the sweetness and fervor of his lyrical ·vein. Halleck answered very happily :

" I do not rise to speak," he said, " for if I were to stand up I could say nothing. I must keep my seat and talk to you without ceremony." And then he went on, speaking modestly and charmingly of his own writings. I cannot, at this distance of time, recollect how he treated the subject, but I well remember that he spoke so well that we could willingly have listened to him the whole evening.

It is now five-and-thirty years, the life of one of the generations of mankind, since I contributed to a weekly periodical, published in this city, an estimate of the poetical genius of Halleck. Of course nobody now remembers having read it, and, as it was written after his most remarkable poems had been given to the public, and as I could say nothing different of them now, I will, with the leave of the audience, make it a part of this paper.

" Halleck is one of the most generally admired of all our poets, and he possesses what no other does, a decided local popularity. He is the favorite poet of the city of New York, where his name is cherished with a peculiar fondness and enthusiasm. It furnishes a standing and ever-ready allusion to all who would speak of American literature, and is familiar in the mouths of hundreds who would be seriously puzzled if asked to name any other American poet. The verses of others may be found in the hands of persons who possess some tincture of polite literature— young men pursuing their studies, or young ladies with whom the age of romance is not yet past ; but those of Halleck are read by people of the humblest degree of literary pretension, and are equally admired in Bond street and the Bowery. There are numbers who regularly attribute to his pen every anonymous poem in the newspapers, in which an attempt at humor is evident, who 'know him by his style,' and whose delight at the supposed wit is heightened almost to transport, by the self-complacency of having made the discovery. His reputation, however, is not injured by these mistakes, for the verses by which they are occasioned are soon forgotten, and his fame rests firmly on the compositions which are known to be his.

" This high degree of local popularity has, for one of its causes, the peculiar subjects of many of the poems of Halleck, relating, as they do, to persons and things and events, with which everybody in New York is more or less acquainted ; objects which are constantly before the eyes, and matters which are the talk of every fireside. The poems written by him in conjunction with his friend, Doctor Drake, for the *Evening Post*, in the year 1819, under the signature of Croaker & Co., and the satirical poem of *Fanny*, are examples of this happy use of the familiar topics of the day. He will pardon this allusion to works which he has never publicly acknowledged, but which are attributed to him by general consent, since, with-

out them, we might miss some of the peculiar characteristics of his genius.

"Halleck's humorous poems are marked by an
uncommon ease of versification, a natural flow and
sweetness of language, and a careless, Horatian
playfulness and felicity of jest, not, however, imitated
from Horace or any other writer. He finds abundant matter for mirth in the peculiar state of our society, in the heterogeneous population of the city—

> 'Of every race the mingled swarm,'

in the affectations of newly assumed gentility, the ostentation of wealth, the pretensions of successful
quackery, and the awkward attempt to blend with
the habits of trade, an imitation of the manners of
the most luxurious and fastidious nobility in the
world—the nobility of England. Sometimes, in the
midst of a strain of harmonious diction, and soft and
tender imagery, so soft and tender that you willingly
yield yourself up to the feeling of pathos, or to the
sense of beauty it inspires, he surprises you with an
irresistible stroke of ridicule,

> ' As if himself he did disdain,
> And mock the form he did but feign;'

as if he looked with no regard upon the fair poetical
vision he had raised, and took pleasure in showing

8*

the reader that it was but a cheat. Sometimes, the poet, with that aerial facility which is his peculiar endowment, accumulates graceful and agreeable images in a strain of irony so fine, that, did not the subject compel you to receive it as irony, you would take it for a beautiful passage of serious poetry— so beautiful, that you are tempted to regret that he is not in earnest, and that phrases so exquisitely chosen, and poetic coloring so brilliant, should be employed to embellish subjects to which they do not properly belong. At other times, he produces the effect of wit by dexterous allusions to contemporaneous events, introduced as illustrations of the main subject, with all the unconscious gracefulness of the most animated and familiar conversation. He delights in ludicrous contrasts produced by bringing the nobleness of the ideal world into comparison with the homeliness of the actual; the beauty and grace of nature with the awkwardness of art. He venerates the past and laughs at the present. He looks at them through a medium which lends to the former the charm of romance, and exaggerates the deformity of the latter.

" Halleck's poetry, whether serious or sprightly, is remarkable for the melody of the numbers. It is not the melody of monotonous and strictly regular measurement. His verse is constructed to please an ear naturally fine and accustomed to a wide range of metrical modulation. It is as different from that painfully balanced versification, that uniform succession of iambics, closing the sense with the couplet, which some writers practise, and some critics praise, as the note of the thrush is unlike that of the cuckoo. Halleck is familiar with those general rules and principles which are the basis of metrical harmony; and his own unerring taste has taught him the exceptions which a proper attention to variety demands. He understands that the rivulet is made musical by obstructions in its channel. You will find in no poet, passages which flow with a more sweet and liquid smoothness; but he knows very well that to make this smoothness perceived and to prevent it from degenerating into monotony, occasional roughnesses. must be interposed.

"But it is not only in humorous or playful poetry that Halleck excels. He has fire and tenderness and manly vigor, and his serious poems are equally admirable with his satirical. What martial lyric can be finer than the verses on the death of Marco Bozzaris! We are made spectators of the slumbers of the Turkish oppressor, dreaming of 'victory in his guarded tent;' we see the Greek warrior ranging his true-hearted band of Suliotes in the forest shades ; we behold them throwing themselves into the camp ; we hear the shout, the groan, the sabre stroke, the death shot falling thick and fast, and in the midst of all, the voice of Bozzaris bidding them to strike boldly for God and their native land. The struggle is long and fierce ; the ground is piled with Moslem slain ; the Greeks are at length victorious ; and, as the brave chief falls bleeding from every vein, he hears the proud huzza of his surviving comrades, announcing that the field is won, and he closes his eyes in death,

> ‘ Calmly, as to a night's repose.’

"This picture of the battle is followed by a dirge over the slain hero—a glorious outpouring of lyrical eloquence, worthy to have been chanted by Pindar or Tyrtæus over one of his ancestors. There is in this poem a freedom, a daring, a fervency, a rapidity, an affluence of thick-coming fancies, that make it seem like an inspired improvisation, as if the thoughts had been divinely breathed into the mind of the poet, and uttered themselves, voluntarily, in poetic numbers. We think, as we read it, of

> ‘ ——The large utterance of the early gods.’

"If an example is wanted of Halleck's capacity

for subjects of a gentler nature, let the reader turn to
the verses written in the album of an unknown lady,
entitled *Woman*.   In a few lines, he has gathered
around the name of woman a crowd of delightful
associations—all the graces of her sex, delightful pictures of domestic happiness and domestic virtues,
gentle affections, pious cares, smiles and tears, that
bless and heal,

> ' And earth's lost paradise restored,
> In the green bower of home.'

" *Red Jacket* is a poem of a yet different kind ; a
poem of manly vigor of sentiment, noble versification,
strong expression, and great power in the delineation
of character—the whole dashed off with a great appearance of freedom, and delightfully tempered with
the satirical vein of the author.   Some British periodical, lately published, contains a criticism on American literature, in which it is arrogantly asserted, that
our poets have made nothing of the Indian character,
and that Campbell's *Outalissi* is altogether the best
portraiture of the mind and manners of an American
savage, which is to be found in English verse.   The
critic must have spoken without much knowledge of
his subject.   He certainly could never have read
Halleck's *Red Jacket*.   Campbell's *Outalissi* is very
well.   He is ' a stoic of the woods,' and nothing

more; an Epictetus put into a blanket and leggins, and translated to the forests of Pennsylvania; but he is no Indian. *Red Jacket* is the very savage of our wilderness. *Outalissi* is a fancy sketch of few lineaments. He is brave, faithful and affectionate, concealing these qualities under an exterior of insensibility. *Red Jacket* has the spirit and variety of a portrait from nature. He has all the savage virtues and savage vices, and the rude and strong qualities of mind which belong to a warrior, a chief, and an orator of the aboriginal stock. He is set before us with sinewy limbs, gentle voice, motions graceful as a bird's in air, an air of command inspiring deference; brave, cunning, cruel, vindictive, eloquent, skilful to dissemble, and terrible, when the moment of dissembling is past, as the wild beasts or the tempests of his own wilderness.

" A poem which, without being the best he has written, unites many of the different qualities of Halleck's manner, is that entitled *Alnwick Castle.* The rich imagery, the airy melody of verse, the grace of language which belong to his serious poems, are to be found in the first half of the poem, which relates to the beautiful scenery and venerable traditions of the old home of the Percys; while the author's vein of gay humor, fertile in mirthful allusion, appears in

the conclusion, in which he descends to the homely
and peaceful occupations of its present proprietors.

"Whoever undertakes the examination of Halleck's poetical character, will naturally wish for a
greater number of examples from which to collect an
estimate of his powers. He has given us only samples of what he can do. His verses are like passages of some noble choral melody, heard in the
brief interval between the opening and shutting of
the doors of a temple. Why does he not more frequently employ the powers with which he is so eminently gifted? He should know that such faculties
are invigorated and enlarged, and rendered obedient
to the will by exercise. He need not be afraid of not
equalling what he has already written. He will excel himself, if he applies his powers, with an earnest
and resolute purpose, to the work which justice to
his own fame demands of him. There are heroes of
our own history who deserve to be embalmed for immortality, in strains as noble as those which celebrate
the death of Marco Bozzaris ; and Halleck has shown
how powerfully he can appeal to our sense of patriotism, in his *Field of the Grounded Arms*, a poem
which has only been prevented from being universally popular by the peculiar kind of verse in which it
is written."

This is what I wrote of Halleck thirty-five years ago. Since that time the causes which gave him a local popularity in New York have, in a great measure, ceased to exist. A new generation has arisen to whom the persons and most of the things which were the objects of his playful satire are known but by tradition. Eminent poets have appeared in our country and acquired fame among us, and divided with him the attention and admiration of the public. His best things, however, are still admired, I think, as much as ever in the city which, for the greater part of his life, he made his abode.

Of his literary habits less is known than of those of most literary men of his time. During the latter years of his life, and, I think, for some time previous, he manifested but little inclination to go into society, on account, I believe, of a difficulty of hearing which made its appearance in middle life and increased somewhat as he grew older. He did not like to make those with whom he was talking repeat what had been said, and often ingeniously contrived to keep up a spirited conversation when he was obliged to guess the words addressed to him. His leisure, we may presume—a good deal of it, at least—was studiously passed, since his conversation showed that his reading was extensive, and his opinions of authors were al-

ways ready, and promptly and decidedly expressed.
I remember hearing him say that he could think of no
more fortunate lot in life than the possession of a well
stored library with ample leisure for reading.   He
was not unskilled in the modern languages of Europe, and once he said to me that he had learned Portuguese in order that he might read the *Lusiad* in the
original.   That poem, in Mickle's translation, is as little like the work of Camoens as Pope's *Iliad* is like
the *Iliad* of Homer.   Mickle has made it declamatory
where Camoens is simple, and all the rapidity of the
narrative is lost in the diffuse verses of the translator.

Halleck was fortunate in a retentive verbal memory, and recited fine passages from other poets with
great spirit and feeling.   He could not, as he remarked, remember what he did not like, and only chose to
dwell upon such as combined a certain melody of versification with beauty of thought.   "There is no poetry," he was wont to say, "without music.   It must
have the grace of rhythm and cadence."   He was not
quite satisfied with much of the poetry of the present
day.   "He thought," says Mr. Tuckerman, "that
much of current verse was the offspring of ingenuity
rather than inspiration,—that sentiment often lost its
wholesome fervor in diluted or perverse utterance."
I too have heard him object to the elaborately beauti-

ful verse of a popular English poet, that it was not manly, and to that of an English poetess of great and original genius, that it was not womanly. He delighted in great or affecting thoughts given with a transparent clearness of expression, and where he found obscurity, vagueness, or harshness, he withheld his admiration.

He was fond of maintaining unexpected opinions, which he often did with much ingenuity and art. He argued in favor of a monarchy and an Established Church. "The ship of state," he used to say, "must be governed and navigated like any other ship without consulting the crew. What would become of the stanchest bark in a gale, if the captain were obliged to call all hands together and say: 'All you who are in favor of taking in sail, will please to say, Aye?'" Before he left New York he began to declare his preference of the Roman Catholic Church over other denominations of Christians, though his manner of stating the argument in its favor might not perfectly satisfy its friends. "It is a church," he was wont to say, "which saves you a deal of trouble. You leave your salvation to the care of a class of men trained and set apart for the purpose; they have the charge both of your belief and your practice, and as long as you satisfy them on these points you need give yourself no anxiety about either." It was difficult always to be certain how far he was in earnest when he talked on these subjects.

On one occasion his habit of maintaining unusual opinions in a manner between jest and earnest, had a consequence which his friends regretted. Seth Cheney, the estimable artist who died in 1856, drew portraits of the size of life, in crayon, using no colors, with extraordinary skill in transferring to the sheet before him the finest and most elevated expression of which the countenance of his sitter was capable. He always wrought with a certain creative enthusiasm, like that of the poet. His best portraits, at the same time that they are good likenesses, have something angelic in their aspect. It is told of Dana the poet, that after looking with wonder at one of these drawings, the likeness of a lady more eminent for goodness than for beauty, he said: " It is our friend as she will be at the resurrection." Cheney could never bring himself to receive as sitters those for whom he did not entertain a decided respect, and for that reason declined to take the likeness of certain men distinguished in public life. Halleck once sat to him, but the artist found the frame of mind which he brought to his task disturbed by the free and sportive manner in which his sitter spoke of certain grave matters, and one morning when Halleck came as usual, Cheney said to him : " I have finished your likeness." " You have been expeditious," said the poet. " Yes," returned Cheney, " I put it in the fire this morning." That was the last of Halleck's sittings to Cheney; but if the poet had not jested so unseasonably we should probably have had one of Cheney's finest heads, for Halleck, with his beaming countenance, was a capital subject for such an artist.

Halleck was much besieged, as authors of note, particularly poets, are apt to be, with applications from persons desirous of appearing in print, to read their manuscript verses and give his opinion of their merits. I have heard him say that he never turned them away with an unfriendly answer. I suppose that, regarding poets as a sensitive tribe, keenly alive to unfavorable criticism, he spared them as much as he could, though I doubt very much whether they obtained from him any opinion worth the trouble they had taken. If what I write should fall under the eye of any persons of either sex, poetically inclined and ambitious of renown, I would strongly advise them against sending their verses to a poet for his judgment. In the first place, it does not follow that because he passes for a poet, he is therefore a competent critic ; in the second place, they may be sure that he will have little time to look at their verses; and thirdly, he will naturally be so desirous to treat their case tenderly that his opinion will be of little value. I have always counselled persons of this class, if they *must* come before the public, not to seek the opinion of individuals, but to get their verses printed in the periodicals that will accept them, and thus appeal to the reading world at large, which is the only proper judge of poetic merit.

The conversation of Halleck was remarkably sprightly and pointed. If there had been any friend to take note of what he said, a volume of his pithy and pleasant sayings might have been compiled, as entertaining as anything of the kind which has appeared since Boswell's Johnson. His letters were of a like character with his familiar talk, and were full of playful turns and witty allusions.

He reached a good old age, dying on the nineteenth of November, 1867, at the age of seventy-seven. Towards the latter part of his life he was subject to a painful disease, from which he seems to have suffered only in occasional paroxysms, since it was but a few days before his death that he wrote to his friend Mr. Verplanck, saying that he would like to meet his old friends in New York at dinner at some old-fashioned place, such as Windust's, and that he would like his younger friend, Mr. F. S. Cozzens, to make the arrangements for the purpose. His wish, so far as depended on his friends here, was about to be fulfilled, when in the midst of their preparations they were shocked by the news of his death.

He was spared the suffering which is the lot of many to whom, in their departure from this life, are appointed long days and nights of pain. To him might be applied with tolerable truth the lines of Milton.

> " So shalt thou live, till like ripe fruit thou drop
>   Into thy mother's lap, or be with ease
>   Gathered, not harshly plucked, for death mature."

But the lines which follow soon after these do not describe the old age of Halleck :

> " —and for the air of youth
>   Hopeful and cheerful, in thy blood will reign
>   A melancholy damp of cold and dry
>   To weigh thy spirits down,"

since he retained to the last the vivacious faculties and quick emotions of his earlier life. His age was not unvisited by the warnings which usually accompany that season of life, but his death was easy, and his last hours were solaced by the affectionate cares of that sister to whose side he had returned when he saw the shadows of the hills lengthen across his path in the evening sunshine.

When I look back upon Halleck's literary life, I cannot help thinking that if his death had happened forty years earlier, his life would have been regarded as a bright morning prematurely óvercast. Yet Halleck's literary career may be said to have ended then. All that will hand down his name to future years had already been produced. Who shall say to what cause his subsequent literary inaction was owing? It was not the decline of his powers; his brilliant conversation showed that it was not. Was it then indifference to fame? Was it because he put an humble estimate on what he had written, and therefore resolved to write no more? Was it because he feared lest what he might write would be unworthy of the reputation he had been so fortunate as to acquire?

I have my own way of accounting for his literary silence in the latter half of his life. One of the resemblances which he bore to Horace consisted in the length of time for which he kept his poems by him that he might give them the last and happiest touches. Having composed his poems without committing them to paper, and retaining them in his faithful memory, he revised them in the same manner, mur-

muring them to himself in his solitary moments, re-
covering the enthusiasm with which they were first
conceived, and in this state of mind heightening the
beauty of the thought or of the expression. I remember that once, in crossing Washington Park, I
saw Halleck before me, and quickened my pace to
overtake him. As I drew near, I heard him crooning
to himself what seemed to be lines of verse, and as
he threw back his hands in walking, I perceived that
they quivered with the feeling of the passage he was
reciting. I instantly checked my pace and fell back,
out of reverence for the mood of inspiration which
seemed to be upon him, and fearful lest I should in-
tercept the birth of a poem destined to be the delight
of thousands of readers.

In this way I suppose Halleck to have attained
the gracefulness of his diction, and the airy melody
of his numbers. In this way I believe that he
wrought up his verses to that transparent clearness
of expression which causes the thought to be seen
through them without any interposing dimness, so
that the thought and the phrase seem one, and the
thought enters the mind like a beam of light. I
suppose that Halleck's time being taken up by the
tasks of his vocation, he naturally lost by degrees
the habit of composing in this manner, and that he

found it so necessary to the perfection of what he wrote, that he adopted no other in its place.

Whatever was the reason that Halleck ceased so early to write, let us congratulate ourselves that he wrote at all. Great authors often overlay and almost smother their own fame by the voluminousness of their writings. So great is their multitude, and so rich is the literature of our language, that, for frequent reading, we are obliged to content ourselves with mere selections from the works of the best and most beloved of our poets, even those who have not written much. It is only a few of their works that dwell and live in the general mind. Gray, for example, wrote little, and of that little, only one short poem, his *Elegy*, can be fairly said to survive in the public admiration, and that poem I have sometimes heard called the most popular in our language.

In what I have said it will be seen that I have principally limited myself to what I personally knew of Halleck. I merely designed to add my humble tribute to those which sorrowing hands had laid on his grave. Our friend is gone, and to those of us who knew him the world seems the dimmer for his departure. The light of that bright eye is quenched; its socket is filled with dust; that voice is heard no more in lively sallies of wit, or repeating in tones full of emotion the verses of the poets whom he loved. When such a man, a man of so bright and active an intellect, dies, the short period of our existence on earth, even when prolonged to old age, presses sadly on our minds, and we instinctively seek relief in the doctrine of the soul's immortality. We ask ourselves how that conscious intelligence, of which the bodily organs are manifestly so imperfect a medium, can be resolved, along with them, into the grosser elements of which they are compounded; how a mind so creative, so keenly alive to the beauty of God's works, and so wonderfully dexterous in combining the materials which these works supply into forms which have in them somewhat of that transcendant beauty, can fail to partake of the endless existence of the Divinity whom it thus imitates. We connect the creative in man with the imperishable and undying, and reverently trust the spirit to the compassionate cares of Him who breathed it into the human frame.

GULIAN CROMMELIN VERPLANCK.

GULIAN CROMMELIN VERPLANCK.

A DISCOURSE ON HIS LIFE, CHARACTER AND WRITINGS, DE-
LIVERED BEFORE THE NEW YORK HISTORICAL SOCIETY,
MAY 17, 1870.

The life of him in honor of whose memory we are
assembled, was prolonged to so late a period, and to
the last was so full of usefulness, that it almost
seemed a permanent part of the organization and the
active movement of society here.   His departure has
left a sad vacuity in the framework which he helped
to uphold and adorn.   It is as if one of the columns
which support a massive building had been suddenly
taken away ; the sight of the space which it once occupied troubles us, and the mind wearies itself in the
unavailing wish to restore it to its place.

In what I am about to say, I shall put together
some notices of the character, the writings, and the
services of this eminent man, but the portraiture
which I shall draw will be but a miniature.   To do it
full justice a larger canvas would be required than
the one I propose to take.   He acted in so many
important capacities ; he was connected in so many
ways with our literature, our legislation, our jurispru-

dence, our public education, and public charities, that it would require a volume adequately to set forth the obligations we owe to the exertion of his fine faculties for the general good.

Gulian Crommelin Verplanck was born in Wall street, in the city of New York, on the 6th of August, 1786. The house in which he was born was a large yellow mansion, standing on the spot on which the Assay Office has since been built. A little beyond this street, so that it was but a step into the country, lay the island of New York in all its original beauty. His father, Daniel Crommelin Verplanck, was a respectable citizen of the old stock of colonists from Holland, who for several terms was a member of Congress, and whom I remember as a short, stout old gentleman, commonly called Judge Verplanck, from having been a judge of the County Court of Duchess. In that county he resided during the latter years of his life on the patrimonial estate, where the son, ever since I knew him, was in the habit of passing a part of the summer. It had been in the family of the Verplancks ever since their ancestor, Gulian Verplanck with Francis Rombout, in 1683, purchased it, with other lands, of the Wappinger Indians for a certain amount of money and merchandise, specified in a deed signed by the Sachem Sakoraghuck and other chiefs, the spelling of whose names seems to defy pronunciation. The two purchasers afterwards divided this domain, and to the Verplancks was assigned a tract which they have ever since held.

This fine old estate has a long western border on the Hudson, and extends easterly for four or five miles to the village of Fishkill. About half a mile from the great river stands the family mansion, among its ancient groves—a large stone building of one story when I saw it, with a sharp roof and dormer windows, beside its old-fashioned and well-stocked garden. A winding path leads down to the river's edge, through an ancient forest which has stood there ever since Hendrick Hudson navigated the river bearing his name, and centuries before. This mansion was the country retreat of Mr. Verplanck from the time that I first knew him ; and here it was that his grandfather on the paternal side, Samuel Verplanck, passed much of his time during our Revolutionary War, in which, although he took no share in political measures, his inclinations were on the side of the mother country.

This Samuel Verplanck, by a custom which seems not to have become obsolete in his time, was betrothed, when but seven years old, to his cousin

Judith Crommelin, the daughter of a wealthy banker of the Huguenot stock in Amsterdam. When the young gentleman was of the proper age he was sent to make the tour of Europe, and bring home his bride. He was married in the banker's great stone house, which stood beside a fair Dutch garden, with a wide marble entrance-hall, the counting-room on one side of it, and the drawing-room bright with gilding on the other. When the grandson, in after years, visited Amsterdam, the mansion which had often been described to him by his grandmother, had to him quite a familiar aspect.

The lady from Amsterdam was particularly accomplished, and versed not only in several modern languages, but in Greek and Latin, speaking fluently the Latin of which the Colloquies of her great countryman, Erasmus, furnished so rich a store of phrases for ordinary dialogue. Her conversation is said to have been uncommonly brilliant and her society much sought. During the Revolutionary War her house was open to the British officers, General Howe, and others, accomplished men, of whom she had many anecdotes to relate to her grandson, when he came under her care. For the greater part of this time her husband remained at the country seat in Fishkill, quietly occupied with his books and the

care of his estate.   Meantime, she wrote anxious letters to her father, in Amsterdam, which were answered in neat French.   The banker consoled his
daughter by saying that " Mr. Samuel Verplanck
was a man so universally known and honored, both
for his integrity and scholarly attainments, that in
the end all would be well."   This proved true ; the
extensive estate at Fishkill was never confiscated,
and its owner was left unmolested.

On the mother's side, our friend had an ancestry
of quite different political views.   His grandfather,
William Samuel Johnson, of Stratford, in Connecticut, was one of the revolutionary fathers.   Before the
revolution, he was the agent of Connecticut in England ; when it broke out he took a zealous part in the
cause of the revolted colonies ; he was a delegate to
Congress from his State when Congress sat in New
York, and he aided in framing the Constitution of the
United States.   Afterwards, he was President of Columbia College from the year 1787 to the year 1800,
when, resigning the post, he returned to Stratford,
where he died in 1819, at the age of ninety-two.   His
father, the great-grandfather of the subject of this
memoir, was Dr. Samuel Johnson, of Stratford, one
of the finest American scholars of his day, and the first
President of Columbia College, which, however, he

9*

left after nine years, to return and pass a serene old age at Stratford. He had been a Congregational minister in Connecticut, but by reading the works of Barrow and other eminent divines of the Anglican Church, he became a convert to that church, went to, England, and taking orders, returned to introduce its ritual into Connecticut. He was the friend of Bishop Berkeley, whose arm-chair was preserved as an heir-loom in his family. When in England, he saw Pope, who gave him cuttings from his Twickenham willow. These he brought from the banks of the Thames, and planted on the wilder borders of his own beautiful river, the Housatonic, which at Stratford enters the Sound. They were, probably, the progenitors of all the weeping willows which are seen in this part of the country, where they rapidly grow to a size which I have never seen them attain in any other part of the world.

The younger of these Dr. Johnsons — for they both received the degree of Doctor of Divinity from the University of Oxford—had a daughter Elizabeth, who married Daniel Crommelin Verplanck, the son of Samuel Verplanck, and the only fruit of their marriage was the subject of this memoir. The fair-haired young mother was a frequent visitor with her child to Stratford, where, under the willow trees from

Twickenham, as appears from some of her letters, he learned to walk. She died when he was but three years old, leaving the boy to the care of his grandmother, by whom he was indulgently yet carefully reared.

The grandmother is spoken of as a lively little lady, often seen walking up Wall street, dressed in pink satin and in dainty high-heeled shoes, with a quaint jewelled watch swinging from her waist. Wall street was then the fashionable quarter; the city, still in its embryo state, extending but a little way above it; it was full of dwelling houses, with here and there a church, which has long since disappeared. Over that region of the metropolis where mammon is worshipped in six days out of seven, there now broods on Sunday a sepulchral silence; but then the walks were thronged with churchgoers. The boy was his grandmother's constant companion. He was trained by her to love books and study, to which, however, he seems to have had a natural and inherited inclination. It is said that at a very tender age she taught him to declaim, standing on a table, passages from Latin authors, and rewarded him with hot pound-cake. Another story is, that she used to put sugar-plums near his bedside, to be at hand in case he should take a fancy to them in the night. But, as he was not spoiled by indulgence, it is but fair to conclude that her method of educating him was tempered by firmness on proper occasions — a quality somewhat rare in grandmothers. A letter from one of her descendants playfully says :

" It is a picture to think of her, seated at a marvellous Dutch bureau, now in possession of her great-granddaughters, which is filled with a complexity of small and mysterious drawers, talking to the child, while her servant built the powdered tower on her head, or hung the diamond rings in her ears. Very likely, at such times, the child was thrusting his little fingers into the rouge pot, or making havoc with the powder ; and perhaps she knew no better way to bring him to order than to tell him of many a fright of her own in the war ; or she may have gone further back in history, and told the boy how she and his Huguenot ancestors fled from France when the bad King Louis forbade every form of worship but his own."

Dr. Johnson, the grandfather of young Verplanck, on the mother's side, came from Stratford to be President of Columbia College, the year after his grandson was born. To him, in an equal degree with his grandmother, we must give the credit of bringing forward the precocious boy in his early studies. I have diligently inquired what school he attended and who were his teachers, but can hear of no others. His father had married again, and to the lively Huguenot lady was left the almost entire charge of the boy. He was a born scholar; he took to books as other boys take to marbles ; and the lessons which he received in the household sufficed to prepare him for entering college when yet a mere child, at eleven years of age.   He took his first degree four years afterwards, in 1801, one year after his maternal grandfather had returned to Stratford.   To that place he very frequently resorted in his youth, and there, in the well-stored and well-arranged library, he pursued the studies he loved.   The tradition is that he conned his Greek lessons lying flat on the floor with his thumb in his mouth, and the fingers of the other hand employed in twisting a lock of the brown hair on his forehead.   He took no pleasure in fishing or in hunting ; I doubt whether he ever let off a fowling-piece or drew a trout from the brook in his life. He was fond of younger children, and would recreate himself in play with his little relatives, but was no visitor to other families.   His contemporaries, Washington Irving, James K. Paulding, and Governeur Kemble, had their amusements and frolics, in which he took no part.   According to Mr. Kemble, the elder men of the time held up to the youths the example of young Verplanck, so studious and accomplished, and so ready with every kind of knowledge, and withal of such faultless habits, as a model for their imitation.

I have said that his relatives on the mother's side were of a different political school from his high tory grandmother. From them he would hear of the inalienable rights of the people, and the duty, under certain circumstances, of revolution ; from her he would hear of the obligation of loyalty and obedience. The Johnsons would speak of the patriotism, the wisdom, and the services of Franklin ; the grandmother of the virtues and accomplishments of Cornwallis. The boy, of course, had to choose between these different sides, and he chose the side of his country and of the people.

I think that I perceive in these circumstances how it was that the mind of Verplanck was educated to that independence of judgment, and that self-reliance, which in after life so eminently distinguished it. He never adopted an opinion for the reason that it had been adopted by another. On some points— on more, I think, than is usual with most men—he was content not to decide, but when he formed an opinion it was his own. He had no hesitation in differing from others if he saw reason ; indeed, he sometimes showed that he rather liked to differ, or chose at least, by questioning their opinions, to intimate that they were prematurely formed. Another result of the peculiar political education which I have described, was the fairness with which he judged of the characters and motives of men who were not of his party. I saw much, very much of him while he was a member of Congress, when political animosities were at their fiercest, and I must say that I never knew a party man who had less party rancor, or who was more ready to acknowledge in his political opponents the good qualities which they really possessed.

After taking his degree he read law in the office of Josiah Ogden Hoffman, an eminent member of the New York bar, much esteemed in social life, whose house was the resort of the best company in New York. His first public address, a Fourth of July oration, was delivered when he was eighteen years of age. It was printed, but no copy of it is now to be found. In due season he was admitted to the bar, and opened an office for the practice of law in New York. A letter from Dr. Moore, formerly President of Columbia College, relates that Verplanck and himself took an office together on the east side of Pearl street, opposite to Hanover Square. "Little business as I had then," proceeds the Doctor, "he seemed to have still less. Indeed, I am not aware that he had, or cared to have, any legal business whatever. He spent much of his time out of the office and was not very studious when within; but it was evident that he read or had read elsewhere to good purpose; for though I read more Greek than law, and thought myself studious, I had occasion to discover more than once that he was a better Grecian than I, and could enlighten my ignorance." From other sources I learn that in his legal studies he delighted in the reports of law cases in Norman French, that he was fond of old French literature, and read Rabelais in the perplexing French of the original. It is mentioned in some accounts of his life that he was elected in 1811 to the New York House of Assembly by a party called the Malcontents, but I have not had the means of verifying this account, nor am I able to discover what were the objects for which the party called malcontents was formed. In this year an incident occurred of more importance to him than his election to the Assembly.

On the 8th of August, 1811, the Annual Com-

mencement of Columbia College was held in Trinity
Church.   Among those who were to receive the degree of Bachelor of Arts was a young man named
Stevenson, who had composed an oration to be delivered on the platform.   It contained some passages
of a political nature, insisting on the duty of a representative to obey the will of his constituents.   Political parties were at that time much exasperated
against each other, and Dr. Wilson of the College, to
whom the oration was submitted, acting, it was
thought, at the suggestion of Dr. John Mason, the
eloquent divine, who was then Provost of the College,
struck out the passages in question and directed that
they should be omitted in the delivery.   Stevenson
spoke them notwithstanding, and was then privately
informed by one of the professors that his degree
would be denied him.   Yet when the diplomas were
delivered, he mounted the platform with the other
graduates and demanded the degree of Dr. Mason.
It was refused because of his disobedience.   Mr.
Hugh Maxwell, afterwards eminent as an advocate,
sprang upon the platform and appealed to the audience against this denial of what he claimed to be
the right of Stevenson.   Great confusion followed,
shouts, applauses and hisses, in the midst of which
Verplanck appeared on the platform, saying : " The

reasons are not satisfactory ; Mr. Maxwell must be supported," and then he moved " that the thanks of the audience be given to Mr. Maxwell for his spirited defence of an injured man." It was some time before the tumult could be allayed, the audience taking part with the disturbers ; but the result was that Maxwell, Verplanck, and several others were prosecuted for riot in the Mayor's Court. De Witt Clinton was then Mayor of New York. In his charge to the jury he inveighed with great severity against the accused, particularly Verplanck, of whose conduct he spoke as a piece of matchless impudence, and declared the disturbance to be one of the grossest and most shameless outrages he had ever known. They were found guilty ; Maxwell, Verplanck, and Stevenson were fined two hundred dollars each, and several others less. An appeal was entered by the accused but afterwards withdrawn. I have heard one of our judges express a doubt whether this disturbance could properly be considered as a riot, but they did not choose to avail themselves of the doubt if there was any, and submitted.

There is this extenuation of the rashness of these young men, that Mr. Mason, to whom was attributed the attempt to suppress certain passages in Stevenson's oration, was himself in the habit of giving free expression to his political sentiments in the pulpit. He belonged to the Federal party, Stevenson to the party then called Republican.

I have said the accused submitted; but the phrase is scarcely accurate. Verplanck took his own way of obtaining redress, and annoyed Clinton with satirical attacks for several years afterwards. Some of these appeared in a newspaper called the *Corrector;* but those which attracted the most attention, were the pamphlets styled *Letters of Abimelech Coody, Ladies' Shoemaker*, the first of which was published in 1811, addressed to Dr. Samuel Latham Mitchell.

The war went on until Clinton or some friend was provoked to answer in a pamphlet entitled *An Account of Abimelech Coody and other celebrated Worthies of New York, in a Letter from a Traveller*. The writer satirizes not only Verplanck, but James K. Paulding and Washington Irving, of whose History of New York he speaks disparagingly. In what he says of Verplanck he allows himself to refer to his figure and features as subjects of ridicule. This war I think was closed by the publication of *The Bucktail Bards*, as the little volume is called, which contains *The State Triumvirate, a Political Tale*, and the *Epistles of Brevet Major Pindar Puff*. These I have heard spoken of as the joint productions of Verplanck and Rudolph Bunner, a scholar and a man of wit. *The State Triumvirate* is in octosyllabic verse, and in the manner of Swift, but the allusions are obscure, and it is a task to read it. The notes, in which the hand of Verplanck is very apparent, are intelligible enough, and are clever, caustic and learned. The Epistles, which are in heroic verse, have striking passages, and the notes are of a like incisive character. De Witt Clinton, then Governor of the State, valued himself on his devotion to science and literature, but he was sometimes obliged, in his messages and public discourses, to refer to compends which are in everybody's hands, and his antagonists made this the subject of unsparing ridicule.

In the family of Josiah Ogden Hoffman, lived Mary Eliza Fenno, the sister of his wife, and daughter of John Ward Fenno, originally of Boston, and afterwards proprietor of a newspaper published in Philadelphia, entitled the *Gazette of the United States*. Between this young lady and Verplanck there grew up an attachment, and in 1811 they were married. I have seen an exquisite miniature of her by Malbone, taken in her early girlhood when about fifteen years old—beautiful as an angel, with light chestnut hair and a soft blue eye, in the look of which

is a touch of sadness, as if caused by some dim presentiment of her early death.   I remember hearing
Miss Sedgwick say that she should always think the
better of Verplanck for having been the husband of
Eliza Fenno.   Several of her letters, written to him
before their marriage, are preserved, which, amidst
the sprightliness natural to her age, show a more
than usual thoughtfulness.   She rallies him on being adopted by the mob, and making harangues at
ward meetings.   She playfully chides him for wandering from the apostolic church to hear popular
preachers and clerks that sing well; which she regards as crimes against the memory of his ancestors—an allusion to that part of the family pedigree
which traced his descent in some way from the royal
line of the Stuarts.   She rallies him on his passion
for old books, remarking that some interesting works
had just appeared which must be kept from him till
he reaches the age of threescore, when they will be
fit for his perusal.   She writes to him from Boston,
that he is accounted there an amazingly plain-spoken
man—he had called the Boston people heretics.   She
writes to him in Stratford, imagining him in Bishop
Berkeley's arm-chair, surrounded by family pictures
and huge folios.   These letters were carefully preserved by her husband till his death, along with vari-

ous memorials of her whom he had lost ; locks of her sunny brown hair, the diamond ring which he had placed on her finger when they were engaged to each other, wrapped in tresses of the same bright hair, and miniatures of her, which the family never heard of till he died ; all variously disposed among the papers in the drawers of his desk ; so that whenever he opened it, he might be reminded of her, and her memory might become a part of his daily life. With these were preserved some letters of his own, written to her about the same time, and of a sportive character. In one of these he laments the passing away of the good old customs, and simple ways of living in the country, supplanted by the usages of town life. Everybody was then reading *Cœlebs in Search of a Wife*, and Verplanck, who had just been looking over some of the writings of Wilberforce, sees in it resemblances to his style, which led him to set down Wilberforce as the author.

He lived with his young wife five years, and she bore him two sons, one of whom died at the age of thirty, unmarried, and the other has become the father of a numerous family. Her health failing he took her to Europe, in the hope that it might be restored by a change of air and scene, but after languishing a while she died at Paris, in the year 1817.

She sleeps in the cemetery of Perc La Chaise, among monuments inscribed with words strange to her childhood, while he, after surviving her for sixty-three years, yet never forgetting her, is laid in the ancestral burying ground at Fishkill, and the Atlantic Ocean rolls between their graves.

He remained in Europe a little while after this event, and having looked at what the continent had to show him, went over to England. In his letters to his friends at home he spoke pathetically of the loss of her who was the blessing of his life, of the delight with which, had she lived, she would have looked at so many things in the Old World now attracting his attention ; and of the misfortune of his children to be deprived of her care and guidance. In one of his letters he speaks enthusiastically of the painter, Allston, with whose genius he was deeply impressed as he looked on the grand picture of Daniel interpreting the Dream of Belshazzar, then begun but never to be finished. In the same letter he relates this anecdote :

" You may expect another explosion of mad poetry from Lord Byron. Lord Holland, who returned. from Geneva, a few days ago, told Mr. Gallatin that he was the bearer of a considerable cargo of verses from his lordship to Murray the publisher, the subject not known. That you may have a higher relish for the new poem, I give you a little anecdote which is told in London. Some time ago Lord Byron's books were sold at auction, where a gentleman purchased a splendid edition of Shakspeare. When it was sent home a volume was missing. After several fruitless inquiries of the auctioneer the purchaser went to Byron. 'What play was in the volume?' asked he. 'I think Othello.' 'Ah! I remember. I was reading that when Lady Byron did something to vex me. I threw the book at her head and she carried it out of the room. Inquire of some of her people and you will get your book."

While abroad, Verplanck fell in with Dr. Mason, who had refused Stevenson his degree. The two travellers took kindly to each other, and the unpleasant affair of the college disturbance was forgotten.

In 1818, after his return from Europe, he delivered before this Society the noble Anniversary Discourse in which he commemorates the virtues and labors of some of those illustrious men who, to use his words, "have most largely contributed to raise or support our national institutions, and to form or elevate our national character." Las Casas, Roger Williams, William Penn, General Oglethorpe, Professor Luzac, and Berkeley are among the worthies whom he celebrates. It has always seemed to me that this is one of the happiest examples in our language of the class of compositions to which it belongs, both as regards the general scope and the execution, and it is read with as much interest now as when it was first written.

Mr. Verplanck was elected in 1820 a member of the New York House of Assembly, but I do not learn that he particularly distinguished himself while in that body. In the year following he was appointed, in the General Theological Seminary of the Episcopal Church, Professor of the Evidences of Revealed Religion and Moral Science in its relations to Theology. For four years he performed the duties of this Professorship, with what ability is shown by his Treatise on the Evidences of Christianity, the fruit of his studies during this interval. It is principally a clear and impressive view of that class of proofs of the Christian religion which have a direct relation to the intellectual and moral wants of mankind. For he was a devout believer in the Christian gospel, and cherished religious convictions for the sake of their influence on the character and the life. This work was published in 1824, about the time that he resigned his Professorship.

It was in 1824, that, on a visit to New York, I first

became acquainted with Verplanck.   On the appearance of a small volume of poems of mine, containing
one or two which have been the most favorably received, he wrote, in 1822, some account of them for
the *New York American*, a daily paper which not
long before had been established by his cousin, Johnson Verplanck, in conjunction with the late Dr.
Charles King.   He spoke of them at considerable
length and in the kindest manner.   As I was then
an unknown literary adventurer, I could not but be
grateful to the hand that was so cordially held out to
welcome me, and when I came to live in New York,
in 1825, an intimacy began in which I suspect the advantage was all on my side.

It was in 1825 that he published his Essay on the
Doctrine of Contracts, in which he maintained that
the transaction between the buyer and seller of a
commodity should be one of perfect frankness and an
entire absence of concealment ; that the seller should
be held to disclose everything within his knowledge
which would affect the price of what he offered for
sale, and that the maxim which is compressed into the
two Latin words, *caveat emptor*—the maxim that the
buyer takes the risk of a bad bargain—is not only a
selfish but a knavish and immoral rule of conduct,
and should not be recognized by the tribunals.   The

question is ably argued on the grounds of an elevated morality—but I have heard jurists object to the doctrine of this essay, that if it were to prevail it would greatly multiply the number of lawsuits.

In 1825, Mr. Verplanck was elected one of the three Representatives in Congress, to which this city was then entitled. He immediately distinguished himself as a working member. This appellation is given in Congress to members who labor faithfully in Committees, consider petitions and report upon them, investigate claims, inquire into matters referred to their judgment, frame bills and present them through their Chairman. Besides these, there are the talking members who take part in every debate, often without knowing anything of the question, save what they learn while the debate is proceeding, and the idle members, who do nothing but vote—generally, I believe, without knowing anything of the question whatever; but to neither of these classes did Verplanck belong. He was a diligent, useful, and valued member of the Committee of Ways and Means, and at an important period of our political history was its Chairman.

Then arose the great controversy concerning the right of a State to refuse obedience at pleasure to any law of Congress, a right contended for under the name of nullification by some of the most eminent men of the South, whose ability, political influence, and power of putting a plausible face on their heresy, gave their cause at first an appearance of great strength, and seemed to threaten the very existence of the Union.

With their denial of the binding force of any law of Congress which a State might think proper to set aside, these men combined another argument. They denied the power of Congress under the Constitution, to levy duties on imported merchandise for the purpose of favoring the home manufacturer, and maintained that it could only lay duties for the sake of raising a revenue. Mr. Verplanck favored neither this view nor their theory of nullification. He held that the power to lay duties being given to Congress, without reservation by the Constitution, the end or motive of laying them was left to the discretion of the Legislature. He showed also that the power to regulate commerce given to that body in the Constitution, was, from an early period in our history, held to imply a right by laying duties, to favor particular traffics, products or fabrics.

This view of the subject was presented with great skill and force in a pamphlet entitled *A Letter to Colonel William Drayton, of South Carolina*, published in 1831. Mr. Verplanck was through life a friend to the freedom of exchange, but he would not use in its favor any argument which did not seem to him just. His pamphlet was so ably reasoned that William Leggett said to him, in my presence, "Mr. Verplanck, you have convinced me ; I was till now, of a different opinion from yours, but you have settled the question against me. I now see that whatever may be the injustice of protective duties, Congress has the constitutional right to impose them."

In was while this controversy was going on that President Jackson issued his proclamation warning those who resisted the revenue laws that their resistance was regarded as rebellion, and would be quelled at the bayonet's point. Mr. Calhoun and his friends were not prepared for this : indeed, I do not think that in any of his plans for the separate action of the slave States, he contemplated a resort to arms on either side. They looked about them to find some plausible pretext for submission, and this the country was not unwilling to give. It was generally admitted that the duties on imported goods ought to be reduced, and Mr. McLane, Secretary of the Treasury, and Mr. Verplanck, Chairman of the Committee of Ways and Means, each drew up a plan for lessening the burdens of the tariff.

Mr. McLane had just returned from a successful mission to Great Britain, and had the advantage of considerable personal popularity. He was a moderate protectionist, and with great pains drew up a scheme of duties which kept the protection of home manufactures in view. Some branches of industry, he thought, were so far advanced that they would bear a small reduction of the duty; others a still larger; others were yet so weak that they could not prosper unless the whole existing duty was retained. The scheme was laid before Congress, but met with little attention from any quarter; the southern politicians regarded it with scorn, as made up of mere cheese-parings. Mr. Verplanck's plan of a tariff was more liberal. He was not a protectionist, and his scheme contemplated a large reduction of duties—as large as it was thought could possibly be adopted by Congress—yet so framed as to cause as little inconvenience as might be to the manufacturers. It was thought that Mr. Calhoun and his friends would readily accept it as affording them a not ignoble retreat from their dangerous position.

While these projects were before Congress, Mr. Littell, a gentleman of the free-trade school, and now editor of the *Living Age*, drew up a scheme of revenue reform more thorough than either of the others.

It proposed to reduce the duties annually until, at the end of ten years the principle of protection, which was what the southern politicians complained of, should disappear from the tariff, and a system of duties take its place which should in no case exceed the rate of twenty per cent. on the value of the commodity imported. The draft of this scheme was shown to Mr. Clay: he saw at once that it would satisfy the southern politicians ; he adopted it, brought it before Congress, urged its enactment in several earnest speeches, and by the help of his great influence over his party it was rapidly carried through both Houses, under the name of the Compromise Tariff, to the astonishment of the friends of free-trade, the mill owners, the Secretary of the Treasury, the Committee of Ways and Means, and, I think, the country at large. I thought it hard measure for Mr. Verplanck that the credit of this reform should be taken out of his hands by one who had always been the great advocate of protective duties ; but this was one of the fortunate strokes of policy which Mr. Clay, when in the vigor of his faculties, had the skill to make. He afterwards defended the measure as inflicting no injury upon the manufacturers, and it never appeared to lessen the good will which his party bore him.

About this time I was witness to a circumstance

which showed the sagacity of Mr. Verplanck in estimating the consequences of political measures. Mr. Van Buren had been sent by President Jackson as our Minister to the British Court while Congress was not in session, and the nomination yet awaited confirmation by the Senate. It led to a long and spirited debate, in which Mr. Marcy uttered the memorable maxim : "To the victor belong the spoils of the enemy," which was so often quoted against him. I was in Washington, dining with Mr. Verplanck, when the vote on this nomination was taken. As we were at the table, two of the Senators, Dickinson, of New Jersey, and Tazewell, of Virginia, entered. Verplanck, turning to them asked eagerly : "How has it gone?" Dickinson, extending his left arm, with the fingers closed, swept the other hand over it, striking the fingers open, to signify that the nomination was rejected.

"There," said Verplanck, "that makes Van Buren President of the United States." Verplanck was by no means a partisan of Van Buren, but he saw what the effect of that vote would be, and his prediction was, in due time verified.

While in Congress, Mr. Verplanck procured the enactment of a law for the further security of literary property. To use his own words, it " gave additional security to the property of authors and artists in their works, and more than doubled the term of legal protection to them, besides simplifying the law in va-,rious respects." It was passed in 1831, though Mr. Verplanck had begun to urge the measure three years before, when he brought in a bill for the purpose, but party strife was then at its height, and little else than the approaching elections were thought of by the members of Congress. When party heat had cooled a little, he gained their attention, and his bill became a law. If we had now in Congress a member so much interested for the rights of authors and artists, and at the same time so learned, so honored and persevering, we might hope that the inhospitable usage which makes the property of the American author in Great Britain and of the British author in the United States the lawful prize of whosoever chooses to apropriate it to himself, would be abolished.

A dinner was given to Verplanck on his return from Washington, in the name of several literary gentlemen of New York; but the expense was, in fact, defrayed by a generous and liberal-minded bookseller, Elam Bliss, who held authors in high veneration and only needed a more discriminating perception of literary merit to make him, in their eyes at least, a perfect bookseller. On this occasion Mr.

10*

Verplanck spoke well and modestly of the part he had taken in procuring the passage of the new law; mentioned with especial honor the " first and ablest champion " who had then " appeared in this cause," the Hon. Willard Phillips, who had discussed the question in the *North American Review;* referred to the opinions of various eminent publicists, and pointed out that our own Constitution had recognized the right of literary property while it left to Congress the duty of securing it. He closed with an animated view of what American literature ought to be and 'might be under circumstances favorable to its wholesome and vigorous growth. We listened with delight and were proud of our Representative.

During Mr. Verplanck's fourth and last term in Congress he became separated from his associates of the Democratic party by a difference in regard to the Bank of the United States. General Jackson had laid rough hands on this institution and removed to the State banks the public money which had till then been entrusted to its keeping. Many of our best men had then a high opinion of the utility of the Bank, and thought much better of its management than, as afterwards appeared, it deserved. The Whig party declared itself in favor of the Bank. Mr. Calhoun and the Southern politicians of his immediate school joined them on this question, and Mr. Verplanck, who regarded the bank with a friendly eye, found himself on the same side, which proved to be the minority. The time arrived for another election of members of Congress from this city. The Democratic party desired to re-elect Mr. Verplanck, if some assurance could be obtained from him that he would not oppose the policy of the Administration in regard to the Bank. That party understood very well his merits and his usefulness, and made a strong effort to retain him, but he would give no assurance, even to pursue a neutral course, on the bank question, and accordingly his name was reluctantly dropped from their list of nominations. A long separation ensued between him and those who up to that time had been his political associates.

In 1834, the Whig party, looking for a strong candidate for the mayoralty of the city, offered the nomination to Verplanck, who accepted it. On the other side, the Democrats brought forward Cornelius W. Lawrence, a man of popular manners and unquestioned integrity. Those were happy days when, in voting for a mayor, the citizen could be certain that he would not vote amiss, and that whoever succeeded in the election, the city was sure of an honest man for its chief officer. One would have thought that this consideration might make the election a quiet one, but it was not so ; the struggle was for party supremacy, and it was violent on both sides. At that time the polls were kept open for three days, and each day the excitement increased : disorders took place ; some heads were broken, and at last it appeared that Lawrence was elected mayor by a majority of about two hundred votes.

While in Congress, Verplanck had leisure, during the interval between one session and another, for literary occupations. He wrote about one-third of an annual collection of miscellanies entitled the *Talisman*, which was published by Dr. Bliss in the year 1827 and the two following years. To these volumes he contributed the *Peregrinations of Petrus Mudd*, a humorous and lively sketch, founded on the travels of a New Yorker of the genuine old stock, who, when he returned from wandering over all Europe and part of Asia, set himself down to study geography in order to know where he had been. Of the graver articles he wrote *De Gourges*, a chapter from the history of the Huguenot colonists of this country, *Gelyna, a Tale of Albany and Ticonderoga*, and several others. In conjunction with Robert C. Sands, a writer of a peculiar vein of quaint humor, he contributed two papers to the collection, entitled *Scenes in Washing-*

ton, of a humorous and satirical character.   He dis-
liked the manual labor of writing and was fond of
dictating while another held the pen.   I was the third
contributor to the *Talisman*, and sometimes acted as
his amanuensis.   In estimating Verplanck's literary
character, these compositions, some of which are
marked by great beauty of style and others by a rich
humor, should not be overlooked.   The first volume
of the *Talisman* was put in type by a young Englishman named Cox, who, while working at his desk as a
printer, composed a clever review of the work, which
appeared in the *New York Mirror*, and of which
Verplanck often spoke with praise.

In 1833, Verplanck collected his public discourses
into a volume.   Among these is one delivered in August of that year, at Columbia College, in which he
holds up to imitation the illustrious examples of great
men educated at that institution.   In one of those
passages of stately eloquence which he knew so well
how to frame, he speaks of the worth of his old adversary, De Witt Clinton, the first graduate of the College
after the peace of 1783, and pays due " honor to that
lofty ambition which taught him to look to designs of
grand utility, and to their successful execution as his
arts of gaining or redeeming the confidence of a generous and public-spirited people."   In the same dis-

course he pronounced the eulogy of Dr. Mason, who had died a few days before. In the same year, Verplanck, at Geneva College, delivered an address on the "Right Moral Influence and Use of Liberal Studies," and the next year, at Amherst College, another on the converse of that subject, namely, the " Influence of Moral Causes upon Opinion, Science and Literature." In 1836, he gave a discourse on " The Advantages and Dangers of the American Scholar." Of these addresses let me say, that I know of no compositions of their class which I read with more pleasure or more instruction. Enlarged views, elevated sentiments, a hopeful and courageous spirit, a wide knowledge of men and men's recorded experience, and a manly dignity of style, mark them all as productions of no common mind.

After separating from the Democratic party, Mr. Verplanck was elected by the Whigs, in 1837, to the Senate of the State of New York, while that body was yet a Court for the Correction of Errors,—a tribunal of the last resort,—and in that capacity decided questions of law of the highest magnitude and importance. Nothing in his life was more remarkable than the new character in which he now appeared. The practised statesman, the elegant scholar and the writer of graceful sketches, the satirist, the critic, the theologian,

started up a profound jurist.   During the four years
in which he sat in this court, he heard the arguments
in nearly every case which came before it, and delivered seventy-one opinions—not simply his written
conclusions, but elaborate judgments founded on the
closest investigation of the questions submitted, the
most careful and exhaustive examination of authorities, and a practical, comprehensive and familiar acquaintance with legal rules and principles, even those
of the most technical nature, which astonished those
who knew that he had never appeared for a client
in court, nor sat before in a judicial tribunal.   I
use in this the language of an able lawyer, Judge
Daly, who has made this part of Verplanck's labors a
subject of special study.

As examples of his judicial ability, I may instance
his examination of the whole structure of our State
and Federal Government in the case of Delafield
against the State of Illinois, where the question came
up whether an individual could sue a State; his survey of the whole law of marine insurance and the principles on which it is founded, in the case of the American Insurance Company against Bryan; his admirable statement of the reasons on which rests the
law of prescription, or right established by usage, in
the case of Post against Pearsall; his exposition of the

extent of the right which in this country the owners of land on the borders of rivers and navigable streams have in the bed of the river, in Kempshall's case—a masterly opinion, in which the whole court concurred. I might also mention the great case of Alice Lispenard, in which he considered the degree of mental capacity requisite to make a will, a case involving a vast amount of property in this city, decided by his opinion. There is also the case of Smith against Acker, relating to the taint of fraud in mortgages of personal property, in which he carried the court with him against the Chancellor and overturned all the previous decisions. Not less important is his elaborate, learned and exhaustive opinion in the case of Thompson against the People, decided by a single vote and by his opinion,—in which he examined the true nature of franchises conferred on individuals in this country by the sovereign power, the right to construct bridges over navigable streams, and the proper operation of the writ of *quo warranto*. These opinions of Verplanck form an important part of the legal literature of our State. If he had made the law his special pursuit, and been placed on the bench of one of our higher tribunals, there is no degree of judicial eminence to which he might not have aspired. The Standing Committee of the Diocese of New York, of which he was a member, in their resolutions expressive of sorrow for his death, spoke of him as one whose judicial wisdom and familiarity with the principles and practice of the law, made his counsels of the highest value.

In 1844, after, I doubt not, some years of previous study, appeared the first number of Verplanck's edition of Shakspeare, issued by Harper & Brothers. The numbers appeared from time to time till 1847, when the work was completed. He made some corrections of the text but never rashly; he selected the notes of other commentators with care; he added some excellent ones of his own, and wrote admirable critical and historical prefaces to the different plays. This edition has always seemed to me the very one for which the general reader has occasion.

Almost ever since the American Revolution a Board of Regents of the University of the State of New York has existed, on which is laid the duty of visiting and superintending in a general way our institutions of education above the degree of Common Schools. It consists of twenty-three members, including the Governor and Lieutenant-Governor, the Secretary of State and the Superintendent of Public Instruction; the other nineteen members are appointed by the Legislature. The Board assists at the incorporation of all colleges and academies, looks into their condition, interposes in certain specified cases, receives reports from them and makes annual reports to the Legislature, and confers by diploma such degrees as are granted by any college or university in Europe.   Mr. Verplanck was appointed a member of this Board in 1826, in place of Matthew Clarkson, who had been a Regent ever since 1787.   In 1855 he was appointed Vice-Chancellor of the University, and to the time of his death punctually attended the meetings of the Board, shared in its discussions and bore his part in its various duties.   In 1844 the State Library was placed under the superintendence of the Regents.   Mr. Verplanck was immediately put on the Library Committee, where his knowledge of books and editions of books made his services invaluable.   There were then about ten thousand volumes in the collection, and many of these consisted of broken sets.   Under the care of the Regents—Mr. Verplanck principally, who gave it his particular attention—it has grown into a well selected, well arranged library of more than eighty-two thousand volumes.   About the same time the State Cabinets of Natural History were put under the care of the Board, and these have equally prospered, every year adding to their extent, until now the Regents publish annually, catalogues of the additions made to them from various sources, and, occasionally, papers communicated by experts in natural history.

Every year in the month of August a University Convocation is held at Albany, to which are invited all the leading teachers and professors of our colleges and academies, and carefully prepared papers relating to education are read.   At the first of these conventions, in 1863, Mr. D. J. Pratt, now the Assistant Secretary of the Board, had read a paper on " Language as the Chief Educator and the noblest Liberal Art," in which he dwelt upon the importance of studying the ancient classic authors in their original tongues.   Mr. Verplanck remarked that in what he had to say he would content himself with relating an anecdote respecting the first Napoleon, which he had from a private source, and which had never been in print.   The Emperor wishing to keep himself advised of what was passing in the University of France, yet without attracting public attention, was wont on certain occasions to send to the University a trustworthy and intelligent person from his household, who was to bring back a report.   This man at one time reported that the question of paying more attention to the mathematical sciences had been agitated.   On this Napoleon exclaimed with emphasis :

" Go to the Polytechnic for mathematics, but classics, classics, classics for the University." At another time Verplanck, still occupied with his favorite studies, gave the convention an address on the pronunciation of the Latin language, in which he came to the conclusion that of all the branches of the Latin race, the Portuguese, in their pronunciation of Latin, make the nearest approach to that of the ancient Romans. He was desired by the members of the Board to write out the address for publication, but this was never done. Verplanck, as I have already remarked, was an unwilling scribe, and did not like to handle the pen.

The Annual Report of the Regents, which are voluminous documents, give much the same view of the arrangements for public education in the State as is obtained of a country by looking down upon it from an observatory. Every college, every academy, every school, not merely a private enterprise, and above the degree of common schools, makes its yearly report to the Regents, and these are embodied in the general report which they make to the legislature, so that the whole great system, with all its appendages, its libraries, its revenues, its expenditures, the number of its teachers and its pupils, and the opportunities of instruction which it gives, lies before the eye of the reader.   It now comprehends twenty Colleges of Literature and Science, three Law Departments, two Medical Colleges, two hundred or more Academies, or schools of that class, besides the Normal school at Albany.

In his discourse delivered before this Society in 1818, Mr. Verplanck had apostrophized his native country as the Land of Refuge.   He could not then have foreseen how well in aftertimes it would deserve this name, nor what labors and responsibilities the care of that mighty throng who resort to our shores for work and bread would cast upon him.   Shortly before the year 1847 the number of emigrants from Europe arriving in our country had rapidly and surprisingly increased.   The famine in Ireland had caused the people of that island to migrate to ours in swarms like those which the populous North poured from her frozen loins to overwhelm the Roman Empire.   In the ten years from 1845 to 1854 inclusive, more than a million and a half of Irish emigrants left the United Kingdom.   The emigration from Germany had also prodigiously increased and promised to become still larger.   All these were exposed, and the Germans in a particular manner, on account of their ignorance of our language, to the extortions of a knavish class, called runners, and of the keepers of boarding-houses, who often defrauded them of all that they possessed, and left them to charity. Most of those who, after these extortions, had the means, made their way into the interior and settled upon farms, but a large number remained to become members of the almshouse, or to starve and sicken in crowded and unwholesome rooms. Mr. Kapp, for some time a Commissioner of Emigration, relates, in his interesting work on Emigration, an example of the manner in which these poor creatures were cheated. An emigrant came to a boarding-house keeper to pay his bill: "It is eighteen dollars," said the landlord. "Why," said the emigrant, "did you not agree to board me for sixpence a meal and threepence for a bed?" "Yes," was the answer, " and that is just seventy-five cents a day; you have been here eight days, and that makes just eighteen dollars."

These things had become a grievous scandal, and it was clear that something must be done to protect the emigrant from pillage, and the country from the burden of his support. The Act of May, 1847, was therefore passed by the New York Legislature. It named six gentlemen of the very highest character, Gulian C. Verplanck, James Boorman, Jacob Harvey, Robert B. Minturn, William F. Havemeyer, and David C. Colden, who were to form a Board of

Commissioners of Emigration, charged with the oversight and care of this vast influx of strangers from the Old World. To these were added the Mayors of New York and Brooklyn, and the Presidents of the German Society and the Irish Emigrant Society. Every master of a vessel was, within twenty-four hours of his arrival, to give this Board a list of his passengers, with a report of their origin, age, occupation, condition, health and other particulars, and either give bonds to save the community from the cos: of maintaining them in case they became paupers, or pay for each of them the sum of two dollars and a half. The payment of money has been preferred, and this has put into the hands of the Commissioners a liberal revenue, faithfully applied to the advantage of the emigrants.

Mr. Havemeyer was chosen President of the Board, but resigned the office after a few months, and was succeeded in it by Mr. Verplanck, who held it till the day of his death. Under the management of the Commissioners, the Bureau of Emigration, becoming with almost every year more perfectly adapted to its purpose, has grown to vast dimensions, till it is now like one of the departments of government in a great empire. Whoever passes by Ward's Island, where the tides of the East River and the Sound meet and rush swiftly to and fro through their narrow channels, will have some idea of what the Board has done, as he sees the domes and spires of that great cluster of buildings, forming a vast caravanserai in which the poorer class of emigrants are temporarily lodged, before they can be sent into the interior or find employment here. Here are barracks for the men, a spacious building for the women and children, a nursery for children of a tender age, Catholic and Protestant chapels, a dispensary, workshops, a lunatic asylum, fever wards, surgical wards, storehouses, residences of the physicians and other persons employed in the care of the place, and outhouses and offices of various kinds. Here, too, rise the stately turrets of the spacious new hospital styled the Verplanck Emigrant Hospital, in honor of the great philanthropist, for such his constant and noiseless labors in this department of charity entitle him to be called.

The Commissioners found that they could not protect the emigrants from imposition without a special landing-place from which they could wholly exclude the rascal crew who cheated them. It took eight years to obtain this from the New York Legislature, but at last, in 1855, it was granted, and the old fort at the foot of Manhattan Island, called Castle

Garden, was leased for this purpose. This is now the Emigrants' Landing, the gate of the New World for those who, pressing westward, throng into it from the Old.   Night and day it is open, and through this passage the vast tide of stranger population, which is to mingle with and swell our own, rushes like the current of the Bosphorus from the Black Sea hurrying towards the Propontis and the Hellespont to fill the great basin of the Mediterranean.   What will be the condition of mankind when the populations of the two hemispheres, the East and the West, shall have found, as they must, a common level, and when the human race, now struggling for room in its ancient abodes, shall look in vain for some unoccupied region where a virgin soil is waiting to reward the laborer with bread ?

As he enters Castle Garden the emigrant undergoes inspection by a competent physician, and if he be aged, sick, or in any way disabled, the master of the vessel must give a special bond for his maintenance.   He is introduced into the building—here he finds one department in which he is duly registered, another from which he receives such information as a stranger requires, another from which his luggage is dispatched to its destination, another at which attend clerks, skilled in the languages of continental Europe, to write his letters, another at which railway tickets are procured without danger of extortion, another at which fair arrangements are made with boarding-houses, another from which, if sick or destitute, he is sent to Ward's Island, and half a dozen others important as helps to one who has no knowledge of the usages of the country to which he has come. I refer to these arrangements, among a multitude of others, in order to show what administrative talent and what constant attention were necessary to ensure the regular and punctual working of so vast a system. To this duty Mr. Verplanck, aided by able and disinterested associates like himself, gave the labors of a third of a century, uncompensated save by the consciousness of doing good. The composition of this Board has just been changed by the Legislature of the State, in such a manner as unfortunately to introduce party influences, from which, during all the time of Mr. Verplanck's connection with it, it had been kept wholly free.

Yet Mr. Verplanck had his party attachments, though he never suffered them to lead him out of the way he had marked for himself. He would accompany a party, but never follow it. His party record is singular enough. He was educated a Federalist, but early in life found himself acting against the Federal party. He was with the Whigs in supporting General Harrison for the Presidency, and claimed the credit of suggesting his nomination. Mr. Clay he would never support on account of his protectionist principles, and when that gentleman was nominated by the Whigs he left them and voted for Mr. Polk, though he was disgusted by the trick which obtained the vote of Pennsylvania for Mr. Polk under the pretence of his being a protectionist. Subsequently he supported General Taylor, the Whig candidate for the Presidency; but the nomination of Mr. Buchanan, in 1857, saw him once more with the Democrats, from whom he did not again separate. When the proposal to make government paper a legal tender for debts was before Congress, he opposed it with great zeal, writing against it in the Democratic journals. I agreed with him that the measure was an act of folly, for which I could find no excuse, but he almost regarded it as a public crime. He vehemently disapproved, also, of the arbitrary arrests made by our government during the war, some of which, without question, were exceedingly ill advised. His zeal on these points, I think, made him blind to the great issues involved in our late civil war, and led his usually clear and liberal judgment astray.

I have not yet mentioned various capacities in which he served the public without any motive but to minister to the public welfare. He was from a very early period a Trustee of the Society Library, in which he took great interest, delighting to make additions to its stock of books, and passing much time in its alcoves and its reading-rooms. He was one of the wardens of Trinity Church, that mistress of mighty revenues. He was for some years one of the governors of the New York Hospital, and I remember when he made periodical visits to the Insane Asylum at Bloomingdale, as one invested with authority there. During the existence of the Public School Society he was one of its Trustees,—from 1834 to 1841,—and rendered essential service to the cause of public education.

His useful life closed on the eighteenth of March last. For some months before this date his strength had declined; and when I met him from time to time it seemed to me that his features had become sharper and his frame more attenuated; yet I perceived no diminution of mental vigor. He took the same interest in the events and questions of the day as he had done years before, his apprehension seemed as quick, and all the powers of his mind as active.

On the Wednesday before his death he attended one of those weekly meetings which he took care never to miss, that of the Commissioners of Emigration. But in one of his walks on a rainy day he had taken a cold which resulted in a congestion of the lungs. On Thursday evening he lay upon a sofa, conversing from time to time, after his usual manner, until near midnight. On Friday morning, when his body servant entered the room and looked at him, he perceived a change and called his grandson, who, with a granddaughter, had constantly attended him during the past winter. The grandson immediately went for his physician, Dr. Carnochan, who, however, was not to be found, and whose assistant, a young man, came in his stead. Mr. Verplanck, in a way which was characteristic of him, studied the young man's face for a moment and then asked: "From what college were you graduated?" The reply was—"Paris;" on which Mr. Verplanck turned away as if it did not much please him, and in a moment afterward expired. He was spared the previous suffering which so many are called to endure. His son had visited him from time to time, and was with him the day before his death; yet this event was unexpected to all the family. His father, in his old age, had as suddenly passed away, having fallen dead by the wayside.

The private life of our friend was as beautiful as his public life was useful and beneficent. He took great interest in the education of his grandchildren; inquired into their studies, talked with them of the books they read, and sought with great success to make them fond of all good learning, directing their attention to all that was noble in literature and in art. His mind was a storehouse of facts in history and biography, on which he drew for their entertainment, and upon occasion diversified the graver narratives with fairy tales and stories of wonder from the *Arabian Nights*. He made learning pleasant to them by taking them on Saturdays to places of amusement, from which he contrived that they should return not only amused but instructed. In short, it seemed as if, in his solicitude for the education of his descendants, he sought to repay the cares bestowed upon his early youth by his grandfather of Stratford, of whom he said in his discourse delivered at Amherst College, that his best education was bestowed by the more than paternal care of one of the wisest and most excellent sons of New England. Long after he was an old man he would make pleasant summer journeys with these young people, and look to their comfort and safety with the tenderest solicitude.

Christmas was merry Christmas at the old family

mansion in Fishkill.   He caused the day to be kept with many of the ancient usages, to the great satisfaction of the younger members of the household. He was fond of observing particular days and seasons, and marking them by some pleasant custom of historical significance—for with all the ancient custom and rites and pastimes pertaining to them he was as familiar as if they were matters of to-day.   It distressed him even to tears when, last Christmas, he found that his health did not allow him to make the journey to Fishkill as usual.   He made much of the birthdays of his grandchildren, and taught them to observe that of Shakspeare by adorning the dwelling with flowers mentioned in those aërial verses of the Winter's Tale,

> "——daffodils,
> That come before the swallow dares and take
> The winds of March with beauty; violets dim,
> But sweeter than the lids of Juno's eyes
> Or Cytherea's breath; pale primroses
> That die unmarried," etc., etc.

For many years past he had divided his time pretty equally between Fishkill and New York, visiting the homestead in the latter part of the week and returning in time to attend the weekly meetings of the Commissioners of Emigration.   While in the country he was a great deal in the open air, superintending the patrimonial estate, which he managed with ability as a man of business, giving a careful attention even to the minutest details. But he was most agreeably employed in his large and well-stored library. Here were different editions of the Greek and Latin classics, some of them rare and enriched with sumptuous illustrations—thirty different ones of Horace and nearly as many of Virgil. With the Greek tragedians he was as familiar as with our own Shakspeare. In this library he wrote for the Crayon his entertaining paper on *Garrick and his portrait*, and his charming little volume entitled *Twelfth Night at the Century Club*. Here also he wrote several papers respecting the true interpretation of certain passages in Virgil, which were published in the *Evening Post*. It is to be regretted that he did not collect and publish his literary papers, which would form a very agreeable miscellany. He seemed, however, almost indifferent to literary fame, and when he had once sent forth into the world an essay or a treatise, left it to its fate as an affair which was now off his hands.

On Sunday morning he was always at the old church in the village of Fishkill, one of the most attentive and devout worshippers there. It is an ancient building of homely architecture, looking now just as it did

a century ago, with a big old pulpit and sounding
board in the midst of the church, which the people
would have been glad to remove, but refrained, because Mr. Verplanck, whom they so venerated, preferred that it should remain.

The patrimonial mansion at Fishkill had historical
associations which must have added to the interest
with which our friend regarded it.   Mr. Tuckerman
relates, in the *North American Review*, though without naming the place or the persons, a story in which
they were brought out in a singular manner.   He was
there fifteen or twenty years since, a guest at Verplanck's table.   He describes the June sunshine,
which played through the shifting branches of tall
elms, on the smooth oaken floor of the old dining-
room, the plate of antique pattern on the sideboard,
and the portraits of revolutionary heroes on the walls.
As they sat down to dinner, an old lady, bowed with
years and with a restless, yet serene look, entered
and took a seat beside Mr. Verplanck.   A servant
adjusted a napkin under her chin and the dinner proceeded.   A steamer was passing up the river and a
band on board struck up a martial air.   The old lady
trembled, clasped her hands, and, raising her eyes,
exclaimed, "Ah! all intercession is vain.   André
must die."   Mr. Verplanck made a sign to the com-

pany to listen, and calling the lady Aunt, addressed her with some kind inquiry, on which she went on to speak of the events and personages of the Revolution as matters of the present day. She repeated rapidly the names of the English officers whom she had known, "described her lofty head-dress of ostrich feathers, which caught fire at the theatre, and repeated the verses of her admirer who was so fortunate as to extinguish it." She dwelt upon the majestic bearing of Washington, the elegance of the French, the dogmatism of the British officers; the by-words, the names of gallants, belles and heroes; the incidents, the questions, the etiquette of those times seemed to live again in her tremulous accents, which gradually became feeble, until she fell asleep! "It was," continued the narrator, "like a voice from the grave." This old lady was a Miss Walton, a sister of Judge Verplanck's second wife.

When he found time for the studies by which his mind was kept so full of useful and curious knowledge, I cannot well conceive. He loved to protract an interesting conversation into the small hours of the night, and he was by no means, as it is said most long-lived men are, an early riser. An anecdote related by a gentleman of the New York bar will serve to illustrate, in some degree, his desultory habits during that part of his time which was passed in New York. This gentleman gave a dinner at Delmonico's, then in William Street, to a professional brother from another city, who was in town only for the day. Mr. Verplanck, Judge William Kent, and one or two other clever lawyers, were of the party. I will allow him to tell the story in his own words.

"We of course," he says, "had a delightful evening, for our stranger guest was a diamond; Kent was never more charming and witty; Mr. —— never more stately and brilliant, and Verplanck was in his most genial mood, full of his peculiarly interesting, graceful and instructive conversation. The spirit of the hour was unrestrained and cordial. We had a good time, and it was not early when the dispersion began. Verplanck and Kent remained with us after the others withdrew, and as midnight approached, Kent also departed. After a while Verplanck and I went forth and sauntered along in the darkness through the deserted streets, among the tenantless and gloomy houses, till we reached the point where his path would diverge for Broadway and up-town, and mine for Fulton Ferry and Brooklyn Heights. Instead of leaving me the good philosopher volunteered to keep on with me to the river, and when we reached the river, proposed to remain with me until the boat arrived, and then proposed to cross the river with me.   We were, I think, the only passengers, and his conversation continued to flow as fresh and interesting as at the dinner-table until we reached the Brooklyn shore.   He declined to pass the rest of the night at my house, and while I waited with him till the boat should leave the wharf to take him back, the night editor of the *Courier and Enquirer*, a clever and accomplished gentleman, came on board on the way to his nocturnal labors.   I introduced them to each other, they were at once in good accord, I saw them off and went homeward.   A day or two after I learned that when they reached the New York shore, Verplanck volunteered to stroll down to the *Courier* office with the editor, accepted his invitation to walk in, ascending with him to his room in the attic, and, to the editor's great delight and edification, remained with him, conversing, reading and ruminating until broad daylight.   There was a charm in Mr. Verplanck's conversation that was distinctive and peculiar.   It was ‘green pastures and still waters.’ "

Our friend had, it is true, a memory which faithfully retained the acquisitions made in early life, but, in some way or other, was continually enlarging

them. I think I have never known one whose
thoughts were so much with the past, whose memory
was so familiar with the words and actions of those
who inhabited the earth before us, and who so loved
.and reverenced the worthy examples they have given
us, yet who so much interested himself in the present and was so hopeful of the future. There was
no tendency of this shifting and changeful age which
he did not observe, no new discovery made, no new
theory started, no untrodden path of speculation
opened to human thought, which did not immediately
engage his attention, and of which he had not something instructive to say. He was as familiar with the
literature of the day as are the crowd of common
readers who know no other; yet he suffered not the
brilliant novelties of the hour to wean his admiration
from the authors whose reputation has stood the test.
of time. He was generous, however, to rising merit,
and took pleasure in commending it to the attention
of others.

His learning was not secular merely; his library
was well stocked with works on theology; he was
familiar with the questions discussed in them; the
New Testament, in the original, was a part of his
daily reading; he had examined the dark or doubtful
passages of Scripture, and they who were much in

his society needed no more satisfactory commentator. Not long since he sent to the Society Library for a theological work rather out of date. "It is the first time that work was ever called for," said the librarian, smiling, as he took it from the shelf and aired the leaves a little.

His kindness to his fellow-men was shown more in deeds than in words—for of words of compliment he was particularly sparing; and he loved to do good by stealth. A letter from his pastor, the Rev. Dr. Shelton, says : "He was very kind and affectionate when he thought he discovered merit in anybody, however humble; and though he dropped never so much as a hint to the individual himself, he was pretty sure to speak a good word for him in quarters where it would have an influence. A great many never knew whom they had to thank for this. Here he recommended some one for a place, there he picked up a book or a set of books for some distant library. In this way he went about doing good, and, not given to impulse, was systematically benevolent." A letter from another hand speaks of the clergymen whom he had put in the way of getting a parish, the youths for whom he had procured employment—favors quietly conferred, when perhaps the person benefited had forgotten the application or given up the pursuit. He preserved carefully all that related to those persons in whom he took a kindly interest. "Never," says Dr. Shelton, "did a juvenile letter come to him that he did not carefully put away. Whole packages of them are found among his papers; if they had been State documents they could not have been more important in his eyes."

I have spoken of the hopefulness of his temper. This was doubtless in a great degree constitutional, for he is said to have been an utter stranger to physical fear, preserving his calmness on occasions when others would be in a fever of alarm. He loved our free institutions, he had a serene and steady confidence in their duration, and his published writings are for the most part eloquent pleas for freedom, political equality and toleration. Even the shameless corruption which has seized on the local government of this city, did not dismay or discourage him. He maintained, in a manner which it was not easy to controvert, that the great cities of Europe are quite as grossly misgoverned, and that every overgrown community like ours must find it a difficult task to rid itself of the official leeches that seek to fatten on its blood.

In looking back upon the public services of our friend, it occurs to me that his life is the more to be held up as an example, inasmuch as, though possessed of an ample fortune, he occupied himself as diligently in gratuitous labors for the general good as other men do in the labors of their profession. In the dispensation of his income he leaned, perhaps, to the side of frugality; but his daily thought and employment were to make his fellow-men happier and better; yet I never knew a man who made less parade of his philanthropy. He rarely, and never, save when the occasion required it, spoke of what he had done for others. I never heard, I think no man ever heard, anything like a boast proceed from his lips, nor did he practice any, even the most innocent expedients, to attract attention to his public services. Not that I suppose him insensible to the good will and good word of his fellow-men. He valued them, doubtless, as every wise man must, but sought them not, except as they might be earned by the unostentatious performance of his duty. If they came they were welcome, if not, he was content with the testimony of his own conscience and the approval of Him who seeth in secret.

It may be said that in almost every instance the place of those who pass from the stage of life is readily supplied from among the multitude of those who are entering upon it; the well-graced actor who makes his exit is succeeded by another, who soon shows that he is as fully competent to perform the part as his predecessor.   But when I look for one to supply the place of our friend who has departed, I confess I look in vain.   I ask, but vainly, where we shall find one with such capacities for earning a great name, such large endowments of mind and acquisitions of study united with such modesty, disinterestedness and sincerity, and such steady and various labors for the good of our race conjoined with so little desire for the rewards which the world has to bestow on those who render it the highest services.   But though we sorrow for his departure and see not how his honored place is to be filled, let us congratulate ourselves and the community in which we live, that he was spared to us so many years.   His day was like one of the finest days in the season of the summer solstice, bright, unclouded, and long.

Farewell—thou who hast already entered upon thy reward! happy in this, that thou wert not called from thy beneficent labors before the night.   Thou hadst already garnered an ample harvest; the sickle was yet in thy hand; the newly reaped sheaves lay on the field at thy side, when, as the beams of the setting sun trembled on the horizon, the voice of the Master summoned thee to thine appointed rest.   May

all those who are as nobly endowed as thou, and who
as willingly devote themselves to the service of God
and mankind, be spared to the world as long as thou
hast been.

MISCELLANEOUS ADDRESSES.

THE PRESS BANQUET TO KOSSUTH.

THE PRESS BANQUET TO KOSSUTH.

ADDRESS AT THE BANQUET GIVEN BY THE NEW YORK PRESS
TO LOUIS KOSSUTH, DECEMBER 9, 1851.

GENTLEMEN :—Before announcing the third regular toast, which is a very short one, allow me to say a very few words.

Let me ask you to imagine that the contest in which the United States asserted their independence of Great Britain had closed in disaster and defeat; that our armies, through treason and a league of tyrants against us, had been broken and scattered; that the great men who led them, and who swayed our councils, our Washington, our Franklin, the venerable President of the American Congress, and their illustrious associates, had been driven forth as exiles. If there had existed at that day, in any part of the civilized world, a powerful republic, with institutions resting on the same foundations of liberty which our own countrymen sought to establish, would there have been in that republic any hospitality too cordial, any sympathy too deep, any zeal for their glorious but unfortunate cause too fervent or too active to be shown towards these illustrious fugitives? Gentlemen, the case I have supposed is before you. The Washingtons, the Franklins of Hungary, her sages, her legislators, her warriors, expelled by a far worse tyranny than was ever endured here, are wanderers in foreign lands. Some of them are within our own borders; one of them sits with his companions as our guest to-night, and we must measure the duty we owe them by the same standard which we would have had history apply, if our ancestors had met with a fate like theirs.

I have compared the exiled Hungarians to the great men of our own history. Difficulty, my brethren, is the nurse of greatness, a harsh nurse, who roughly rocks her foster-children into strength and athletic proportion. The mind, grappling with great aims and wrestling with mighty impediments, grows by a certain necessity to their stature. Scarce any thing so convinces me of the capacity of the human intellect for indefinite expansion in the different stages of its being, as this power of enlarging itself to the height and compass of surrounding emergencies. These men have been trained to greatness by a quicker and surer method than a peaceful country and a tranquil period can know.

But it is not merely, or even principally, for their personal qualities, that we honor them; we honor them for the cause in which they so gloriously failed. Great issues hung upon that cause, and great interests of mankind were crushed by its downfall. I was on the continent of Europe when the treason of Görgey laid Hungary bound at the feet of the Czar. Europe was at that time in the midst of the reaction; the ebb tide was rushing violently back, sweeping all that the friends of freedom had planned into the black bosom of the deep. In France the liberty of the press was extinct; Paris was in a state of siege; the soldiery of that Republic had just quenched in blood the freedom of Rome; Austria had suppressed liberty in Northern Italy; absolutism was restored in Prussia; along the Rhine and its tributaries, and in the towns and villages of Wirtemberg and Bavaria, troops, withdrawn from the barracks and garrisons, filled the streets and kept the inhabitants quiet with the bayonet at their breasts. Hungary, at that moment, alone upheld—and upheld with a firm hand and dauntless heart—the blazing torch of liberty. To Hungary were turned up the eyes, to Hungary clung the hopes of all who did not despair of the freedom of Europe.

I recollect that while the armies of Russia were

moving, like tempest from the north, upon the Hungarian host, the progress of events was watched with the deepest solicitude by the people of Germany. I was at that time in Munich, the splendid capital of Bavaria. The Bavarians seemed for the time to have put off their usual character, and scrambled for the daily prints, wet from the press, with such eagerness that I almost thought myself in America. The news of the catastrophe at last arrived; Görgey had betrayed the cause of Hungary, and yielded to the demands of the Russians. Immediately a funeral gloom settled, like a noon-day darkness, upon the city. I heard the muttered exclamations of the people, " It is all over ; the last hope of European liberty is gone."

Russia did not misjudge. If she had allowed Hungary to become independent and free, the reaction in favor of absolutism had been incomplete : there would have been one perilous example of successful resistance to despotism ; in one corner of Europe a flame would have been kept alive at which the other nations might have rekindled among themselves the light of liberty. Hungary was subdued ; but does any one who hears me believe that the present state of things in Europe will last ? The despots themselves scarcely believe it; they rule in constant fear, and, made cruel by their fears, are heaping chain on chain around the limbs of their subjects.

They are hastening the event they dread. Every added shackle galls into a more fiery impatience, those who are condemned to wear it. I look with mingled hope and horror to the day—the hope, my brethren, predominates — a day bloodier, perhaps, than we have seen since the wars of Napoleon; when the exasperated nations shall snap their chains and start to their feet. It may well be that Hungary, made less patient of the yoke by the remembrance of her own many and glorious struggles for independence, and better fitted than other nations, by the peculiar structure of her institutions, for founding the liberty of her citizens on a rational basis, will take the lead. In that glorious and hazardous enterprise; in that hour of her sore need and peril, I hope she will be cheered and strengthened with aid from this side the Atlantic; aid given, not with a parsimonious hand; not with a cowardly and selfish apprehension lest we should not err on the safe side—wisely, of course. I care not with how broad and comprehensive a regard to the future—but in large, generous, effectual measure.

And you, our guest, fearless, eloquent, large of heart and of mind, whose one thought is the salvation of oppressed Hungary, unfortunate, but undiscouraged, struck down in the battle of liberty, but great in defeat, and gathering strength for triumphs to come; receive the assurance at our hands, that in this great attempt of man to repossess himself of the rights which God gave him, though the strife be waged under a distant belt of longitude, and with the mightiest despotisms of the world, the Press of America will take part—*will* take do I say?—already takes part with you and your countrymen.

Enough of this, I will detain you from the accents to which I know you are impatient to listen only just long enough to pronounce the toast of the evening:

LOUIS KOSSUTH.

THE IMPROVEMENT OF NATIVE FRUITS.

THE IMPROVEMENT OF NATIVE FRUITS.

ADDRESS DELIVERED BEFORE THE NEW YORK HORTICUL-
TURAL SOCIETY AT THE EXHIBITION SEPTEMBER 26, 1856.

MR. PRESIDENT AND MEMBERS OF THE HORTICULTURAL SO-
CIETY:

If I have committed, as I fear I may have done, an imprudence in yielding to a request that I should address you at this time, the splendid show of fruits and flowers on the tables of the Society will, I hope, withdraw your attention from my deficiencies. I shall be short; but to be brief is not always the way to escape being tiresome.

The last exhibition of this Society was held in what was formerly called the season of roses and strawberries, the earliest and most delicious fruit of the year, and the most beautiful and most agreeably fragrant of flowers. Twenty-three hundred years ago,—I believe it was nearer twenty-four hundred,—the Greek poet Anacreon called the rose the Queen of Flowers. Since his time the botanist and the florist have explored every nook of the globe, wherever, in

the hottest or coldest climates, the green blood flows
in vegetable veins,—wherever buds swell and blossoms open—and have brought home, to embellish our
conservatories and gardens, every flower distinguished by beauty of form or tint, delicacy of texture or
grateful perfume, flowers worthy of Paradise, to use
a phrase of Milton; yet, among them all, the Rose
has not found a peer. She has never been dethroned, and is still the sovereign of the flowers.

In Anacreon's time and long after, down to the
time when Moore, the translator of Anacreon, composed his song, entitled the " Last Rose of Summer,"
there was an especial season of roses. One flush of
bloom came over the rose-trees, and then the delicate leaves were strewn withered on the ground;
the fruit appeared in its stead,. and there were no
more roses for that year; the summer must pass into
autumn, the autumn into winter, and even the spring
must approach its close before roses were again
gathered in our gardens. But it is no longer so, as
your tables this day bear witness. See what horti-
culture has done; how it has prolonged the gentle
reign of this Queen of Flowers! The florist comes,
he takes the roses of warmer climates, which are unaccustomed to our seasons, he crosses them with the
hardier growth of our northern gardens, and obtains

plants which endure our winters in the open air, and bloom continually from the beginning of June to the setting in of the winter frosts. There is now no last rose of summer,—summer goes out in a cloud of roses; they spring up under the departing footsteps of autumn. Some poet speaks ironically of roses in December; what he meant as an extravagance has become the literal truth. I have gathered roses in my garden on Long Island on the twentieth of December; last year I broke them from their stems on the tenth. It is curious to see the plant go on putting forth its flowers and rearing its clusters of buds as if without any presentiment of approaching winter, till, in the midst of its bloom, it is surprised by a frost nipping all its young and tender shoots at once, like a sudden failure overtaking one of our men of commerce in the midst of his many projects.

With the strawberry, the horticulturist has wrought nearly equal wonders. If we were in France now, your tables would show that there is a second season of strawberries. There the gardener finds means to delay the production of fruit at the usual period. When the summer heats are overpast, and a temperature like that of June returns, he encourages the blossoms to open and the fruit to mature, and in September and October the markets of

Paris are fragrant with strawberries, an abundant and cheap dessert, even for humble tables.

These, my friends, are the triumphs of the art you cultivate, but it has yet to achieve peculiar triumphs in our own country. Of the cultivated vegetable productions which we inherit from the Old World, we have yet to produce or procure varieties suited to our soil and climate; we have yet to introduce new fruits and flowers from foreign countries, and we have yet to improve and draw forth into new and desirable varieties, such as are the indigenous growth of our soil. On each of these points I shall say a few words, though not, I hope, so many as to weary you.

In our country the peach-tree perishes by a sort of marasmus, while the tree is yet in the promise of its growth. Two or three years' bearing are all that we can expect from it, and it then becomes sickly and dies prematurely, or is torn from the ground as worthless; and if a new supply is desired, other trees must be planted in another spot. We call our peaches the best in the world, and with good reason, but this is the fate of the tree. There is a remedy, if we could but discover it. On Long Island in the hedge rows, or among heaps of stones, in neglected spots, never turned by the spade or torn by the plough, you may see peach-trees, self-planted, which flourish in full vigor, with leaves of the darkest and glossiest green, bearing fruit every year, and surviving generation after generation of their brethren of the gardens. In the soil and situation of these places exist the qualities which are necessary to the health of the peach-tree. What are they? Can the practical gardener determine? Can the chemist? The question is worthy of long and most careful research.

The peach-tree is said to have come originally from Persia; the botanists recognize that country as its birth-place, and give it the name of *persica*. But it is more than probable that it had a remoter and more Eastern origin, since in China it has been cultivated from time immemorial. From China comes the flat peach, a remarkable production, with the stone on one side and the fleshy part of the peach on the other. There must have existed a long and intimate familiarity between the gardener and the peach-tree, before it yielded to his whims, and gave its fruit so strange a shape to gratify them. Are there no healthy and enduring varieties of the peach to be procured from China out of which other healthy varieties may be bred? Has the Chinese horticulturist, in the practice of thousands of years, discovered

12*

no method of preventing the disease by which the tree with us perishes at the very period when it should be most vigorous and productive?

The apricot in our country, blooming at an early season, suffers by the spring frosts, which cause its fruit to drop in the germ, and often render the tree barren. In the East, its native country, it is cultivated over an immense variety of latitudes. Damascus lies among orchards of the apricot, lofty trees like those of the forest, with dark stately stems and spreading branches; and I have scarce ever seen a more beautiful sight than the banks of the Barada, a river of Anti-Lebanon, in its green, narrow valley, overhung in the month of March with apricot-trees in bloom, vieing in height with the poplars among which they stood. Yet, far to the north of Damascus, far to the north of the vale of the Barada, groves of this tree clothe the cool declivities of Caucasus, and they grow on the mountains of northern China, in a climate of fierce and sudden vicissitudes of heat and cold. Our varieties of the apricot may have been procured from too southern a latitude or from a climate of very great uniformity. It is hardly possible that prolific varieties, suited to the most inconstant climate, should not be found somewhere in Asia, to the western half of which, the fruit of the apricot in a dried state is, what the prune is to France and Germany.

I will leave this point here, which might be further illustrated by numerous examples, particularly by the cherry, of which many of the varieties most prized in Europe, become worthless under the warm and showery skies of our June, by decaying the instant they ripen; and by the plum, which in some districts, where the tree flourishes with uncommon vigor, loses all its fruit by the stings of an insect pest called the circulio.   I proceed to speak of the vegetable productions of other countries, which we might advantageously introduce into our own.   Eastern Asia, situated like these Atlantic States, on the eastern coast of a large continent, and possessing, like them, a climate subject to great extremes of heat and cold, is the region to which we must look for the most important contributions of this kind.   Whatever, among the growths of the vegetable kingdom, will bear the hard winter of that region, and, at the same time, requires the heat of its summer to ensure its perfection, will, of course, flourish here in the same latitudes as there.   Japan and Northern China are now opened to our commerce, and we may freely transfer all that is worth so distant a conveyance to our fields and gardens.   The Dutch and English florists have already adopted many of their flowering plants: the camellia of Southern Japan, is one of the fairest ornaments of our conservatories; Japan lilies and China roses bloom in our gardens; the Japan quince and Chinese pear embellish our shrubberies; but in fruits and esculents, as yet, we owe them little.

Although the Chinese make no wine, they have excellent table grapes; the French missionary Huc commends them highly; and a gentleman, long a resident in Southern China, once informed me that the finest come to Canton from about the 37th degree of north latitude. It is a variety of the common grape of the Old World: but whatever may be its quality, it is of course a variety certain to flourish here as well as in the kindred climate of China. The European vine—at least the varieties of it which are cultivated in Europe—cannot, it seems to be agreed on all hands, be naturalized here so as to escape the mildew on its fruit, when it grows in the open air. We should immediately make the experiment of adopting the Chinese varieties in their place. The lamps by which the dwellings and streets of China are lighted at night, are fed with oil pressed from the fruit of a tree which grows all over the country. The chasers of the whale on our coast every year pursue their game into more remote seas, and every year bring back diminished cargoes of oil.   Ere long it may be well to bethink ourselves of resorting to the vegetable oils used by the Chinese, and of procuring a supply by the same means.   The evergreens of China, if introduced here, where the stock of hardy evergreens is small, would form a most desirable ornament of the grounds about our dwellings.   Among these is a kind of palm, of the genus *chamærops*, which endures an intense degree of cold, and makes a singular appearance, bearing on its tropical looking leaves in the winter season loads of snow.   Here are large opportunities for inquiry and experiment, and one office of societies like yours in this country will, I am convinced, at no distant day, be to send a horticultural mission to eastern Asia.

The last point on which I propose to touch would open, if I chose to enter it, a vast field of speculation and conjecture.   If we had only our native fruits to cultivate ; if we had but the crab-apple of our forests, and the wild plum of our thickets from which to form our orchards ; if we had only the aboriginal flowers of our woods and fields to domesticate in our gardens, what haste should we make to mellow the harsh juices of the fruits and to heighten and vary the beauty of the flowers !   We neglect what is native, because we have the vegetable productions of the

Old World already improved to our hands. Yet many of these were as little promising, when the gardener first tried his art upon them, as the crude fruits of our woodlands. The pear-tree in the woods of Poland and on the dry elevated plains of Russia, where it grows wild, is horrid with thorns, and produces a small fruit of the austerest and most ungrateful flavor. Under culture, it lays aside its thorns, and becomes the parent of an infinitely varied family of fruits, filled with ambrosial juices for the refreshment of almost every month in the year. I have somewhere read the assertion that the grape of Europe and the East was, even in its original state, a fruit of excellent quality. I think this is a mistake. I believe that I have twice seen that grape lapsed to its primitive condition. Some years since, while travelling from Rome to Naples, on the Via Labiana, the diligence broke down ; the passengers were detained several hours while it was repairing, and I took the opportunity to explore the surrounding country. I climbed a hill where, on one side of the way, was a vineyard, with grapes white and purple, just ripe, and almost bursting with their saccharine juices ; while on the other side was an unfenced pasture ground, half overgrown with bushes, on which the wild vines clambered, apparently self-sown. I tried the grapes on both sides of the way ; the cultivated sorts were of the high flavor and intense sweetness common to the grapes of Italy ; the fruit of the wild vine was small, of the size of our pigeon grape, with large seeds, a thick skin and meagre juices.   In the same journey I had an opportunity to make a similar comparison in another place, and became convinced that the European grape, in its wild or primitive state, is not remarkable for any particular excellence.

In the improvement of our own native fruits we have done something ; the Virginia strawberry is the parent of a numerous family called the Scarlets ; the blackberry has given birth to the Lawton variety ; the grape of our woods is the parent of the Isabella and the Catawba ; and our wild gooseberry has been improved into the Houghton.   Beyond this I think we have hardly gone.   Of our flowers, we can, I believe, only boast to have domesticated and made double the Michigan rose.   There is yet an ample field for experiment, with every hope of success.   The American grape naturally runs into varieties of different sizes, colors, degrees of sweetness, and seasons of maturity.   The richness of our woods, in regard to these varieties, are yet far from being exhausted.   I remember, when a youth, while wandering in the woodlands of the eastern part of Massachusetts, where the wild vines trailed from tree to tree, I found a grape of very peculiar characteristics—of an amber color, an oval shape, a thin, slightly astringent skin like that of the European grape, and flesh of a brittle firmness, somewhat like that of the Frontignan. I am satisfied that varieties may yet be obtained from the American grape of an excellence of which we have now hardly any idea. The American plum exists in a great number of varieties of different size, color and flavor; yet nothing has been done to improve it, by seedlings carefully produced and selected. I see nothing to prevent it from passing, under skilful treatment, into as many pleasant varieties as the domestic plum, for which, as naturalists tell us, we are indebted to Syria. At this season the paw-paw, sometimes called the custard-apple, a name expressive of its qualities, is ripening under its dark green leaves in the thickets of the West. It is a fruit which, like the fresh fig, is pronounced by many whose palates are unaccustomed to it, to be insipid; but like the fig, it is mucilaginous and nutritive. Transplanted to our gardens, and made prolific,—which may perhaps be a difficult, but, I suppose, is not an impossible task—it would, I doubt not, become a popular and very desirable fruit. It is wonderful

with what facility—what certainty, I had almost said
—Nature complies with the wishes of the assiduous
cultivator ; and how, after persevering solicitation, she
supplies the quality of which he is in search.   I have
now finished what I intended, very briefly, to say on a
very important subject, which deserves to be treated
both more at large and more intelligently than I am
able to do it.

The earliest occupation of man, we are told,—
his task in a state of innocence,—was to tend and
dress the garden in which his Maker placed him.   I
cannot say that as men addict themselves to the
same pursuit, they are raised nearer to the state of
innocence; but this I will say, that few pursuits so
agreeably interest without ever disturbing the mind,
and that he who gives himself to it sets up one bar-
rier the more against evil thoughts and unhallowed
wishes.   The love of plants is a natural and wholesome instinct.   Through that, perhaps, quite as much
as through any other tendency of our natures, the
sense of beauty, the grateful perception of harmony
of color and of grace and fair proportion of shape, enter the mind and wean it from grosser and more sen-
sual tastes.   The Quakers, who hesitate to cultivate
some of the fine arts, indulge their love of beauty
without scruple or restraint in rearing flowers and

embellishing their grounds. I never read description of natural scenery, nor expressions of delight at the beauty of vegetable products more enthusiastic than those in the travels of old Bartram, the Quaker naturalist, recording his wanderings in Florida. The garden of the two Bartrams, father and son, near Philadelphia, filled with the plants and trees gathered on their journeys, still remains the pride and ornament of the city.

You, my friends, who are the members of the Horticultural Society, are engaged in a good work, the work of cherishing the relations of acquaintanceship and affection, too apt to be overlooked and forgotten in a city life, with the vegetable world in the midst of which God placed us, and on which he made us so essentially dependent. So far as you occupy your minds with these natural and simple tastes, you keep yourselves unperverted by the world, and preserve in sight a reminiscence of the fair original garden.

MUSIC IN THE PUBLIC SCHOOLS.

MUSIC IN THE PUBLIC SCHOOLS.

AN ADDRESS DELIVERED AT THE CLOSE OF A SERIES OF LECTURES BY RICHARD STORRS WILLIS, DECEMBER 29, 1856.

I have been asked to say a word or two on the general subject of the series of lectures to which you have listened. If I shall suggest anything that will enforce the views which the lecturer has so ably taken, I shall esteem myself fortunate.

Many persons entertain doubts in regard to the expediency of making music a branch of the education acquired in our common schools. Until these doubts are removed, we shall miss what is most desirable—the hearty and efficient coöperation of those who entertain them. There are a few considerations in favor of the affirmative side of this question which, I think, can hardly be too strongly urged.

It is admitted, by those who have thought much on the subject, that the people of our country allow themselves too little relaxation from business and its cares. If this be so—and for my part I think there is no doubt of it—they will find in the cultivation of music a recreation of the most innocent and unobjectionable kind. The effect of music is to soothe, to tranquillize; a series of sweet sounds, skilfully modulated, occupies the attention agreeably and without fatigue; it refreshes us like rest. I recollect a remarkable passage in Milton's Paradise Lost, expressive of his idea of the power of music. He describes a group of fallen angels endeavoring to divert their thoughts from the misery to which they had reduced themselves, and says:

> "—the harmony
> Suspended hell; and took with ravishment
> The audience."

Milton was not only the greatest epic poet who has lived since Homer, but he was a schoolmaster, and devised for his pupils a plan of education in which the fatigues of study were wisely interspersed by intervals of music.

Many persons relax from labor and care by the use of narcotics. Music is a better resource. A tune is certainly better than a cigar. Others, for want of some more attractive employment, addict themselves to the pleasures of the table. Music is certainly better than conviviality. In this respect the cultivation of music comes in aid of health.

In another respect vocal music—which is likely to be the kind of music principally taught in the

Common Schools—promotes the health of the body.
If you observe the physical conformation of those
who are accustomed to sing in public, you will perceive that they are remarkable for a full development
of the chest. This is in part, no doubt, the gift of
nature, for breadth and depth of the chest give power
and fulness of voice; but in part it is the effect of
practice, and the chest is opened and expanded by
the exercise of singing. I have no question, for my
part, that complaints of the lungs would be less frequent than now if vocal music were universally cultivated. It is an undisputed truth that those organs
of the body which are most habitually exercised are
preserved in the soundest and healthiest state.

Not only health, but morals, are promoted by the
cultivation of music. It is not only a safeguard
against sickly and unwholesome habits, as I have
shown, but against immoral ones also. If we provide
innocent amusements, we lessen the temptation to
seek out vicious indulgences. Refined pleasures, like
music, stand in the way of grosser tastes. If we fill
up our leisure innocently, we crowd out vices, almost
by mechanical pressure; we leave no room for
them.

It is no trivial accomplishment to speak our language in pleasing tones and with a clear articulation.

our countrymen are accused of speaking English in a slip-shod manner, and a nasal and rather shrill tone of voice. If vocal music be properly taught, the pupil is made to avoid these faults, and to combine the smoothest and most agreeable sounds with the most absolutely distinct articulation of the words. On this point, the gentleman to whom we have just listened, has dwelt with a force to which I can add nothing. Yet I may be allowed to say that they who have been trained to avoid disagreeable tones and an imperfect and slovenly articulation in singing, will see their deformity in reading and conversation, and will be very apt to avoid them there also.

In making music a branch of common education, we give a new attraction to our common schools. Music is not merely a study, it is an entertainment; wherever there is music there is a throng of listeners. We complain that our common schools are not attended as they ought to be. What is to be done? Shall we compel the attendance of children? Rather let us, if we can, so order things, that children shall attend voluntarily—shall be eager to crowd to the schools; and for this purpose nothing can be more effectual, it seems to me, than the art to which the ancients ascribed such power that, according to the fables of their poets, it drew the very stones of the earth from their beds and piled them in a wall around the city of Thebes.

It should be considered, moreover, that music in schools is useful as an incentive to study. After a weary hour of poring over books, with perhaps some discouragement on the part of the learner, if not despair at the hardness of his task, a song puts him in a more cheerful and hopeful mood ; the play of the lungs freshens the circulation of the blood, and he sits down again to his task in better spirits and with an invigorated mind. Almost all occupations are cheered and lightened by music. I remember once being in a tobacco manufactory in Virginia where the work was performed by slaves who enlivened their tasks with outbursts of psalmody. " We encourage their singing," said one of the proprietors ; " they work the better for it." Sailors pull more vigorously at the rope for their ' Yo heave ho!' which is a kind of song. I have heard the vine-dressers in Tuscany, on the hill-sides, responding to each other in songs, with which the whole region resounded, and which turned their hard day's work into a pastime.

If music be so important an art, it is important that it should be well taught. It is a sensible maxim that whatever is worth doing at all, is worth doing well. Suitable teachers of music for the common

13

schools, as we have heard from our friend, are exceedingly difficult to be found; persons who along with a competent knowledge, a willingness, to teach the mere rudiments of the art, and an acquaintance with the best methods of imparting them, possess a pure and unexceptionable taste. The only certain method of procuring a supply of such teachers certainly seems to be the one pointed out by the lecturer—that of training them for instruction at the normal schools. Such is now the rage for making accomplished pianists of all our young ladies, that a class of teachers has been raised up whose merit I do not doubt, but who are altogether too ambitious for the common schools. We need a class for an humble, but more useful ministration—teachers of home music, the importance of which has been so well set forth. It costs no more to be taught music well than to be taught ill, but the difference to the pupil is everything.

I speak as one unlearned in the science of music, and am glad that I have the good fortune to agree in so many points with one so thoroughly versed in its principles and so conversant with its practical details as our lecturer. There is a numerous class—the majority of my countrymen—who, in this respect, are much like myself. They have a perception of the beauty of sweet sounds artfully modulated, and of time in music; they perceive the disagreeableness of a discord, but they do not understand complicated harmonies; they do not perceive niceties to which better instructed or more sensitive organs are acutely alive; they take no delight in difficulties overcome, for of these difficulties they have a very imperfect conception, and they are somewhat bewildered in listening to compositions which justly pass for prodigies of art. They have a partiality for the human voice, as the most expressive instrument of music which they are acquainted with, and they desire that the sentiment of the air to which they listen should be interpreted to their minds by intelligible words. But that it is not the words alone which interest them, is proved by the fact that they listen with pleasure to common-place words when they are united to music. For my part, I find that the music transfigures the words, invests them with a sort of supernatural splendor, making them call up deeper emotions and conveying more vivid images. The class of whom I am speaking require for their enjoyment of music a certain simplicity—certain aids which bring it down to their level. And yet, on that level, not only taste, but art and genius, if we are to judge music by the same rules which we apply to the other fine arts, may find an ample field for their exercise. Some of the finest productions of literature are those which are written with the greatest simplicity, and address themselves to the greatest number of minds. I suppose, therefore, that I may conclude what I have to say with an acknowledgment to the lecturer in behalf of that large class to which I belong, for having so well stated our wants, and so clearly pointed out, in his admirable vindication of Home Music, the means of providing for them.

SCHILLER.

SCHILLER.

AN ADDRESS DELIVERED AT THE COOPER INSTITUTE ON THE OCCASION OF THE SCHILLER FESTIVAL, NOVEMBER 11, 1859.

I am sensible that, after the eloquent words which have been just uttered by the countrymen of the great poet whose birth we commemorate, and uttered in the noble language in which he wrote, I can say little that will interest this assembly. My own shortcomings, however, will be more than made up for by the gentlemen who, I understand, are to speak after me, and I therefore engage that I will not attempt to hold your attention long.

It might seem a presumptuous, if not an absurd proceeding for an American to speak of the literary character of Schiller in the presence of Germans, who are familiar with all that he has written to a degree which cannot be expected of us, and by whom the spirit of his writings, to the minutest particular, must be far more easily, and, we may therefore suppose, should be more thoroughly, apprehended. Yet let me be allowed to say that the name of Schiller, more than that of any other poet of his country, and for the very reason that he was a great tragic poet, belongs not to the literature of his country alone, but to the literature of the world. The Germans themselves have taught us this truth in relation to the tragic poets. In no part of the world is our Shakspeare more devoutly studied than in Germany; nowhere are his writings made the subject of profounder criticism, and the German versions of his dramas are absolute marvels of skilful translation.

We may therefore well say to the countrymen of Schiller: " Schiller is yours, but he is ours also. It was your country that gave him birth, but the people of all nations have made him their countryman by adoption. The influences of his genius have long since overflowed the limits within which his mother tongue is spoken, and have colored the dramatic literature of the whole world. In some shape or other, with abatements, doubtless, from their original splendor and beauty, but still glorious and still powerful over the minds of men; his dramas have become the common property of mankind. His personages walk our stage, and, in the familiar speech of our firesides, utter the sentiments which he puts into their mouths. We tremble alternately with fear and hope; we are moved to tears of admiration, we are melted to tears of pity; it is Schiller who touches the master chord to which our hearts answer. He compels us to a painful sympathy with his Robber Chief; he makes us parties to the grand conspiracy of Fiesco, and willing lieges of Fiesco's gentle consort Leonora; we sorrow with him for the young, magnanimous, generous, unfortunate Don Carlos, and grieve scarcely less for the guileless and angelic Elizabeth; he dazzles us with the splendid ambition and awes us with the majestic fall of Wallenstein; he forces us to weep for Mary Stuart and for the Maid of Orleans; he thrills us with wonder and delight at the glorious and successful revolt of William Tell. Suffer us, then, to take part in the honors you pay to his memory, to shower the violets of spring upon his sepulchre, and twine it with the leaves of plants that wither not in the frost of winter."

We of this country, too, must honor Schiller as the poet of freedom. He was one of those who could agree with Cowper in saying that, if he could worship aught visible to the human eye or shaped by the human fancy, he would rear an altar to Liberty, and bring to it, at the beginning and close of every day, his offering of praise. Schiller began to write when our country was warring with Great Britain for its independence, and his genius attained the maturity of its strength just as we had made peace with

13*

our powerful adversary and stood upon the earth a full-grown nation. It was then that the poet was composing his noble drama of *Don Carlos*, in which the Marquis of Posa is introduced as laying down to the tyrant, Philip of Spain, the great law of freedom. In the drama of the *Robbers*, written in Schiller's youth, we are sensible of a fiery, vehement, destructive impatience with society, on account of the abuses which it permits; an enthusiasm of reform, almost without plan or object; but in his works composed afterwards we find the true philosophy of reform calmly and clearly stated. The Marquis of Posa, in an interview with Philip, tells him, at the peril of his life, truths which he never heard before; exhorts him to lay the foundations of his power in the happiness and affections of his people, by observing the democratic precept, that no tie should fetter the citizen save respect for the rights of his brethren, as perfect and as sacred as his own, and prophesies the approaching advent of freedom, which unfortunately we are looking for still—that universal spring which should yet make young the nations of the earth.

Yet was Schiller no mad innovator. He saw that society required to be pruned, but did not desire that it should be uprooted—he would have it reformed, not laid waste. What was ancient and characteristic

in its usages and ordinances, and therefore endeared
to many, he would, where it was possible, improve
and adapt to the present wants of mankind. I remember a passage in which his respect for those devices of form and usage by which the men of a past
age sought to curb and restrain the arbitrary power
of their rulers, is beautifully illustrated   I quote
it from the magnificent translation of *Wallenstein*
made by Coleridge. Let me say here that I know
of no English translation of a poem of any length
which, a few passages excepted, so perfectly repro-
duces the original as this, and that if the same hand
had given us in our language the other dramas of
this author, we should have had an English Schiller
worthy to be placed by the side of the German.
" My son," says Octavio Piccolomini, addressing the
youthful warrior Max—

> " My son, of those old narrow ordinances
> Let us not hold too lightly. They are weights
> Of priceless value, which oppressed mankind
> Tied to the volatile will of the oppressor.
> For always formidable was the league
> And partnership of free power with free will."

And then, remarking that what slays and destroys
goes directly to its mark, like the thunderbolt and the
cannon-ball, shattering everything that lies in their
way, he claims a beneficent circuitousness for those

ancient ordinances which make so much of the ma-
chinery of society.

> " My son, the road the human being travels,
> That on which Blessing comes and goes, doth follow
> The river's path, the valley's playful windings,
> Curves round the corn-field and the hill of vines,
> Honoring the holy bounds of property,
> And thus, secure, though late, leads to its end."

Schiller perceived the great truth that old laws, if
not watched, slide readily into abuses, and knew that
constant revision and renovation are the necessary
conditions of free political society; but he would
have the revision made without forgetting that the
men of the present day are of the same blood with
those who lived before them. He would have the
new garments fitted to the figure that must wear
them, such as nature and circumstances have made
it, even to its disproportions. He would have the old
pass into the new by gradations which should avoid
violence, and its concomitants, confusion and misery.

The last great dramatic work of Schiller—and
whether it be not the grandest production of his
genius I leave to others to judge—is founded on the
most remarkable and beneficent political revolution
which, previous to our own, the world had seen—an
event the glory of which belongs solely to the Teu-
tonic race—that ancient vindication of the great right

of nationality and independent government, the revolt of Switzerland against the domination of Austria, which gave birth to a republic now venerable with the antiquity of five hundred years. He took a silent page from history, and, animating the personages of whom it speaks with the fiery life of his own spirit, and endowing them with his own superhuman eloquence, he formed it into a living protest against foreign dominion which yet rings throughout the world. Wherever there are generous hearts, wherever there are men who hold in reverence the rights of their fellow-men, wherever the love of country and the love of mankind coexist, Schiller's drama of *William Tell* stirs the blood like the sound of a trumpet.

It is not my purpose to dwell on the eminent literary qualities which make so large a part of the greatness of Schiller, and which have been more ably set forth by others than they can be by me. It is not for me to analyze his excellences as a dramatic poet; I will not speak of his beautiful and flowing lyrics, the despair of translators; I will say nothing of his noble histories, written, like his dramas, for all mankind—for it was his maxim that he who wrote for one nation only proposed to himself a poor and narrow aim. These topics would require more time than you could give me, and I should shrink with dismay from a task of such extent and magnitude. Let me close with observing that there is yet one other respect in which, as a member of the great world of letters, Schiller is entitled to the veneration of all mankind.

He was an earnest seeker after truth; a man whose moral nature revolted at every form of deceit; a noble example of what his countrymen mean when they claim the virtue of sincerity for the German race. He held with Akenside that

> "————Truth and Good are one,
> And Beauty dwells in them;"

that on the ascertainment and diffusion of truth the welfare of mankind largely depends, and that only mischief and misery can spring from delusions and prejudices, however enshrined in the respect of the world and made venerable by the lapse of years. The office of him who labored in the field of letters, he thought, was to make mankind better and happier, by illustrating and enforcing the relations and duties of justice, beneficence and brotherhood by which men are bound to each other; and he never forgot this in anything which he wrote. Immortal honor to him whose vast powers were employed to so worthy a purpose, and may the next hundredth anniversary of his birth be celebrated with even a warmer enthusiasm than this!

A BIRTHDAY ADDRESS.

A BIRTHDAY ADDRESS.

DELIVERED IN THE ROOMS OF THE CENTURY CLUB, IN REPLY TO ONE OF THE HON. GEORGE BANCROFT, ON THE OCCASION OF MR. BRYANT'S SEVENTIETH BIRTHDAY, NOVEMBER 3, 1864.

I thank you Mr. President, for the kind words you have uttered, and I thank this good-natured company for having listened to them with so many tokens of assent and approbation. I must suppose, however, that most of this approbation was bestowed upon the orator rather than upon his subject. He who has brought to the writing of our national history a genius equal to the vastness of the subject, has of course more than talent enough for humbler tastes. I wonder not, therefore, that he should be applauded this evening for the skill he has shown in embellishing a barren topic.

I am congratulated on having completed my seventieth year. Is there nothing ambiguous, Mr. President, in such a compliment? To be congratulated on one's senility! To be congratulated on having reached that stage of life when the bodily and mental powers pass into decline and decay! "Lear" is made by Shakspeare to say:

> " Age is unnecessary."

And a later poet, Dr. Johnson, expressed the same idea in one of his sonorous lines:

> " Superfluous lags the veteran on the stage."

You have not forgotten, Mr. President, the old Greek saying:

> "Whom the gods love die young."—

nor the passage in Shakspeare:

> —" Oh, sir, the good die first,
> And they, whose hearts are dry as summer dust,
> Burn to the socket."

Much has been said of the wisdom of Old Age. Old Age is wise, I grant, for itself, but not wise for the community. It is wise in declining new enterprises, for it has not the power nor the time to execute them; wise in shrinking from difficulty, for it has not the strength to overcome it; wise in avoiding danger, for it lacks the faculty of ready and swift action, by which dangers are parried and converted into advantages. But this is not wisdom for mankind at large, by whom new enterprises must be undertaken, dangers met and difficulties surmounted. What a

world would this be if it were made up of old men!—
generation succeeding to generation of hoary ancients who had but half a dozen years or perhaps half
that time to live! What new work of good would be
attempted! What existing abuse or evil corrected!
What strange subjects would such a world afford for
the pencils of our artists—groups. of superannuated
graybeards basking in the sun through the long days
of spring, or huddling like sheep in warm corners in
the winter time; houses with the timbers dropping
apart; cities in ruins; roads unwrought and impassable; weedy gardens and fields with the surface feebly
scratched to put in a scanty harvest; feeble old men
climbing into crazy wagons, perhaps to be run away
with, or mounting horses, if they mounted them at all,
in terror of being hurled from their backs like a stone
from a sling. Well it is that in this world of ours the
old men are but a very small minority.

Ah, Mr. President, if we could but stop this rushing tide of time that bears us so swiftly onward and
make it flow towards its source; if we could cause
the shadow to turn back on the dial-plate! I see before me many excellent friends of mine worthy to live
a thousand years, on whose countenances years have
set their seal, marking them with the lines of thought
and care and causing their temples to glisten with

the frosts of life's autumn. If to any one of these could be restored his glorious prime, his golden youth, with its hyacinthine locks, its smooth unwrinkled brow, its fresh and rounded cheek, its pearly and perfect teeth, its lustrous eyes, its light and agile step, its frame full of energy, its exulting spirits, its high hopes, its generous impulses—and add all these to the experience and fixed principles of mature age, I am sure, Mr. President, that I should start at once to my feet and propose that in commemoration of such a marvel and by way of congratulating our friend who was its subject, we should hold such a festivity as the Century has never seen nor will ever see again. Eloquence should bring its highest tribute, and Art its fairest decorations to grace the festival; the most skilful musicians should be here with all manner of instruments of music, ancient and modern; we would have sackbut and trumpet and shawm, and damsels with dulcimers, and a modern band three times as large as the one that now plays on that balcony. But why dwell on such a vain dream, since it is only by passing through the dark valley of the shadow of death that man can reach his second youth.

I have read, in descriptions of the old world, of the families of Princes and Barons, coming out of their castles to be present at some rustic festivity, such as a wedding of one of their peasantry. I am reminded of this custom by the presence of many literary persons of eminence in these rooms, and I thank them for this act of benevolence. Yet I miss among them several whom I wished rather than ventured to hope that I should meet on this occasion. I miss my old friend Dana, who gave so grandly the story of the Buccaneer in his solemn verses. I miss Pierpont, venerable in years, yet vigorous in mind and body, and with an undimmed fancy; and him whose pages are wet with the tears of maidens who read the story of Evangeline; and the author of Fanny and the Croakers, no less renowned for the fiery spirit which animates his Marco Bozzaris; and him to whose wit we owe the Biglow Papers, who has made a lowly flower of the wayside as classical as the rose of Anacreon; and the Quaker poet whose verses, Quaker as he is, stir the blood like the voice of a trumpet calling to battle; and the poetess of Hartford, whose beautiful lyrics are in a million hands; and others whose names, were they to occur to me here as in my study, I might accompany with the mention of some characteristic merit. But here is he whose aerial verse has raised the little insect of our fields, making its murmuring journey from flower to flower, the humble-bee, to a dignity equal to that of Pindar's eagle : here is the Autocrat of the Breakfast Table—author of that most spirited of naval lyrics, beginning with the line :

    "Aye, tear her tattered ensign down ! "

Here, too, is the poet who told in pathetic verse the story of Jeptha's daughter ; and here are others, worthy compeers of those I have mentioned, yet greatly my juniors, in the brightness of whose rising fame I am like one who has carried a lantern in the night, and who perceives that its beams are no longer visible in the glory which the morning pours around him.   To them and to all the members of the Century, allow me, Mr. President, to offer the wish that they may live longer than I have done in health of body and mind and in the same contentment and serenity of spirit which has fallen to my lot.   I must not overlook the ladies who have deigned to honor these rooms with their presence.   If I knew where, amid myrtle bowers and flowers that never wither, gushed from the ground the fountain of perpetual youth so long vainly sought by the first Spanish adventurers on the North American continent, I would offer to the lips of every one of them a beaker of its fresh and sparkling waters, and bid them drink unfading bloom.

But since that is not to be, I will wish what, perhaps, is as well, and what some would think better, that the same kindness of heart which has prompted them to come hither to-night, may lend a beauty to every action of their future lives. And to the Century Club itself—the dear old Century Club—to whose members I owe both the honors and the embarrassments of this occasion—to that association, fortunate in having possessed two such presidents as the distinguished historian who now occupies the chair, and the eminent and accomplished scholar and admirable writer who preceded him, I offer the wish that it may endure, not only for the term of years signified by its name—not for one century only, but for ten centuries—so that hereafter, perhaps, its members may discuss the question whether its name should not be changed to that of the Club of a Thousand Years, and that these may be centuries of peace and prosperity, from which its members may look back to this period of bloody strife, as to a frightful dream soon chased away by the beams of a glorious morning.

FREEDOM OF EXCHANGE.

FREEDOM OF EXCHANGE.

SPEECH AT A DINNER GIVEN TO MR. BRYANT, IN NEW YORK,
JANUARY 30, 1868.

MR. CHAIRMAN AND GENTLEMEN:

An honor like this requires from me a particular
acknowledgment, which yet I hardly know how to
make in fitting terms. Conferred as it is by men
whom I so much value and respect, and who possess
in so high a degree the esteem of their fellow-citizens, I can not but feel that it would amply reward
services infinitely greater than I can pretend to have
rendered to any cause. What I have done in applying the principles of human liberty to the exchange
of property between man and man and between nation and nation, has been very easy to do. It was
simply to listen to my own convictions, without any
attempt to reason them away, and to follow whither-
soever they might lead me. In this manner I have
been saved a good deal of trouble, some perplexity
and bewilderment, some waste of ingenuity, if I had
any to waste, and perhaps no little remorse.

Another circumstance has made my task easy. I had only to walk in a path smoothed and lighted by some of the best thinkers of the age—impartial, unprejudiced men, who had no object in view but the simple discovery of truth. It was not difficult to walk in such a path. Grand and noble intellects held their torches over it, and I could not well step astray with such guidance. Besides, I had only to follow in the way which the world is going. The tendency of enlightened public opinion in all countries is towards the freedom of trade. There is no difficulty in swimming with the current. I saw that the navigation was safe, and let my boat float with the stream, while others laboriously tried to stem it or lay moored to the shore wondering which way they ought to go. We shall have them all with us yet, Mr. Chairman, a merry fleet of all manner of craft, bound on the same easy voyage.

Another circumstance which has made the task of Free Trade more easy, is the involuntary admiss'ons which the protectionists make of the fallacy of their system. A capitalist in New England, owning cotton or woollen mills, however great his attachment to the protective system, has no idea of employing any part of his capital in raising wheat in the fields close to his mills, that he may save the expense to him and his work-people of bringing it from the distant West. He brings it from a thousand miles away, and sends back his fabrics in exchange, at the very moment that he is procuring laws to be passed which will prevent us, the consumers, from buying iron and cloth and paper from Europe, that we may, as they say, save the expense of freight. When we make a new acquisition of territory, they do not object that we are to have Free-Trade with the new region. On the contrary, they rejoice in a wider market. This they did when Texas was taken into the Union. They made no opposition to the acquisition of California on the ground that all revenue laws which shut out the trade of that wide region would now be repealed. When we talk of annexing Canada, they do not object that we and the Canadians will then be no longer independent of each other.

In this they are in the right; in this they tacitly admit the advantage of Free-Trade. Whatever other objection may be made to the acquisition of new territory, the enlargement of our borders by the addition of new and extensive provinces is a great commercial and industrial advantage, because it makes the exchange of commodities between them and us perfectly free.

Yet there is a certain plausibility in what the protectionists say when they talk of home industry and a home market—a plausibility which misleads many worthy and otherwise sensible people—sensible in all other respects, and whom as men I admire and honor. There are clever men among them, who bring to their side of the question a great array of facts, many of which, however, have no real bearing upon its solution. There is a plausibility, too, in the idea that the sun makes a daily circuit around the earth, and if there were any private interests to be promoted by maintaining it, we should have thousands believing that the earth stands still while the sun travels round it. " See for yourself," they would say. Will you not believe the evidence of your own senses? The sun comes up in the East every day before your eyes, stands over your head at noon, and goes down in the afternoon in the west. Why, you admit the fact when you say the sun rises, the sun sets, the sun is up, the sun is down. What a fool was Galileo, what nonsense is the system of Copernicus, what trash was written by Sir Isaac Newton!"

I remember a case in point—an anecdote which I once heard in Scotland. A writer to the signet, that is to say, an attorney, named Moll, who knew very little, except what related to the drawing up of law-papers, once heard a lecture on astronomy, in which some illustrations were given of the daily revolution of the earth on its axis. The attorney was perplexed and bewildered by this philosophy, which was so new to him, and one day, his thoughts frequently recurring to the subject, he looked up from his law-papers, and said: "The young mon says the warld turns roond. It's vera extraordinar'. I've lived in this place sax-and-thretty years, and that grass-plot presarves the same relative poseetion to the house that it had sax-and-thretty years sin'; and yet the young mon says the warld turns roond. It's vera extraordinar'." Here was a man who was not to be taken in by this nonsense about the earth revolving on its axis; and if there were any real or imaginary pecuniary advantage to be gained by denying it, Mr. Moll would have a whole army of his way of thinking, many of them far wiser and better informed in other respects than he.

Perhaps, Mr. Chairman and gentlemen, you will allow me to make use of another familiar illustration. You have heard of a man attempting to lift himself from the ground by the waistband of his pantaloons. Now, if anything were to be gained by it, a very respectable *a priori* argument might be made in favor of the possibility of the feat. One might say: "You can lift two hundred pounds; your weight is but one hundred and sixty. A power of gravitation equal to one hundred and sixty pounds holds you down to the earth. You have only to apply a counteracting force a little greater than this and you will be lifted into the air. Take hold of your waistband, therefore, with both hands, and pull vigorously. If you do not lift yourself up at the first trial you must pull harder." All that might sound very plausible to one who had no experience to guide him.

This country has been persuaded to attempt the feat of lifting itself from the ground by the waistband, for nearly half a century past, with occasional short relaxations of the efforts prompted by a return of common sense. When the first pull was made, and was ineffectual, we were told to try another, and then another still more vigorous, and another and another; and now what do we see? The garment of which the waistband forms a part is torn to shreds and tatters, presenting what Pope, alluding to a similar accident, somewhere calls a "dishonest sight," mortifying to the pride of philosophy.

It is most true that a man can be raised from the ground by the waistband; but he cannot do the feat himself—another must perform the office. The force must come from without. One strong man may raise another in this way, and be raised by him in turn.

In this case there is an interchange of good offices—freedom of trade. No man even with the strength of Samson, can go into a room by himself and endeavor to perform the feat alone, without coming forth from the undertaking in rags, his nether garment full of ghastly rents, inviting the entrance of the January wind. So no nation can enrich itself by excluding foreign commerce ; the more perfect it makes the exclusion, the more certain it is to impoverish itself.

Mr. Chairman and gentlemen ; There is a great law imposed upon us by the necessities of our condition as members of human society, the law of mutual succor, the interchange of benefits and advantages, the law of God and nature, commanding us to be useful to each other. It is the law of the household ; it is the law of the neighborhood ; it is the law of different provinces included under the same government, and well would it be for mankind if it were in an equal degree recognized as a law to be sacredly regarded by the great community of nations in their intercourse with each other. Were that law to be repealed, the social state would lose its cohesion and fall in pieces. There is not a pathway across the fields, nor a highroad, nor a guide-post at a turn of the way, nor a railway from city to city or from State to State, nor a sail upon the ocean, which is not an illustration of this

14*

law. It is proclaimed in the shriek of the locomotive. It is murmured in the ripple of waters divided by the prow of the steamer. The nation by which it is disregarded, or which endeavors to obstruct it by artificial barriers against the free intercourse of its citizens with those of other countries, revolts against the order of nature and strikes at its own prosperity.

THE ELECTRIC TELEGRAPH.

THE ELECTRIC TELEGRAPH.

SPEECH AT A DINNER GIVEN TO SAMUEL BREESE MORSE, DECEMBER, 29, 1868.

I speak, Mr. President, in behalf of the press. To the press the electric telegraph is an invention of immense value. Charles Lamb, in one of his papers, remarks that a piece of news, which, when it left Botany Bay was true to the letter, often becomes a lie before it reaches England. It is the advantage of the telegraph that it gives you the news before circumstances have had time to alter it. The press is enabled to lay it fresh before the reader. It comes to him like a steak hot from the gridiron, instead of being cooled and made flavorless by a slow journey from a distant kitchen. A battle is fought three thousand miles away, and we have the news while they are taking the wounded to the hospital. A great orator rises in the British Parliament, and we read his words almost before the cheers of his friends have ceased. An earthquake shakes San Francisco, and we have the news before the people who have rushed into the street have returned to their houses. I am afraid that the columns of the daily newspapers would now seem flat, dull, and stale to the readers were it not for the communications of the telegraph.

But while the telegraph does this for the press, the press in some sort returns the obligation. Were it not for the press, the telegram, being repeated from mouth to mouth, would, from the moment of its arrival, begin to lose something of its authenticity. Every rumor propagated orally at last becomes false. Mr. President, you are familiar with the personification of Rumor by the poets of antiquity—at first of dwarfish size, and rapidly enlarging in bulk till her feet sweep the earth and her head is among the clouds. The press puts Rumor into a straight jacket, swaddles her from head to foot, and so restrains her growth. It transcribes the messages of the telegraph in their very words, and thus prevents them from being magnified or mutilated into lies. It protects the reputation of the telegraph for veracity. You know, Mr. President, what a printer's devil is. It is the messenger who brings to the printer his copy—that is to say, matter which is to be put into type. Some petulant, impatient author, I suppose, who was negligent in furnishing the required copy, must have given him that name; although he is so useful that he is entitled to be called the printer's angel, the original word for angel and messenger being the same. Our illustrious guest, Mr. President, has taken portions of the great electric mass, which in its concentrated form becomes the thunderbolt ; he has drawn it into slender threads, and every one of these becomes in his hands an obedient messenger—a printer's devil, carrying with the speed of a sunbeam volumes of copy to the type-setter.

In the Treatise on Bathos, Pope quotes, as a sample of absurdity not to be surpassed, a passage from some play, I think one of Nat. Lee's, expressing the modest wish of a lover :

> " Ye gods, annihilate both space and time,
> And make two lovers happy. "

But 'see what changes a century brings forth. What was then an absurdity, what was arrant nonsense, is now the statement of a naked fact. Our guest has annihilated both space and time in the transmission of intelligence. The breadth of the Atlantic, with all its waves, is as nothing ; and in sending a message from Europe to this continent, the time, as computed by the clock, is some six hours less than nothing.

There is one view of this great invention of the

electric telegraph which impresses me with awe. Beside us at this board, along with the illustrious man whom we are met to honor, and whose name will go down to the latest generations of civilized man, sits the gentleman to whose clear-sighted perseverance and to whose energy—an energy which knew no discouragement, no weariness, no pause—we owe it that the telegraph has been laid which connects the Old World with the New through the Atlantic Ocean. My imagination goes down to the chambers of the middle sea, to those vast depths where repose, the mystic wire on beds of coral, among forests of tangle, or on the bottom of the dim blue gulfs strewn with the bones of whales and sharks, skeletons of drowned men, and ribs and masts of foundered barks, laden with wedges of gold never to be coined, and pipes of the choicest vintages of earth never to be tasted. Through these watery solitudes, among the fountains of the great deep, the abode of perpetual silence, never visited by living human presence and beyond the sight of human eye, there are gliding to and fro, by night and by day, in light and in darkness, in calm and in tempest, currents of human thought borne by the electric pulse which obeys the bidding of man. That slender wire thrills with the hopes and fears of nations; it vibrates to every emotion that can be awakened by any event affecting the welfare of the human race. A volume of contemporary history passes every hour of the day from one continent to the other. An operator on the continent of Europe gently touches the keys of an instrument in his quiet room, a message is shot with the swiftness of light through the abysses of the sea, and before his hand is lifted from the machine the story of revolts and revolutions, of monarchs dethroned and new dynasties set up in their place, of battles and conquests and treaties of peace, of great statesmen fallen in death, lights of the world gone out and new luminaries glimmering on the horizon, is written down in another quiet room on the other side of the globe.

Mr. President, I see in the circumstances which I have enumerated a new proof of the superiority of mind to matter, of the independent existence of that part of our nature which we call the spirit, when it can thus subdue, enslave, and educate the subtlest, the most active, and, in certain of its manifestations the most intractable and terrible of the elements, making it in our hands the vehicle of thought—and compelling it to speak every language of the civil-

ized world. I infer the capacity of the spirit for
a separate state of being, its indestructible essence
and its noble destiny, and I thank the great discoverer whom we have assembled to honor for this
confirmation of my faith.

THE METROPOLITAN ART MUSEUM.

THE METROPOLITAN ART MUSEUM.

ADDRESS DELIVERED AT A MEETING IN THE UNION CLUB
HOUSE, NOVEMBER 23, 1869.

We are assembled, my friends, to consider the
subject of founding in this city a Museum of Art, a repository of the productions of artists of every class,
which shall be in some measure worthy of this great
metropolis and of the wide empire of which New
York is the commercial centre. I understand that
no rivalry with any other project is contemplated, no
competition, save with similar institutions in other
countries, and then only such modest competition as
a museum in its infancy may aspire to hold with
those which were founded centuries ago, and are enriched with the additions made by the munificence of
successive generations. No precise method of reaching this result has been determined on, but the object
of the present meeting is to awaken the public, so far
as our proceedings can influence the general mind, to
the importance of taking early and effectual measures
for founding such a museum as I have described.

Our city is the third great city of the civilized.

world. Our republic has already taken its place among the great powers of the earth ; it is great in extent, great in population, great in the activity and enterprise of her people. It is the richest nation in the world, if paying off an enormous national debt with a rapidity unexampled in history be any proof of riches ; the richest in the world, if contented submission to heavy taxation be a sign of wealth ; the richest in the world, if quietly to allow itself to be annually plundered of immense sums by men who seek public stations for their individual profit be a token of public prosperity. My friends, if a tenth part of what is every year stolen from us in this way, in the city where we live, under pretence of the public service, and poured profusely into the coffers of political rogues, were expended on a Museum of Art, we might have, deposited in spacious and stately buildings, collections formed of works left by the world's greatest artists, which would be the pride of our country. We might have an annual revenue which would bring to the Museum every stray statue and picture of merit, for which there should be no ready sale to individuals, every smaller collection in the country which its owner could no longer conveniently keep, every noble work by the artists of former ages, which by any casualty, after long remaining on the walls of some ancient building, should be again thrown upon the world.

But what have we done—numerous as our people are, and so rich as to be contentedly cheated and plundered, what have we done towards founding such a repository? We have hardly made a step towards it. Yet, beyond the sea there is the little kingdom of Saxony, with an area even less than that of Massachusetts, and a population but little larger, possessing a Museum of the Fine Arts, marvellously rich, which no man who visits the continent of Europe is willing to own that he has not seen. There is Spain, a third-rate power of Europe and poor besides, with a Museum of Fine Arts at her capital, the opulence. and extent of which absolutely bewilder the visitor. I will not speak of France or of England, conquering nations, which have gathered their treasures of art in part from regions overrun by their armies ; nor yet of Italy, the fortunate inheritor of so many glorious productions of her own artists. But there are Holland and Belgium, kingdoms almost too small to be heeded by the greater powers of Europe in the consultations which decide the destinies of nations, and these little kingdoms have their public collections of art, the resort of admiring visitors from all parts of the civilized world.

But in our country, when the owner of a private gallery of art desires to leave his treasures where they can be seen by the public, he looks in vain for any institution to which he can send them. A public-spirited citizen desires to employ a favorite artist upon some great historical picture ; there are no walls on which it can hang in public sight. A large collection of works of art, made at great cost, and with great pains, gathered perhaps during a lifetime, is for sale in Europe. We may find here men willing to contribute to purchase it, but if it should be brought to our country there is no edifice here to give it hospitality.

In 1857, during a visit to Spain, I found in Madrid a rich private collection of pictures, made by Medraza, an aged painter, during a long life, and at a period when frequent social and political changes in that country dismantled many palaces of the old nobility of the works of art which adorned them. In that collection were many pictures by the illustrious elder artists of Italy, Spain and Holland. The whole might have been bought for half its value, but if it had been brought over to our country we had no gallery to hold it. The same year I stood before the famous Campana collection of marbles, at Rome, which was then waiting for a purchaser—a noble collection, busts and statues of the ancient philosophers, orators and poets, the majestic forms of Roman senators, the deities of ancient mythology,

" The fair humanities of old religion,"

but if they had been purchased by our countrymen and landed here, we should have been obliged to leave them in boxes, just as they were packed.

Moreover, we require an extensive public gallery to contain the greater works of our own painters and sculptors. The American soil is prolific of artists. The fine arts blossom not only in the populous regions of our country, but even in its solitary places. Go where you will, into whatever museum of art in the Old World, you find there artists from the new, contemplating or copying the master-pieces of art which they contain. Our artists swarm in Italy. When I was last at Rome, two years since, I found the number of American artists residing there as two to one compared with those from the British isles. But there are beginners among us who have not the means of resorting to distant countries for that instruction in art which is derived from carefully studying works of acknowledged excellence. For these a gallery is needed at home, which shall vie with those abroad, if not in the multitude, yet in the merit, of the works it contains.

15

Yet further, it is unfortunate for our artists, our painters especially, that they too often find their genius cramped by the narrow space in which it is constrained to exert itself. It is like a bird in a cage which can only take short flights from one perch to another and longs to stretch its wings in an ampler atmosphere. Producing works for private dwellings, our painters are for the most part obliged to confine themselves to cabinet pictures, and have little opportunity for that larger treatment of important subjects which a greater breadth of canvas would allow them, and by which the higher and nobler triumphs of their art have been achieved.

There is yet another view of the subject, and a most important one. When I consider, my friends, the prospect which opens before this great mart of the western world, I am moved by feelings which I feel it somewhat difficult clearly to define. The growth of our city is already wonderfully rapid; it is every day spreading itself into the surrounding region, and overwhelming it like an inundation. Now that our great railway has been laid from the Atlantic to the Pacific, Eastern Asia and Western Europe will shake hands over our republic. New York will be the mart from which Europe will receive a large proportion of the products of China, and will become not only a centre of commerce for the New World, but for that region which is to Europe the most remote part of the Old.   A new impulse will be given to the growth of our city, which I cannot contemplate without an emotion akin to dismay.   Men will flock in greater numbers than ever before to plant themselves on a spot so favorable to the exchange of commodities between distant regions; and here will be an aggregation of human life, a concentration of all that ennobles and all that degrades humanity, on a scale which the imagination cannot venture to measure. To great cities resort not only all that is eminent in talent, all that is splendid in genius, and all that is active in philanthropy; but also all that is most dexterous in villany, and all that is most foul in guilt.   It is in the labyrinths of such mighty and crowded populations that crime finds its safest lurking-places : it is there that vice spreads its most seductive and fatal snares, and sin is pampered and festers and spreads its contagion in the greatest security.

My friends, it is important that we should encounter the temptations to vice in this great and too rapidly growing capital by attractive entertainments of an innocent and improving character.   We have libraries and reading-rooms, and this is well; we have also spacious halls for musical entertainments, and that also is well; but there are times when we do not care to read and are satiate with the listening to sweet sounds, and when we more willingly contemplate works of art. It is the business of the true philanthropist to find means of gratifying this preference. We must be beforehand with vice in our arrangements for all that gives grace and cheerfulness to society. The influence of works of art is wholesome, ennobling, instructive. Besides the cultivation of the sense of beauty—in other words, the perception of order, symmetry, proportion of parts, which is of near kindred to the moral sentiments—the intelligent contemplation of a great gallery of works of art is a lesson in history, a lesson in biography, a lesson in the antiquities of different countries. Half our knowledge of the customs and modes of life among the ancient Greeks and Romans is derived from the remains of ancient art.

Let it be remembered to the honor of art that if it has ever been perverted to the purposes of vice, it has only been at the bidding of some corrupt court or at the desire of some opulent and powerful voluptuary whose word was law. When intended for the general eye no such stain rests on the works of art. Let me close with an anecdote of the influence of a well-known work. I was once speaking to the poet

Rogers in commendation of the painting of Ary Scheffer, entitled *Christ the Consoler*. "I have an engraving of it," he answered, "hanging at my bed-side, where it meets my eye every morning." The aged poet, over whom already impended the shadow that shrouds the entrance to the next world, found his morning meditations guided by that work to the Founder of our religion.

THE MERCANTILE LIBRARY.

THE MERCANTILE LIBRARY.

AN ADDRESS DELIVERED ON THE FIFTIETH ANNIVERSARY
OF THE FOUNDING OF THE NEW YORK MERCANTILE LI-
BRARY, NOVEMBER 9, 1870.

I esteem myself fortunate in being able to congratulate the Mercantile Library Association upon
having arrived at its fiftieth anniversary. Forty-five
years ago, when I came to live in New York, it was
in its early infancy. The public-spirited gentlemen
by whom it was founded, I remember, expected much
from it in the future. They hoped, and the hope was
not vain, that it would greatly aid in forming the
minds of the younger part of the mercantile class to
liberal tastes and to generous views of their duty to
their country and to mankind, and that it would be
in some measure a safeguard against the temptations
which beset young men in a populous city. Those
who then sat by its cradle, if they survive, are now
aged men; those whose birth was coeval with its
origin, are men of mature age, who have passed the
zenith of life; the books which were collected in its
first years, to form the beginning of what is now a

15*

flourishing library, belong to the literature of a past generation. Yet, in founding this institution, the men of that day left a noble legacy to future times. While other institutions have risen and fallen, it has continued to grow and to extend its beneficial influences with the growth of our city ; not, indeed, in the same proportion, but steadily and with a sure advance, till now its prosperity and duration seem almost beyond the reach of accident. I learn that there is no library in the country which increases so fast as that which belongs to this association, and that within the last ten years it has more than doubled the number of its volumes. If it proceeds at this rate it will eventually have a library which will command the admiration of the world and become the pride of our country.

In the years yet to come, far in the depths of the future, the young men who search among the old books of the library will say to each other, " See with what reading our ancestors entertained themselves many centuries since, and how the language has changed since that time! We can laugh yet at the humor of Irving, in spite of the antiquated diction. What a fiery spirit animates the quaint sentences of the old novelist Cooper! In these verses of Longfellow we still perceive the sweetness of the numbers and the pathos of the thoughts, and wonder not that the maidens of that distant age wept over the pages of Evangeline. Here," they will add, "are the scientific works of that distant age. Clever men were these ancestors of ours ; diligent inquirers, fortunate discoverers of scientific truth, but how far in its attainment below the height which we have since reached ! "

What I have just now imagined supposes our flourishing library to escape destruction by war and by casual fires. Ah, my friends, never may the fate of unhappy Strasburg be ours ! to lie for weeks under a hail storm of iron and a rain of fire, showered from the engines of destruction, which Milton properly makes the guilty invention of the sinning angels, and doomed to see her library, rich with the priceless treasures of past centuries, suddenly turned to ashes. But whatever may be the fate of our library, the association itself is not so easily destroyed. If the library perish, the same spirit which founded at first, will restore it so far as a restoration is possible. The association, I venture to predict, will subsist till this great mart of commerce shall be a mart no longer ; till the mercantile class shall have disappeared from the spot where it stands, and New York shall have dwindled to a fishing town.

But will this ever be? Will our great city share the fate of Tyre and Sidon, whose merchants were princes, and which are now but Arab villages, with a few caiques and here and their a felucca moored in their clear but shallow waters, choked with the ruins of palaces? Will she become like Carthage, once mistress of flourishing colonies, but now a desert; like Corinth, once the seat of a vast commerce— opulent, luxurious, magnificent Corinth—now a mere cluster of houses overlooked by a dismantled and mouldering citadel?

Or to come down to later times, will this city decay like Amsterdam, the mother of New York, and once the centre of the world's commerce? Or like Genoa, surnamed the proud, and Venice, once the mistress of the Adriatic, cities which, after having successively wielded the commerce of the East, and made Italian the language of commerce in all the ports of the Levant, have long since ceased to hold a place among the great marts of the world?

I answer that none of these cities had the same firm and durable basis of commercial prosperity as our New York. It was their enterprise in opening channels of trade; it was their conquests and colonies which gave them their temporary prosperity. They had no broad, well-peopled region around them, under the same government with themselves, whose superabundant products it was their office to exchange with other countries. Their prosperity was built on narrow foundations, and it fell. Our circumstances are different. Here is a republic of vast extent, stretching from the sea which bathes the western coast of Europe to that which washes the eastern shore of Asia—a region of fertile plains, rich valleys, noble forests, mountains big with mines, water-courses whose sands are gold, mighty rivers, railways going forth from our great cities to every point of the compass, and covering an immense territory with their intersections, and not a hinderance to commerce between city and city or between sea and sea, or on our great rivers, or on the borders of the States forming our confederation. This mighty region, alive with an energetic population, is flanked with seaports through which the products sent by us to other countries *must* pass, and through which the merchandise sent us in exchange *must* be received. They are therefore an indispensable part of our national economy. Their prosperity is necessary, inevitable, and will endure while our political organization remains as it now is.

But if it should come to pass that this fortunate order of things is broken up, if this great republic should fall to pieces and become divided into a group of independent commonwealths, each animated by a narrow jealousy of the others ; and if an illiberal legislation should obstruct the channels of trade now so fortunately open over all our vast territory, there are none of our great marts of exchange for whose future prosperity I could answer. Some would fall into a slow decay, some pass into a rapid decline; some would become like Ascalon on the coast of Palestine, once a harbor crowded with shipping, but when I saw it, a desolate spot, where the sea-sand had drifted upon the foundations of temples and palaces, invaded the harvest fields, and moving before the wind had entered the olive groves and piled itself among them to the tops of the trees.

Our security from such unhappy results will, in a good degree, lie in such institutions as this, and in other means of a like character, the object of which is to diffuse knowledge, to open men's eyes to their true interests, and accustom them to large and generous views of the relation of communities to each other and to the world at large. For this reason let us hope for the permanent and increasing prosperity of the Mercantile Library Association.

ITALIAN UNITY.

ITALIAN UNITY.

AN ADDRESS DELIVERED BEFORE A MEETING IN NEW YORK,
JANUARY, 1871.

We are assembled, my friends, to celebrate a new
and signal triumph of liberty and constitutional government—not a victory obtained by one religious denomination over another, but the successful assertion
of rights which are the natural inheritance of every
man born into the world—rights of which no man
can divest himself, and which no possible form
of government should be allowed to deny its subjects. A great nation, the Italian nation, while yet
acknowledging allegiance to the Latin church, has
been moved to strike the fetters of civil and religious
thraldom from the inhabitants of the most interesting
city of the world, in the midst of their exulting accla-
mations. We are assembled to re-echo those accla-
mations.

The government which has just been overthrown
in Rome denied to those who had the misfortune to
be its subjects, every one of the liberties which are
the pride and glory of our own country—liberty of

the press, liberty of speech, liberty of worship, liberty of assembling. It was an iron despotism which, to the scandal of the Christian church, insisted on persecution as a duty, set the example of persecution to other Catholic countries, and wherever it could make itself obeyed, maintained the obligation of re pressing heresy by the law of force.

Take a single example of the manner in which the government was administered. An American lady, an acquaintance of mine, a resident in Rome for several years, was summoned one morning to appear before the police of that city. She went accompanied by the American Consul.

"You are charged," said the police magistrate, "with having sent money to Florence, to be employed in founding a Protestant orphan asylum. What do you say?"

"I did send money for that purpose," was the lady's answer. "I did not ask for it, it was brought to me by some ladies, who requested me to forward it to Florence, and I did so; and I take the liberty to say that it is no affair of yours."

"Of that you are not to judge," replied the magistrate. "See that you never repeat the offence."

Such was the government which to the great joy of the Roman people and the satisfaction of the friends of liberty everywhere, has been overthrown. Was it worthy—I put this question to this assembly—was such a government worthy to subsist even for an hour?

And yet there are those who protest against this change — American citizens, and excellent people among them, who lend their names to a public remonstrance against admitting the people of Rome to the liberties which we enjoy. My friends, is there a single one of these liberties which is not as dear to you as the light of day and the free air of heaven? The liberty of public worship, would you give it up without a mortal struggle? The liberty of discussing openly, in conversation, or by means of the press, in books or in newspapers, every question which interests the welfare of our race—a liberty of which the poor Romans were not allowed even the shadow—this and the liberty of assembling as we now assemble in vast throngs, thousands upon thousands, to give an expression of public opinion the significance of which cannot be mistaken—are not these as dear to you as the crimson current that warms your hearts, and are they not worthy to be defended at the risk of your lives? How is it then that any citizen of our own country, in the enjoyment of these blessings, and prizing them as he must, can protest against their be-

ing conferred upon the Roman people—a people nobly endowed by nature, and worthy of a better lot
than the slavery they have endured for so many generations?

What sort of Protestantism is this? Protestantism
in its worst form of misapplication.   I should as soon
think of protesting against the glorious light of the
sun, of protesting against admitting the sweet air of
the outer world into a dungeon full of noisome damps
and stifling exhalations.   I should as soon think of
remonstrating with Providence against the return of
spring with its verdure and flowers and promise of
harvests, after a long and dreary winter.   Is it possible that those of our countrymen who lend their
names to condemn this act of justice to the Roman
people are aware of what they do?

My friends, I respect profound religious convictions wherever I meet them.   I honor a good life wherever I see it, and I find men of saintly lives in every
religious denomination.   But when I hear it affirmed
that there is a natural alliance between despotism
and Christianity; that the necessary prop and support
of religion is the law of force, and that the Christian
church should be so organized that its head shall be
an absolute temporal monarch, surrounded by a population compelled to be his slaves, I must say to those

who make this assertion, whatever be their personal worth, that their doctrine dishonors Christianity, that it brings scandal upon religion, and blasphemes the holy and gracious memory of the Saviour of the world.

It is now nearly two centuries and a half since Roger Williams established in Rhode Island a commonwealth on the basis of strict religious equality. That was a little light shining upon the world from a distance, and slow has been the progress of the nations in taking that commonwealth for an example. Yet, though slow, the progress of religious liberty has been constant; the day of its triumph has arrived; to-night we celebrate its crowning conquest. It was but a little while since that Austria thrust out the priesthood from that partnership in the political power which it had held for centuries. It is not many years since that at Malaga, in Spain, when a heretic died, his corpse was conveyed to the sea beach, amid the hootings of the populace, and that the soil of Spain might not be polluted by his remains, it was buried in the sand at low-water mark, where the waves sometimes uncovered it and swept it out to sea to become the prey of sharks. Now, the heretic may erect a temple and pay worship in any part of Spain. Not long since there was no part of Italy in which any worship save that of the Latin church was permitted. Now, we owe to an eminent Italian statesman the glorious maxim, " A free church in a free state," and we behold the religious conscience set free from its fetters even in the Eternal city. With the aid of popular education it will remain so forever.

When I think of these changes, I am reminded of that grand allegory in one of the Hebrew prophets, in which we read of a stone cut out of the quarry without hands smiting a gigantic image with a head of gold and legs of iron, and breaking it to pieces, which became like the chaff of the summer threshing-floors, to be carried away by the wind, while the stone that smote the image grew to be, a great mountain and filled the whole earth. Thus has the principle of religious liberty, a stone cut out of the quarry without hands—an inspiration of the Most High—smitten the grim tyranny that held the religious conscience in subjection to the law of force and broken it into fragments, while it is rapidly expanding itself to fill the civilized world. Let us hope that the rubbish left by the demolition of this foul idol. made small as the chaff of the summer threshing-floors and dispersed by the breath of public opinion, may never be gathered up again and reconstituted even in the mildest form it ever wore, while the globe on which we tread shall endure.

THE MORSE STATUE.

THE MORSE STATUE.

There are two lines in the poem of Dr. Johnson's on the *Vanity of Human Wishes*, which have passed into a proverb:

> "See nations slowly wise and meanly just,
> To buried merit raise the tardy bust."

It is our good fortune to escape the censure implied in these lines. We come together on the occasion of raising a statue, not to buried but to living merit—to a great discoverer who yet sits among us, a witness of honors which are but the first fruits of that ample harvest which his memory will gather in the long train of seasons yet to come. Yet we cannot congratulate ourselves on having set an example of alacrity in this manifestation of the public gratitude. If our illustrious friend, to whom we now gladly pay these honors, had not lived beyond the common age of man, we should have sorrowfully laid them on his grave. In what I am about to say I shall not attempt to relate the history of the Electric Telegraph, or discuss the claims of our friend to be acknowledged as its inventor. I took up the other day one of the forty-six volumes of the great biographical dictionary compiled by French authors, and immediately after the name of Samuel Finley Breese Morse I read the words "inventor of the electric telegraph." I am satisfied with this ascription. It is made by a nation which, having no claims of its own to the invention, is naturally impartial. The words I have given may be taken as an expression of the deliberate judgment of the world, and I should regard it as a waste of your time and mine to occupy the few minutes allotted to me in demonstrating its truth. As to the history of this invention, it is that of most great discoveries. Coldly and doubtingly received at first, its author compelled to struggle with difficulties, to encounter neglect, to contend with rivals, it has gradually gained the public favor till at length it is adopted throughout the civilized world.

It now lacks but a few years of half a century since I became acquainted with the man whom this invention has made so famous in all countries. He was then an artist, devoted to a profession in which he might have attained a high rank, had he not, fortunately for his country and the world, left it for a pursuit in which he has risen to a more peculiar eminence. Even then, in the art of painting, his tendency to mechanical invention was conspicuous. His mind, as I remember, was strongly impelled to analyze the processes of his art—to give them a certain scientific precision, to reduce them to fixed rules, to refer effects to clearly-defined causes, so as to put it in the power of the artist to produce them at pleasure and with certainty, instead of blindly groping for them, and, in the end, owing them to some happy accident, or some instinctive effort, of which he could give no account. The mind of Morse was an organizing mind. He showed this in a remarkable manner when he brought together the artists of New York, then a little band of mostly young men, whose profession was far from being honored as it now is, reconciled the disagreements which he found existing among them, and founded an association, to be managed solely by themselves — the Academy of the Arts of Design—which has since grown to such noble dimensions, and which has given to the artists a consideration in the community far higher than was before conceded to them. This ingenuity in organization, this power of combining the causes which produce given effects into a system, and making them act together to a common end, was not long afterward to be exemplified in a very remarkable manner.

The voyage made by Mr. Morse, from Havre to New York, on board the packet-ship Sully, in the year 1832, marks an important era in the history of inventions. In a casual conversation with some of the passengers concerning certain experiments which showed the identity of magnetism and electricity, the idea struck his mind that in a gentle and steady current of the electric fluid there was a source of regular, continued and rapid motions, which might be applied to a machine for conveying messages from place to place, and inscribing them on a tablet at their place of destination. We can fancy the inventor, full of this thought, as he paced the deck of the Sully, or lay in his berth, revolving in his mind the mechanical contrivances by which this was to be effected, until the whole process had taken a definite shape in his imagination, and he saw before him all the countries of the civilized world intersected with lines of his electric wire, bearing messages to and fro with the speed of light.

I have already said that this invention met with a tardy welcome. It was not till three years after this —that is to say, in 1835—that Morse found means to demonstrate to the public its practicability by a telegraph constructed on an economical scale, and set up at the New York University, which recorded messages at their place of destination. The public, however, still seemed indifferent; there was none of the loud applause, none of that enthusiastic reception which it now seems natural should attend the birth of so brilliant a discovery. The inventor, however, saw further than we all, and I think never lost courage. Yet I remember that some three or four years after this he said to me with some despondency: " Wheatstone in England, and Steinheil in Bavaria, who have their electric telegraphs, are afforded the means of bringing forward their methods, while to my invention, of earlier date than theirs, my country seems to show no favor." He persevered, however, and the doubts of those who hesitated were finally dispelled in 1844 by the establishment of a telegraph on his plan between Washington and Baltimore. France and other countries on the European Continent soon adopted his invention and vied with each other in rewarding him with honors. The indifference of his countrymen, which he could not but acutely feel, gave place to pride in his growing fame, and to-day we express our admiration for his genius and our gratitude for the benefit he has conferred upon the world by erecting this statue, which has just been unveiled to the public.

It may be said, I know, that the civilized world is

already full of memorials which speak the merit of
our friend, and the grandeur and utility of his invention. Every telegraphic station is such a memorial;
every message sent from one of these stations to another may be counted among the honors paid to his
name. Every telegraphic wire strung from post to
post, as it hums in the wind, murmurs his eulogy.
Every sheaf of wires laid down in the deep sea, occupying the bottom of soundless abysses, to which
human sight has never penetrated, and carrying the
electric pulse, charged with the burden of human
thought from continent to continent; from the Old
World to the New, is a testimonial to his greatness.
Nor are these wanting in the solitudes of the land.
Telegraphic lines crossing the breadth of our Continent, climbing hills, descending into valleys, thread-
ing mountain passes, silently proclaim the great discovery and its author to the uninhabited desert.
Even now there are plans for putting a girdle of
telegraphic stations around the globe, which in all
probability will never be disused, and will convey a
knowledge of his claims on the gratitude of mankind
to millions who will never see the statue erected to-
day. Thus the Latin inscription in the Church of
St. Paul's, in London, referring to Sir Christopher
Wren, its architect, " If you would behold his mon-

ument, look around you," may be applied in a far more comprehensive sense to our friend, since the great globe itself has become his monument. All this may be said and all this would be undeniably true, but our natural instincts are not thus satisfied. It is not the name of a benefactor merely, it is the person that we cherish, and we require, whenever it is possible, the visible presentment of his face and form to aid us in keeping the idea of his worth before our minds. Who would willingly dispense with the image of Washington as we have it in painting and sculpture, and consent that it should be removed from the walls of our dwellings and from all public places, and that the calm countenance and majestic presence with which we associate so many virtues should disappear and be utterly and forever forgotten ? Who will deny that by means of these resemblances of his person we are the more frequently reminded of the reverence we owe to his memory? So in the present instance, we are not willing that our idea of Morse should be reduced to a mere abstraction. We are so constituted that we insist upon seeing the form of that brow beneath which an active, restless, creative brain devised the mechanism that was to subdue the most wayward of the elements to the service of man and make it his obedient messenger.

We require to see the eye that glittered with a thousand lofty hopes, when the great discovery was made, and the lips that curled with a smile of triumph when it became certain that the lightning of the clouds would become tractable to the most delicate touch. We demand to see the hand which first strung the wire by whose means the slender currents of the electric fluid were taught the alphabet of every living language—the hand which pointed them to the spot where they were to inscribe and leave their messages. All this we have in the statue which has this day been unveiled to the eager gaze of the public, and in which the artist has so skilfully and faithfully fulfilled his task as to satisfy those who are the hardest to please, the most intimate friends of the original. But long may it be, my friends—very long—before any such resemblance of our illustrious friend shall be needed by those who have the advantage of his acquaintance, to refresh the image of his form and bearing as it exists in their minds. Long may we keep with us what is better than the statue—the noble original; long may it remain among us in a healthful and serene old age; late, very late, may He who gave the mind to which we owe the grand discovery to-day commemorated, recall it to His more immediate presence that it may be employed in a higher sphere and in a still more beneficial activity.

SHAKSPEARE.

SHAKSPEARE.

AN ADDRESS ON THE UNVEILING OF SHAKSPEARE'S STATUE
IN THE CENTRAL PARK, MAY 22, 1872.

We have come together, my friends, for the purpose of celebrating the erection of a statue to one of
the most wonderful men that ever lived; a genius
great, far beyond all ordinary greatness, and destined
to hold the admiration of mankind, through century
after century, in tne ages yet to come.

In a part of 'this republic which, within a few
years past, has been added to our Union, lying between the Rocky Mountains and the western sea, are
yet standing a few groves of a peculiar kind of tree,
prodigious in height and bulk, and seemingly produced by nature to show mankind to what size a tree
can attain in a favorable soil and a congenial climate,
with no enemy to lay the axe at its root. The earth,
in its most fertile spots, in its oldest forests, and under its mildest skies, has nothing like them—no
stems of such vast dimensions, no summits towering
so high and casting their shadows so far, putting
forth their new leaves and ripening their seed-vessels

in the region of the clouds. The traveller who enters these mighty groves almost expects to see some huge son of Anak stalking in the broad alleys between their gigantic trunks, or some mammoth or mastodon browsing on the lower branches.

So it is with those great minds which the Maker of all sometimes sends upon the earth and among mankind, as if to show us of what vast enlargement the faculties of the human intellect are capable, if but rarely in this stage of our being, yet at least in that which follows the present life, when the imperfections and infirmities of the material frame, which is now the dwelling of the spirit, shall neither clog its motions nor keep back its growth. Such a great mind was that of Shakspeare. An imagination so creative, a reason so vigorous, a wisdom so clear and comprehensive, taking views of life and character and duty so broad and just and true, a spirit so fiery and at the same time so gentle, such acuteness of observation and such power of presenting to other minds what is observed—such a combination of qualities seems to afford us, as we contemplate it, a glimpse of what, in certain respects, the immortal part of man shall be, when every cause that dims its vision or weakens its energy or fetters its activity or checks its expansion shall be wholly done away, and

that subtler essence shall be left to the full and free
exercise of the powers with which God endowed it.

It has occurred to me, in thinking what I should
say at this time, that the writings of Shakspeare contain proofs that if he had but given his attention to
the work of preparing for usefulness and distinction
in other pursuits than that in which he acquired his
fame, he might have achieved in some of them a renown almost equal to that which attends his dramatic writings.   The dramatic poet who puts into the
mouths of personages whom he would represent as
great beyond the common stature of greatness words
and sentiments corresponding to their exalted character, must, in order to do this, possess an intellectual
character somewhat like theirs, must in some sort
partake of their greatness.   I wonder not, therefore,
that some who have insisted that Shakspeare did not
write the plays attributed to him should, in searching
for the true author, have fixed upon Lord Bacon,
finding in them passages which may be plausibly referred to the father of modern philosophy and the
most profound jurist of his age.   I do not accept
their theory, but I say to myself when I read what
they have quoted from his writings in support of it:
" What a giant among philosophers was lost in this
dramatic poet ! what an able jurist and legislator

allowed the faculties which would have made him such to slumber while he employed himself in writing for the stage !"

So when I read the passages gathered from his plays to show that Shakspeare anticipated Harvey in his knowledge of the circulation of the blood in its channels through the animal frame, my reflection is that here was an embryo physiologist, endowed beyond his fellow-men with an instinctive perception of the interior mechanism of the human body, and the power of detecting its subtle workings, hidden from man for so many ages from the birth of our species. Not the less, nay, perhaps still more remarkable, was the insight of Shakspeare into the different, even the most subtle, forms of mental distemperature, an insight shown in his portraiture of the madness of Hamlet, that of Ophelia and that of King Lear, all how distinctly drawn, yet each how diverse from the others! What a physician might he not have made to an insane asylum! How tenderly and how wisely might he not have ministered to the mind diseased—he who so shrewdly traced its wanderings and was so touched with a feeling of its infirmities! How gently might he not have led it away from its illusions and guided it back to sanity!

Moreover, if Shakspeare had worn the clerical

gown, what a preacher of righteousness he would have become, and how admirably and impressively he would have enforced the lessons of human life—he who put into the mouth of Cardinal Wolsey the pathetic words :

> " Had I but served my God with half the zeal
> I served my king, he would not in mine age
> Have left me naked to mine enemies."

I am sure that if those who deny to Shakspeare the credit of writing his own dramas had thought of ascribing them to the judicious Hooker or the pious Bishop Andrews, instead of Lord Bacon, they might have made a specious show of proof by carefully culled extracts from his writings. Nay, if Jeremy Taylor, whose prose is so full of poetry, had not been born a generation too late, I would engage, in the same way, to put a plausible face on the theory that the plays of Shakspeare, except, perhaps, some passages wickedly interpolated, were composed by the eloquent and devout author of *Holy Living and Dying*.

The fame of our great dramatist fills the civilized world. Among the poets he is what the cataract of Niagara is among waterfalls. As those who cannot take the journey to Niagara that they may behold its vast breadth of green waters plunging from the lofty precipice into the abyss below, content themselves with such an idea of its majesty and beauty as they can obtain from a picture or an engraving, so those who cannot enjoy the writings of Shakspeare in the original English read him in translations, which have the effect of looking at a magnificent landscape through a morning mist. All languages have their versions of Shakspeare. The most eminent men of genius in Germany have been his translators or commentators. In France they began by sneering at him with Voltaire, and they end by regarding him in a transport of wonder with Taine. He stands before them like a mighty mountain, filling with its vastness half the heavens, its head in an eternally serene atmosphere, while on its sides burrow the fox and the marmot, and tangled thickets obstruct the steps of the climber. The French critic, while amazed at the grandeur and variety of its forms, cannot help suffering his attention to wander to the ant-heaps and mole-holes scattered on its broad flanks.

To the great chorus of admiration which rises from all civilized nations, we this day add our voices as we erect to the memory of Shakspeare, in a land distant from that of his birth, yet echoing through its vast extent with the accents of his mother-tongue, the effigy of his bodily form and features. Those who profess to read in the aspect of the individual the qualities of his intellectual and moral character, have always delighted to trace in the face, of which we this day unveil an image to the public gaze, the manifest signs of his greatness. Read what Lavater wrote a hundred years since, and you shall see that he discovers in this noble countenance a promise of all that the critic finds in his writings. Come down to the phrenologists of the present day, and they tell you of the visible indications of his boundless invention, his universal sympathy, his lofty idealism, his wit, his humor, his imagination, and every other faculty that conspired to produce his matchless works.

This counterfeit presentment of the outward form of Shakspeare we offer to-day to the public of New York as an ornament of the beautiful pleasure ground in which they take so just a pride. It has been cast in bronze, a material indestructible by time, in the hope that perchance it may last as long as his writings. It is nobly executed by the artist, and with a deep feeling of the greatness of his subject. One profound regret saddens this ceremony—that our friend Hackett, who was foremost in procuring this expression of our homage to the memory of Shakspeare, is not with us, but sleeps with the great author whose writings he loved and studied, and interpreted both to the ear and the eye.

The spot in which this statue is placed will henceforth be associated with numberless ideas and images called up to the mind of the visitor by the name of Shakspeare. To all whose imagination is easily kindled into activity it will seem forever haunted by the personages whom he created and who live in his dramas: the grave magician Prospero, and his simple-hearted daughter Miranda, and his dainty spirit Ariel, the white-haired Lear, and the loving Cordelia, the jealous Moor and the gentle Desdemona, Imogen and Rosalind, and the majestic shadow of Coriolanus. Before the solitary passer-by will rise the burly figure of the merry knight, Falstaff, and round about this statue will flit the slight forms of Slender and Shallow and Dogberry. To those who chance to tread these walks by moonlight, the ghost of the Royal Dane may shape itself from the vapors of the night and again disappear. But may the sound of battle never be heard here, nor the herbage be trampled by the rude heel of the populace in its fury to disturb the fairy court of Oberon and Titania, and scare the little people from their dances on the greensward.

To memories and associations like these, we devote this spot from henceforth and for ever.

REFORM.

REFORM.

AN ADDRESS DELIVERED AT A MEETING HELD IN THE
COOPER INSTITUTE, SEPTEMBER 23, 1872.

I am glad, my fellow-citizens, to see that this
occasion has brought so many of you together. It is
not for any narrow party purpose that we are assembled ; it is not that we may consult how to advance
the interests of a popular favorite and his associates ;
it is not to pull down his rival and the set of men by
whom his rival is supported. It is by a higher and
nobler motive that you are animated, one in which
all honest men necessarily concur, the wish to secure
to the State, and to all the smaller communities of.
which the State is made up, the benefits of a just,
honest, economical, and in all respects, wise administration of public affairs. You could hardly come together for a more worthy purpose.

It seems an idle remark, because it is perfectly
obvious, that the great mass of the people have no
interest in being badly governed, but that on the
contrary, their interest lies in committing their public
affairs to men who will manage them honestly and

frugally. It is the great mass who suffer when rapacious and knavish men obtain authority and power. The robbers are the few; the robbed are the many. If the many would only come to a mutual understanding and act together, the robbers would never obtain public office, or if by accident they obtained it, would be thrust out the first opportunity. In these matters concert of action is everything, and the rogues know it. As long as the opposition to their designs is divided into many little minorities, they laugh at it. High-handed villany takes its adversaries one after another, by the throat, and strangles them by detail. An army scattered is an army defeated. It has passed into a proverb that in union there is strength; it is just as true that in division there is weakness, and there are none who know this better than the knaves who enrich themselves by plundering the public.

The material world abounds with instances of the power obtained by the combination of forces. I came a few days since from a rural neighborhood which a few weeks before had been visited by a shower of rain more copious and violent than any living person remembered. In two hours the roads leading down the hills were ploughed by it into deep channels for the torrents, and rendered impassable; bridges were swept away; huge stones were rolled down before the waters; and beds of soil, sand, gravel, pebbles and fragments of rock were borne along from field to field and found new owners. Yet this sudden flood was composed of single drops of rain, each one of which as it reached the earth had not force enough to displace the smallest pebble. It was combination, it was concert of action, it was organization that gave them their fearful power. The drops were gathered into rills, the rills into streams, the streams into torrents. By union they became terrible; by union they were made irresistible, and all that man could do was to look on till their work was done.

Just as irresistible and just as sure to accomplish their work will be the men whose interest it is that public affairs shall be frugally and wisely administered, if they can only be brought to combine with one purpose and one system of action. To promote this end we are assembled this evening. Let me not be told that if we keep one set of rogues out of office another will be sure to have their place. That is the moral of an old fable of Æsop, but the moral is a false one. You remember the ingenious parable: A fox among the reeds of a stream was tormented by gnats. A swallow, I think it was, saw his distress and offered to drive them away. "Do not," said the fox, "for if you drive these away a hungrier swarm will come in their place and drain my veins of their last drop of blood." But my friends, all that I infer from . this fable is that official corruption is more than two thousand years old, at least. The lesson which this fable seems to inculcate—that they who plunder the public should not be molested in their guilty work—is absurd. There are in the community men whom you know to be absolutely honest, men of proved integrity, and all that you have to do is to agree upon such men as your candidates for office, and the public interest is safe. Let me relate for your encouragement what has already been done in this city.

It was about forty years ago—when many who now do me the honor of listening to me were in their cradles, but I will not be certain as to the year—that the people of this city of New York were very much dissatisfied with their Common Council, which was then composed of a single board, the Aldermen. Some of the Aldermen had grown rich while in office. They knew sooner than other persons where new streets were to be laid out, and they purchased lands contiguous to those streets, which they afterwards sold at a large advance. One of the Aldermen owned a country seat at the northern extremity of the Third Avenue, and through his influence a great deal of money was expended upon that thoroughfare, making it as hard as a rock, and so smooth and even that, as I heard a gentleman say at the time, there was not on its whole surface a hollow deep enough to hold a pint of water. These now seem small offences, which, compared with the crimes of Tweed and his set, almost whiten into perfect innocence; yet the people of that day were discontented, and declared that they wanted men in office who thought only of the public good. So we all went to work and elected a Common Council of honest men in spite of Æsop and his fable. Let me name some of them: There was Stephen Allen, the very impersonation of downright honesty. There was Myndert Van Schaick, wholly incorruptible and devoted to the public interest. There was Dr. McNevin too much taken up with science to think of making money. There was Dr. Augustine Smith, who brought to the tasks of his office large knowledge and an integrity beyond question. There were other men in the Common Council, worthy by their character to be the associates of these, and there was no complaint of corruption or malversation of any sort in our municipal affairs. We were all proud of our Common Council. It was an honor to belong to such a body of men. I doubt whether the affairs of any

17

municipality since the time of the elder Cato have ever been administered by men so virtuous and intelligent as those to whom I have referred. It was only by slow gradations, and after many years, that our municipal affairs lapsed into that frightful state from which we are now seeking effectually to reclaim them.

This, fellow-citizens, was what we did forty years ago, and something like this, if by the blessing of God we can act heartily and vigorously in concert, we may do now.

SIR WALTER SCOTT.

SIR WALTER SCOTT.

The Scottish residents of this city whose public spirit and reverence for genius have moved them to present to the people of New York the statue of their countryman which has just now been unveiled to the public gaze, have honored me with a request that I should so far take part in these ceremonies as to speak a few words concerning the great poet and novelist, of whose renown they are so justly proud.

As I look round on this assembly I perceive few persons of my own age—few who can remember, as I can, the rising and setting of this brilliant luminary of modern literature. I well recollect the time when Scott, then thirty-four years of age, gave to the world his *Lay of the Last Minstrel*, the first of his works which awakened the enthusiastic admiration that afterwards attended all he wrote. In that poem the spirit of the old Scottish ballads—the most beautiful of their class—lived again. In it we had all their fire, their rapid narrative, their unlabored graces, their pathos, animating a story to which he had given a certain epic breadth and unity. We read with scarcely less delight his poem of *Marmion*, and soon afterward the youths and maidens of our country hung with rapture over the pages of his *Lady of the Lake*. I need not enumerate his other poems, but this I will say of them all, that no other metrical narratives in our language seem to me to possess an equal power of enchaining the attention of the reader, and carrying him on from incident to incident with such entire freedom from weariness. These works, printed in cheap editions, were dispersed all over our country; they found their way to almost every fireside, and their popularity raised up both here and in Great Britain a multitude of imitators now forgotten.

This power over the mind of the reader was soon to be exemplified in a more remarkable manner, and when, at the age of forty-three, Scott gave to the world, without any indication of its authorship, his romance of *Waverley*, all perceived that a new era in the literature of fiction had begun. " Here," they said, " is a genius of a new order. What wealth of materials, what free mastery in moulding them into shape, what invention, humor, pathos, vivid portraiture of character—nothing overcharged or exaggerated yet all distinct, spirited and life-like! Are we not," they asked, "to have other works by the same hand?"

The desire thus expressed was soon gratified. The expected romances came forth with a rapidity which amazed their readers. Some, it is true, ascribed them to Scott as the only man who could write them. "It cannot be," said others; "Scott is occupied with writing histories and poems, and editing work after work which require great labor and research; he has no time for writing romances like these." So he went on, throwing off these remarkable works as if the writing of them had been but a pastime, and fairly bombarding the world with romances from his mysterious covert. It was like what in the neighborhood of this city we see on a fine evening of the Fourth of July, when rocket after rocket rises from the distant horizon and bursts in the air, throwing off to right and left jets of flame and fireballs of every brilliant hue, yet whose are the hands that launch them we know not. So we read and wondered and lost ourselves in conjectures as to the author who ministered to our delight, and when at length, at a public dinner in the year 1827, Scott avowed himself to be the sole author of the *Waverley Novels*, the interest which we felt at this disclosure was hardly less than that with which we heard of the issue of the great battle of Waterloo.

I have seen a design by some artist in which Scott is shown surrounded by the personages whom in his poems and romances he called into being. They formed a vast crowd, face beyond face, each with its characteristic expression—a multitude so great that it reminded me of the throng—the cloud I may call it—of cherubim which in certain pictures on the walls of European churches surround the Virgin Mother. For forty years has Scott lain in his grave, and now his countrymen place in this park an image of the noble brow, so fortunately copied by the artist, beneath which the personages of his imagination grew into being. Shall we say *grew*, as if they sprang up spontaneously in his mind, like plants from a fruitful soil, while his fingers guided the pen that noted down their words and recorded their acts? Or should we imagine the faculties of his mind to have busied themselves at his bidding in the chambers of that active brain, and gradually to have moulded the characters of his wonderful fictions to their perfect form? At all events, let us say that He who breathed the breath of life into the frame of which a copy is before us, imparted with that breath a portion of his own creative power.

And now as the statue of Scott is set up in this beautiful park, which, a few years since, possessed no human associations, historical or poetic, connected with its shades, its lawns, its rocks, and its waters, these grounds become peopled with new memories. Henceforth the silent earth at this spot will be eloquent of old traditions, the airs that stir the branches of the trees will whisper of feats of chivalry to the visitor. All that vast crowd of ideal personages created by the imagination of Scott will enter with his sculptured effigy and remain—Fergus and Flora MacIvor, Meg Merrilies and Dirk Hatteraik, the Antiquary and his Sister, and Edie Ochiltree, Rob Roy and Helen Macgregor, and Baillie Jarvie and Dandie Dinmont, and Diana Vernon and Old Mortality—but the night would be upon us before I could go through the muster roll of this great army. They will pass in endless procession around the statue of him in whose prolific brain they had their birth, until the language which we speak shall perish, and the spot on which we stand shall be again a woodland wilderness.

THE END.